WANTED FOR LIFE

FOR LIFE

LOVE UNDER FIRE

WANTED
FOR LIFE

LOVE UNDER FIRE

ALLISON B. HANSON

To Stacy,
So nice to
meet you!
Allison B H

Entangled Publishing, LLC
2614 South Timberline Road
Suite 105, PMB 159
Fort Collins, CO 80525
Visit our website at www.entangledpublishing.com.

Amara is an imprint of Entangled Publishing, LLC.

Edited by Nina Bruhns
Cover design by KAM Designs
Cover art from Shutterstock and Pixabay

Manufactured in the United States of America

First Edition April 2018

AMARA
an imprint of Entangled Publishing LLC

For my sister, Becky, who is always willing to drop everything to read something for me. You're the best!

Chapter One

San Francisco, California

U.S. Deputy Marshal Angel Larson woke to the coppery smell of blood, and the pale light of approaching dawn seeping through the high-rise glass. She fought through a heavy sense of unease, knowing something was terribly wrong. Angel never slept all night. Especially when she was protecting someone.

The last time she'd slept soundly had been years ago during a stay in the hospital. But that was only because she'd been...sedated.

"Shit." Her rough voice broke through the silence of the room as reality filtered in through the fog. She'd been drugged. Which explained the heaviness in her limbs and the numbness in her brain.

As clarity returned, other facts caught her notice. She was in her protectee's bedroom—more accurately, in Heath Zeller's bed. She was still fully clothed, but her clothing felt wet. No, it was sticky.

Rubbing her temples, she fought to remember what had happened the night before.

She and Heath had attended a media event where he'd teased the press with what was to come from his newest piece of technology to be released in a few months.

The man had upturned the normal stereotype of geeky tech mogul. Heath had a pleasant personality, and a way of speaking that didn't bring on fits of narcolepsy to members of the non-tech world.

He'd used this gift to push his way out of the silicon box and into the hearts and homes of America. His good looks, paired with his hefty bank account, had him listed as most-eligible bachelor on every talk show across the land.

Angel had been assigned the job by her boss, Supervisory Deputy United States Marshal Josiah Thorne. Acting the part of Heath's girlfriend, Aubrey Daniels, was an easy way to stay close enough to protect him while he launched his new product.

Being the only female on Task Force Phoenix came with an extra dose of pressure. Angel prided herself on keeping up with the other deputy marshals. But the scent that greeted her when she'd awoken foretold of her failure to keep Heath Zeller safe.

Sluggishly, she reached out to turn on the light. The sun wasn't moving fast enough.

She wasn't surprised to see all the blood, but her breath caught anyway. Her hands were covered in blood, as were her clothes.

Heath lay next to her, pale and cold. She swallowed down the instant flood of despair, and forced herself to scan the scene. His throat had been cut first, as evident by the arterial spray across the wall. The spatter pattern from his other wounds matched up predictably to the stains on her shirt.

Wiping her hands on her ruined sweatpants, she moved to the safe by the desk. With stiff fingers she touched the correct keys and the lock disengaged. To the casual observer, nothing would seem amiss. The large stack of cash, his diamond cufflinks, and a number of stock certificates were all where they should be.

But something very important was missing—the nondescript-looking cell phone that held the prototype software for Zeller Communication's next step toward global domination.

Someone had gotten away with a priceless piece of technology, and done a damn fine job of setting Angel up for murder.

Chapter Two

Other than that first brief inspection of the scene, Angel avoided looking at Heath's body as she focused on deciding her next step. She could call the police...however, the evidence against her seemed solid. She hadn't discovered any proof that another person had been in the room, and she knew for a fact someone else had been there. Because she hadn't done this.

No doubt, her prints would be the only ones on the knife lying on the floor next to the bed. Someone had done a thorough job positioning her to take the fall. If she'd planned this hit, she would have also paid off a few people to say they'd heard her and Heath arguing at or after the party. No doubt, helpful witnesses would surface as soon as the news broke.

Josiah Thorne, her boss, would get her out of the situation eventually, if he could. But that would take time. Time she didn't have if she was in jail. Or if the cops believed her and she was embroiled in an official investigation. Not if she wanted to launch her own.

Until she knew who did this, dealing with the legal system wouldn't be safe. Whoever set her up were professionals. They knew exactly how to plant evidence so she would be the main suspect. She could only trust Thorne and her small team at Phoenix. They were like family.

Everyone else was an unknown.

She brushed aside the last cobwebs of the sedative and her instincts kicked in. Her next step was to get out of there before she was caught red handed. Literally. For a moment, her heart filled with sadness at the loss of the man lying in the bed. While their relationship had been strictly client/bodyguard, she'd liked and respected him as a person.

He'd told her many times how he trusted her with his life.

And she'd let him down in the worst possible way.

Putting aside the deluge of guilt, she worked out the details of her escape plan. No marshal worth their badge went anywhere without having a bolt plan. Normally, it would include the person she was protecting, but now it was to save herself.

From earlier surveillance of Heath's condo at 181 Fremont, she knew the cameras in all seventeen elevators were well monitored. The two main stairwells, however, only had active cameras on every fifth floor, alternating. No sane person took the stairs in a skyscraper.

She might have been able to hack into the building's security system to mitigate the cameras, but she quickly discovered the intruders who'd set her up had also taken her laptop. All the more reason to find them.

And make them pay.

Changing out of her bloody clothes, she threw them in a bag and pulled on a clean outfit and sneakers. Her platinum blond hair had splashes of red stains through it. She pulled it back and shoved on a ball cap to cover the blood.

She paused by the door before slipping out into the

hall and heading for the stairs. There were only two other residences on this floor and it was still early, but she held her breath as she rushed past the other doors.

Down two floors, she took that corridor to get to the stairwell on the opposite end. Down the next three and across that floor. Heath lived on the sixty-seventh floor. It would have taken a long time to get to the lobby at this rate.

Good thing she wasn't heading for the lobby.

The main entrance was covered by cameras and security. She knew she couldn't simply walk out of the building without being recorded. Fleeing in disguise would make her appear all the more guilty.

She continued down to the fifty-fifth floor—to Heath's safe house. She'd suggested he rent the place under a fake name so he had a place to go in case his apartment was compromised. It wouldn't be linked back to her, and it would take weeks for them to track it back to Heath.

The scent of new paint and drywall hit her as she entered the apartment. Dropping her go-bag, she hurried directly to the shower, wanting to remove the evidence of her failure.

"I'm sorry, Heath. So sorry." A few tears escaped, but she quickly choked them back. U.S. deputy marshals didn't cry. They didn't allow emotions to get in the way of their duty.

The two times she'd broken that rule she'd paid dearly. The first time was when she'd lost perspective on her first partner at the Marshals Service. That mistake had nearly cost her life. She'd quickly learned not to let her heart get involved on the job.

She'd liked Heath, and they'd had a lot of fun playing a happy couple. But it had been a job and nothing more.

She swiped her last tear away and sighed. She knew Heath would have forgiven her if he'd been there. He probably would have told her she couldn't have been any more careful. They'd never eaten or drunk anything that hadn't been inspected by someone she trusted. Even bottled water had been dipped for contaminants.

She'd done everything right. She didn't know how someone had managed to incapacitate her and kill the man she'd been entrusted to protect.

Pink water swirled around her toes before escaping down the drain.

Heath Zeller was gone, and his life's work, his legacy, was in the hands of his murderer. As Angel stood there dripping, she vowed to get it back.

And to do that, she had to find the real killer.

Chapter Three

Two days later, Angel was ready to make her move out of the building. By now, law enforcement would have scoured the footage taken at every exit. The day of the murder and the next, there would have been a strong police presence as they canvased the area and spoke to all of the neighbors.

A patrolman had even knocked on the safe house door to ask if she'd seen anything. She'd shaken her head, causing her newly dyed black locks to fall over her shoulder. She'd pushed her glasses up on her nose to look at the flyer that carried her own picture front and center. She'd nodded seriously and agreed to call the number listed if she remembered anything.

Now, with the police presence cut back, it should have been easier for her to make her escape. But there was one element she hadn't anticipated. Heath Zeller—eligible bachelor and America's brilliant boy-next-door—had been a media sweetheart when he was alive. His murder was being discussed on every channel across the country. And with every report, her photo was shown.

She was the jilted ex-lover, Aubrey Daniels, who'd killed Zeller in a fit of jealousy and was now on the run. Armed and extremely dangerous. Wanted by every law enforcement agency in existence...other than Task Force Phoenix, the only ones who knew the truth.

Angel had spent the last two days working out a plan to get out of the building and away from San Francisco. Using a paper map, she drew a circle around the city showing the distance she could go with the fuel in her SUV's tank and the extra she kept in the back. It didn't help that 50 percent of the circle was in the ocean and therefore useless.

A town had caught her eye. Crystal Grove, Oregon, was within the circle. She shook her head and moved on. No. That wasn't an option.

Fortunately, she wouldn't need it.

She owned three small homes off the grid. Her West Coast property was just outside the circle. It meant she'd have to risk stopping for gas, but once she made it to her cottage, she wouldn't need to go outside again for months. Plenty of time to get things resolved, and hunt down a killer.

With a plan and all the clothing she had with her packed in a small bag, she took out her prepaid emergency phone. She knew she could only risk one phone call, and even that would be layered in code. Calls to her team were undoubtedly being recorded and traced in anticipation of her contact. They would also be watching her team, expecting them to make a move to help her or bring her in.

She dialed the number, having thought out exactly what she wanted to say ahead of time.

"Thorne." Her boss answered on the second ring.

"Hi." She didn't need to identify herself. They'd spoken nearly every day, up until Heath was killed.

"Where are you?" His question was normal protocol. If someone was listening they would think he was doing his best to talk in a rogue deputy marshal.

"I can't tell you that." She played her part. "I didn't do this." Which he well knew.

"You know how it looks. You should come in and discuss it. Tell your side."

She knew Thorne trusted her. From the moment he'd come to get her out of jail seven years ago to offer her a different life with Task Force Phoenix, he'd been a father figure to her.

In many ways he even reminded Angel of her real father. Both tall, steady men with graying hair. They had an air about them that emitted confidence, and made people want to listen to them. Thorne had known her father back before Thorne became Josiah Thorne. Back when he'd had a wife and a baby on the way. Before he'd given up his life for a new one protecting people.

Angel often wondered what kind of strength it took to do something like that—to give up everything and everyone you loved, for the greater good. She hadn't had the option to walk away. Her family was already gone. It had made the decision easier. Thorne had offered her a place on a team that was like a family of orphans, and for that she would be forever grateful. He'd saved her life and given her a purpose.

Her stomach twisted, knowing she'd let him down this time. Heath was dead because she'd failed. She swallowed and continued with a shaky voice.

"I know how it looks, which is why I can't come in yet."

"Where will you go? You can't keep running forever," he said.

"We'll see about that."

"You're too visible. Everyone is looking for you. The second you step out for food or gas, someone will recognize you."

"I have other options." Meaning, her other properties.

"There's nowhere you can hide that we don't already

know about." *Shit*. He was telling her the other properties had been compromised. She was quickly running out of options.

"I'll figure it out."

She hung up the phone and tossed it on the sofa. She consulted her map once more before leaving the apartment. Her gaze moved to Crystal Grove again, which was nestled safely on the inside of the circle.

Her heart sank.

All her choices had just been reduced to one horrible solution.

It was a really, really bad idea. But the only one left.

Walking with purpose, she stepped onto the elevator, strode across the lobby, and out to the street without anyone noticing.

In a parking garage two blocks away, she used the remote to unlock the waiting SUV. Having an emergency vehicle nearby was another standard procedure for Phoenix ops. In addition to the full tank of gas, as a precaution there was also an extra ten-gallon can of fuel in the back. Stopping at a gas station meant risking being noticed or caught on surveillance. Thanks to Heath's fame, the news story wouldn't die down anytime soon. Making every stop even riskier.

She needed help. Even with all her precautions, she was still too visible. It wouldn't take long for law enforcement to realize she'd been in the building the whole time they'd been looking for her.

She was officially on the run, hunted.

She needed a place no one would expect her to go. She needed someone no one would expect her to turn to.

One person kept popping into her mind as she wrestled with the decision.

A year ago, she'd left him without a word.

Would he help her now?

Or would he turn her in the first chance he got…?

Chapter Four

Former DEA agent turned high school math teacher Colton Williamson's headlights flashed across his modest home before he pulled into the one-car garage. He got out of his truck and went in through the mudroom, as he always did.

Except this time someone was waiting for him.

With a very guilty look on his face.

At the sight of brightly colored debris strewn all over the kitchen floor, Colton let out a soft curse. "Dammit, Pudge."

The mammoth German shepherd let out a whine, not even trying to hide the destroyed tennis shoe at his paws.

"If you were going to chew up a pair of my shoes, why didn't you go for those loafers with the tassels? They're an abomination."

Pudge looked away.

"Right. I understand. It would be too embarrassing to be caught chewing on them. How do you think it feels to have to *wear* them?"

Pudge trotted to the back door and gave Colton the look that meant he needed to go out.

"Fine. But we're not done discussing this. I am *not* happy." He opened the door and the dog rushed out. "And if you could go in the back corner like we talked about, that would be great. We're not trying to create a minefield out there."

Still grumbling under his breath, he closed the door and went to get a beer.

He talked to his dog way too much to be considered normal. He was just glad he had a dog so he wouldn't have conversations with himself. Yeah, things were that bad.

When the hell were they going to track down Viktor Kulakov, arrest the bastard, and get his trial over with so Colton could get back to his real life?

He'd been in witness protection for a little over a year and it wasn't getting any easier. He missed his old job in the DEA, and he missed his big, overbearing family even more.

At one time, he'd been annoyed by the constant phone calls from his brothers and their wives trying to fix him up on dates. He'd sometimes avoided calls from his mother when she checked in to see if he'd had a good dinner, not liking the guilt it caused when he had to tell her he'd had pizza for dinner, yet again.

What he wouldn't give to pick up the phone and hear their voices now. He'd love to tell his mother he'd actually learned to cook. And he'd gladly go on a hundred boring dates just so he had someone to talk to.

Not that those dates would go anywhere long term. His heart was unavailable. Mainly due to the fact he hadn't yet gathered up all the pieces after a certain U.S. deputy marshal blew it apart last year.

He shook his head and got a beer.

"Moving on. Moving on," he repeated his mantra out loud. He needed to make a new life for himself here in Crystal Grove. Who knew how long it would take law enforcement to find and arrest Viktor Kulakov? Maybe they never would. Colton just needed to let go of the past and look toward the future. That's what his WITSEC handler told him every time he checked in.

Tonight he had attended a retirement party for one of his fellow high school teachers. As with everything in Colton's life now, it had been totally uneventful.

What kind of party was over by nine o'clock on a Friday night?

He shook his head and flipped on the television. He would spend the evening watching an action movie, and point out all the places where they'd messed up. He should know. Between his time in the military, and the eight years working undercover for the DEA, he knew how to carry a gun and bust in a door for real.

Unfortunately, the closest he'd come to seeing any action since being in WITSEC was his police interview last week about an egging a few houses down.

He was sorely tempted to egg his own home just so he could call them back and help them investigate.

He'd never been bored in his previous life.

In his old job at the DEA, there had never been a dull day. Okay, so his last day may have been a bit more action filled than he ever wanted to face again. But overall, he missed the excitement, and the sense of duty and purpose.

Sure, teaching also had a high level of respectability. Shaping future generations so they didn't all turn out to be ignorant asshats was an important job. But it wasn't one Colton was cut out for.

He needed adrenaline and action in his life. He'd been born into it. His cop father and brothers had pushed him to his limits both physically and mentally while growing up. There was no room for accountants or teachers in the Williamson family.

Next week, the school year would be over and he'd have the entire summer to do...absolutely nothing. While the other teachers looked forward to summer vacation, Colton wondered how he was going to survive.

He flipped through the TV channels, stopping with a gasp at a familiar face on the screen.

"Holy shit," he said, turning up the volume.

"Aubrey Daniels is wanted for the murder of technology mogul Heath Zeller. The coroner has reported the victim's throat was cut, and Mr. Zeller was stabbed multiple times in his sleep. Please be aware this woman is armed and extremely dangerous."

"The hell she is," Colton said to the reporter on the screen. "If she killed that man, I'll eat those loafers myself. Tassels and all."

Still, just because he knew with all certainty she hadn't killed Heath Zeller, it didn't mean she wasn't dangerous. She'd hurt Colton, bad.

He knew her all too well. And her name wasn't Aubrey Daniels. It was U.S. Deputy Marshal Angel Larson.

She'd been the one assigned to protect him as he prepared for Kulakov's trial a year ago in Philadelphia. They'd spent months together in a safe house. There were only so many board games to play, or movies to watch, so eventually they started talking.

She'd shared very little, but the things she'd shared were true. He could tell—or at least he'd thought so. Then one night they got a bit too close. When they ended up in bed the second time, she was adamant it couldn't happen again.

He'd agreed. It couldn't go anywhere, anyway. But as they gave in to their urges again and again, Colton realized it was more than just lust. The itch had been scratched, but he still wanted her. Then, Kulakov escaped custody and the trial was postponed indefinitely, so Colton was told he had to leave Philadelphia and disappear into WITSEC.

With only days left before he would move away to start a new life with a new home and a new name, he'd taken a giant leap.

And fallen flat on his face.

He'd asked Angel to come with him. She'd told him she would think about it. But the next morning she was gone. No note, not a word. There was another agent protecting him, and he never saw Angel again.

Not until her photo popped up on his television tonight.

Maybe he didn't know her as well as he thought.

He considered the possibility of the woman he knew murdering someone in their sleep. He shook his head. Nope. Not remotely possible. Angel might have some major commitment issues, but she was no killer.

Pudge barked at the back door to be let in.

Colton got up and opened the door wide, but his dog stayed sitting on the porch, tail wagging.

"What are you waiting for, an invitation?" he asked in annoyance.

"Actually, that might be nice," came the soft, feminine answer.

His world turned upside down as Angel Larson stepped out of the shadows and his memories, and back into his life.

Chapter Five

Angel hadn't been sure what kind of reception to expect from Colton. Having a gun pulled on her had not been outside the realm of possibility. Still, seeing a Glock 19 pistol instantly appear in his hand made her pulse jump and her own hands reach for the sky.

She only hoped she'd be able to explain before he pulled the trigger.

"You broke my guard dog," he said.

A cautious spurt of relief went through her. "I didn't break him. He works fine. He just loves me. I think he knows I picked him when *you* said he was scrawny."

When Colton had found out he was destined for WITSEC, he'd decided he wanted a companion. She'd suggested a puppy. Later, when he asked her to go into the program with him, she'd realized he wanted more in a companion than long walks and playing catch.

He'd wanted to spend the rest of his life with someone, and okay, she'd panicked.

"Not only did you eat my shoes, but you picked a girl over me?" He frowned at the dog, who didn't look the slightest bit remorseful.

Colton's Glock was still leveled on her, so she stayed still with her hands in the air. "I seem to remember telling you not to purchase a firearm."

He looked down at the pistol and shrugged. "Old habits."

"Your new identification is good, but an overzealous background check could turn up inconsistencies," she reminded him.

"And then what? I'd have to move somewhere else? Get a new identity? What could WITSEC do to me that would be worse than being a math teacher in Crystal Grove, Oregon?"

She'd guessed right away his new identity wouldn't sit well with him. She'd even spoken to his handler about it. The man needed constant action. He would say it was because he didn't like being bored, but that was BS.

She knew the real reason why he lived for danger.

"Are you going to let me in, or should I leave?" she asked, no longer alarmed by the gun. He might be really angry at her, but he wouldn't shoot her. At least, she didn't think so.

He'd probably been pissed after she'd left without a word in the middle of the night, but, surely, he was over that by now. No doubt, she was the only one still wondering what might have happened if she'd stayed…

"That depends," he said. "Are you going to kill me, too?"

He knew her better than that. They'd spent months together, and she'd let him in behind her walls, where no one else was permitted. Granted, she hadn't told him about her past—she didn't talk about that, ever—but she'd told him enough for him to know that she would have gladly put herself in front of that knife to stop someone from killing the person she was protecting.

There had been a time when she wasn't sure she was cut

out for that level of duty, but it had been tested, and she'd proven she would always do the right thing when it came right down to it.

"Seriously?" She made a sound of annoyance and rolled her eyes.

"Where'd you park the white Bronco?" he continued with his comedy routine.

"Ha ha. The silver Explorer is in a storage unit down the street."

She'd pinned everything on his willingness to help her. Her Plan B was to look for an abandoned property and hide out until things died down. But with the level of media coverage the story was getting, that could take months. Or longer.

Besides, abandoned properties usually contained things like rats and spiders. No thanks. She'd go up against a bad guy any day, but a spider? Hell, no.

She needed Colton. In more ways than one. But she was determined to keep things professional this time.

She let out a breath when he lowered the Glock.

"Get in here," he muttered.

Whether he meant her or the dog she wasn't sure, but both of them hightailed it into the house.

Chapter Six

Colton couldn't believe Angel was here, in person, standing in his kitchen.

"How did you even know where I lived? You left before I was assigned," he said as he tucked his weapon back in his pants. How many times had he thought of her since moving here?

Most of the time his thoughts still contained a certain level of irritation. He'd gotten over his anger—mostly. Some thoughts were of a sexual nature—that part of their relationship had been amazing. A few thoughts were just normal ones about where she might be, and if she was happy.

Her hair was dyed black instead of the white-blond it normally was. This color suited her better. It made those icy blue eyes seem a little softer.

"I may or may not have hacked into your file to see where they were moving you," she admitted.

"And why would you have done such a thing?" A hint of a smile played at his lips. Had she looked him up back then so she could find him for more than just a place to hide?

When she didn't answer right away, he didn't push. Pushing her would just make her defensive. Besides, he preferred to keep his fantasy alive—the one where she comes to him and begs for his forgiveness, and admits she made a terrible mistake in leaving him.

"This is the perfect place for me to hide," she explained, "because no one knows I know where you were moved. This is the last place anyone would look for me."

So much for fantasies.

"How long do you plan to stay?" He didn't mind her being here, but it might become inconvenient if she couldn't ever leave the house because she was a wanted criminal.

And it would be nice to know how long he had with her this time.

"Not that long. I just need to figure out who set me up, get the prototype back, and clear my name."

He chuckled. "Sounds like a piece of cake." Fortunately he was still allowed to have sarcasm in WITSEC. "Any leads?"

The familiar surge of excitement rushed through his veins. A puzzle to be solved. Someone to help. He felt alive again. Useful.

"No. Not yet. Can I use your computer?"

He knew from the months she spent with him she was happiest when her fingers were on a keyboard with information scrolling on the screen in front of her. He was surprised she didn't have one with her, or had already fabricated one from a transistor radio and a coconut.

But computers definitely weren't his thing.

"Don't worry, no one will track me back to your IP address," she assured him.

Not that he had a clue what that meant.

He pointed down the hall. "It's in the spare room. First door on the left."

She hurried into the room, Pudge following behind her like a love-struck puppy. Which was exactly what he was.

"What the hell is this?" she said, stopping dead in her tracks.

"What?" he asked, stepping in behind her.

She stared at his computer in disgust, her nose scrunched up in a way that made her look adorable instead of fierce. "This is a *desktop*."

"Um...yeah?" He'd heard that term before. They had desktops in the computer lab at the high school.

"The CPU is *gray*, Colton."

It had been so long since anyone had called him by his real name, he physically flinched. As if someone would overhear and find out who he really was.

"What's wrong with gray?"

"Gray means it's *old*." She sat down at his desk and turned it on. The computer hummed to life.

Sort of.

Normally when he used it, he turned it on before he went to make dinner so it would be up and running by the time he was finished eating.

"Thirty-two bit?" she squeaked after clicking on a few things. "Are you messing with me?"

"I only use it to keep track of my students' grades. I have a spreadsheet I fill out." He'd thought he was a regular tech genius when he'd figured out how to create a formula so it calculated the grade point average automatically.

She picked up the phone line where it connected into the back of the big square thing and her shoulders fell. "Dial-up? You have *dial*-up?" Her blue eyes begged him to tell her he had some other alternative.

Unfortunately he didn't. He wasn't 100 percent sure what other alternatives there even were.

He frowned and crossed his arms. He hadn't used

computers when he was a DEA agent. At six feet four inches, he'd almost always been assigned undercover gigs as a bodyguard or a fighter. Criminals didn't hire someone his size for their computer skills.

"I'm sorry it's not up to your standards," he said as she popped the case off his computer and pulled out something that looked pretty important. He hadn't had a computer in the safe house they'd shared. Not that she would have needed it, since she'd brought three laptops with her.

Back then, she'd told him about some of her assignments where she'd taken a temp job at a company and downloaded evidence off their own computers. Half the time, he didn't know what the hell she was talking about. But intelligent women turned him on and Angel was whip smart.

"I have a chain of IP addresses linking back to an untraceable proxy server," she said, "but I need to be on a net—"

He put up a hand to stop her. "I see your mouth moving, but I don't understand a word you're saying."

He wasn't an idiot. He was actually pretty smart, especially in math—old school—thus the teaching job. He'd just never had an interest in spending all his free time sitting at a desk staring at a screen. He'd always needed to be moving. Doing something. Not sitting.

"Fine. Put the thingy-what's-it back in my computer and log on." He could throw the fancy lingo around, too. "Go online and pick out whatever computer you want."

"Okay. I need to check in with my boss. And I want to see the news footage they've been showing." She looked at him and brightened. "You have a smart phone, right?"

"Yes." He pulled it from his back pocket and handed it over after unlocking it.

Her thumbs flew over the screen and she looked up at him. "You've never launched Safari before?"

"Again, I have no idea what you're saying." Was she just

stringing random words together to frustrate him?

She laughed and pointed at an icon.

"Ah." He shook his head. "I liked the black compass better than the blue one."

When she pressed her lips together, he knew he'd said something funny without meaning to. Before he had a chance to defend himself—yet again—she gasped.

"Oh, no." She let out a breath. "My cover's been blown. They have my real identity."

The worry on her face broke something loose in his chest. Instincts he'd thought were gone kicked in, and he wrapped his arms around her to pull her close.

"It's okay, Angel. I'll protect you," he promised blindly.

A year ago, she'd said the same thing to him. He knew without a doubt she'd meant those words as much as he meant them now. She'd seen him through the hardest thing he'd ever done—leaving behind everything he knew and loved. He'd still been recovering from six gunshot wounds that should have ended his life.

Correction: they *had* ended his life.

Chapter Seven

Angel wasn't sure how it had leaked, but there was her photo on the news section of the browser. The name Angel Larson, not Aubrey Daniels, was printed under it. The write-up said she was a special agent gone rogue, which meant they probably didn't know she actually worked for the U.S. Marshals Service. It also listed her as armed and extremely dangerous.

True enough—though she was only dangerous to two people: the real killer, and the person who had given her up. Were they one and the same?

She needed to get a message to Thorne. He would be worried.

Looking over Colton's prehistoric computer setup, her gaze landed on a printer/copier/fax machine. Only somewhat newer than his tower.

"I have an idea," she said more to herself, knowing discussing her plan would just frustrate him again. Colton was a smart guy with a quick wit. His lack of computer savvy was due to disinterest rather than an inability to comprehend.

That was fine. He had plenty of other skills she appreciated. Although a good number of those skills were off-limits.

She needed to dig up a viable lead so she could be on her way. She wanted to get her life back and let Colton get back to his.

"Are you hungry?" he asked.

She hadn't realized how hungry she was until he mentioned it. Her stomach growled in answer before her mouth had the chance. Pudge lifted his head, which had been resting on her foot.

"Yes, very," she admitted.

"I'll go make dinner while you wreck my system. Please, just save my spreadsheet. If I lose those grades there'll be a hundred and twenty students beating down the door, desperate to graduate in a few days."

"I won't lose anything," she promised as she popped his memory card back in place and snapped on the cover.

For the next few minutes she used his word processing program and added some palm trees from his design software to create a vacation flyer. She included a few phone numbers, which were actually an encrypted code only Thorne would understand.

After removing the return fax number from the program, she let out a breath and sent the fax to Thorne's office. He always complained that the only thing he ever got on his fax machine was vacation offers. It just pissed him off because he was too busy to take a vacation. When he did take a vacation, it wasn't to a tropical island. It was to spend time with his daughter, who was in witness protection herself—a daughter he'd only met several months ago.

Having a fax machine at a federal agency might sound antiquated, but sending a fax over an analog phone line was actually still one of the safest ways to move data. No one could hack into a phone line and read the data.

As she sent out her fax, Colton showed up at the door with plate and a sheepish look.

"That smells delicious. What is it?"

"Eggplant parmesan." He handed it over, looking as if he wanted to say something more.

"Left over from your date this evening?" she asked with a lopsided smile.

Yes, she was fishing to see if he'd had a date. It was Friday night. Though, if he'd been out on a date it hadn't lasted very long. Who came home from a date at nine thirty unless it wasn't going well?

"Retirement party for one of my colleagues."

She sensed something more behind those words, but the food was too good to waste time talking.

"And no. It's not leftovers. I made it from scratch."

"You did?" she mumbled with her mouth full. "It's really good." Still eating, she followed him back out to the kitchen. She was going to want more.

"I've taken up cooking, since I don't have much else to do." He looked a bit embarrassed by that.

It was obvious he'd made the best of his situation. Last year, he'd had the usual concerns about starting over and leaving his life and family behind. But he seemed to be doing better in his new world than she'd expected.

There was a photo hanging on the refrigerator—Colton surrounded by three teenagers wearing matching T-shirts for a math league competition.

The smile on his face told her they'd won, even if she'd missed the trophy.

Humming to himself, he tossed a towel over his shoulder and carried the rest of the food to the table. She sat down next to him and reached for a roll, still warm from the oven. Heaven.

She must have made a yummy noise because when

she opened her eyes, his were focused on her face. She remembered the way his hazel eyes reminded her of a stormy sea when he was aroused.

She swallowed and concentrated on her plate. Maybe her yummy-food noise was too similar to her good-sex sounds. She'd have to watch that from now on.

She couldn't afford to get involved with Colton. Not like that. It had hurt too much the first time she'd had to leave. If she didn't stay focused, she might not survive when she had to leave this time.

And she would definitely need to leave. She couldn't stay here forever, hoping someone else stumbled across the real killer. She needed to figure out who had set her up, and make them pay for what they did to Heath.

Which would mean leaving Colton.

Again.

She glanced over at him. He seemed content. Happy, even. He wasn't looking at her anymore, so she took a moment to study him closer—his strong jaw and light brown hair with hints of gold mixed throughout. He'd been blond when he was younger. She'd seen a photo in his file.

She let out a sigh of regret.

She'd been so selfish when she stormed into his home and disrupted his life.

She swallowed down a bite of food and frowned. "I'm sorry I barged in here and really messed up your evening."

"I'm glad you're here," he said before jumping up to go into the kitchen again.

As much as she might like it, things could not go back to the way they'd been when she was protecting him. They couldn't afford to get personally involved. It had been against the rules before, and any kind of relationship would be highly unwise now.

At any moment, she might need to leave again.

As she finished the best meal she'd eaten in months, she realized it had been a huge mistake to come here. Seeing him again was dredging up memories and emotions best left buried.

But she hadn't had any other choice.

Or maybe she hadn't tried hard enough to come up with other choices…

She told herself she didn't have anywhere else to go, and needed somewhere safe to stay while she figured out her next move.

But maybe that wasn't the real reason.

If she were a stronger person, she'd just admit to herself that she'd wanted to see him again.

If she were a better person, she would have kept her distance to begin with, instead of getting him involved and putting him in danger.

As he walked back into the dining room, their eyes met again…and her heart sank.

She might be a strong person, but she'd never pretended to be a good one.

Chapter Eight

Angel was quiet the rest of the evening. Colton offered her his bed, but she declined, so he made up the sofa with a blanket and pillow, knowing he wouldn't win that argument.

"How are you for weapons?" he asked her.

She pulled out two semi-automatics—her standard issue Glock 40 and a smaller Beretta PX4—and set them on the coffee table. Then she extracted three extra clips from her front pockets.

"So, pretty good then," he joked.

She smiled, but it wasn't her normal smile. Not the smile that haunted him every night when he closed his eyes. Was she scared?

He couldn't blame her if she were. She was a wanted fugitive. But he wanted to put her mind at ease.

"I have a bolt hole in my closet. The floor pulls up and it leads to the crawlspace under the house."

He knew normal people didn't need to think about such things. But he'd created an escape plan before he'd even unpacked his clothes. He figured he was safe for now. Viktor Kulakov thought he was dead. And even if he suspected Colton was still alive, he would have to dig through layers of cover before he would find Colton's real name or his family.

The DEA had made sure his family would be safe. There were too many of them to move into the WITSEC program. Though, some days he selfishly wished they'd been forced to come with him. He hated the idea that his family thought he was dead. They'd lost his dad when they were younger, and now Colton. He wished there was a way to tell them he was alive and well.

Even if he hadn't felt alive in months and didn't consider the unrelenting loneliness as being all that well.

Still, he wasn't dead.

His exit plan meant he had a chance to stay alive if anyone ever did show up wanting to do a better job at killing him than the last time.

"The hatch from under the house leads to the backyard," he said. "When you get to the yard, stick to the fence on the left. Follow it the whole way to the end. There is a small garage across the alley. I own it. There's a vehicle inside. Keys are in the pocket behind the seat. It's stocked. Food, water, ammo. Anything you would need to get away."

She digested all that for a moment, then said, "Thank you, Colton."

He let out a breath. "Thanks for saying my name. It's been so long since I've heard it spoken aloud, it almost doesn't sound like it belongs to me anymore."

Her brows creased. "What is your new name? I don't remember. I just memorized your address."

He'd always thought she'd chosen it on purpose as some kind of silly joke. But maybe not.

"Duncan Willis," he told her, watching her face intently to see if there was a hint of recognition. Nothing.

She scrunched up her nose. "Duncan?"

"It took two whole days for some high school punk to come up with the nickname Dunking Willies."

The laughter spurted out of her, and she covered her mouth with her hand in an effort to keep it in.

"They sometimes add a Scottish accent. *Dunkin' Weelies.*" He used his best brogue to send her into another round of hysterics.

"I'm s-sorry. That's not f-funny," she stammered.

He might have believed her if she wasn't still laughing. "I don't know what this says about your sense of humor."

She snorted. "Are you kidding? Normally I'm in the fifth-grade boy range. I feel like I've matured to high school level."

"You're the epitome of maturity," he drawled.

"Whoa. Hold on a second. Don't go using big words on me." She was still laughing. "I see your mouth moving, but I don't know what you're saying."

He rolled his eyes. "Get some sleep," he ordered to end the mocking.

She nodded, but he knew she wouldn't. Angel didn't sleep. She rested in short spurts, but never slept deeply, or for very long. He'd always wondered if she'd conditioned herself that way for the job, or if it was caused by something else.

He paused by the edge of the living room. Pudge had already claimed a spot next to the sofa. Apparently, he was staying with her. That suited Colton just fine. Angel needed the heightened senses Pudge offered.

"In case you're not here when I wake up, I wish you the best." He took a breath. "It was nice to see you again."

He shouldn't have said that last part, but he couldn't help it. It *had* been nice to see her. It had also been nice to hold her in his arms for that short moment. At the table earlier, he'd wanted to lean over and kiss her so badly he'd actually almost done it.

And when she'd made that moan of satisfaction over the food, his body had reacted to the sound just as it had in the past when he'd elicited a similar response from her.

But not from his cooking.

They'd been great together. The sex had been hot and fun. Their attraction had always seemed to hit them while doing the most mundane things. Once when she'd been cleaning her gun, they'd ended up rolling around on the floor. Another time, he'd been moving laundry from the washer to the dryer and she'd practically attacked him.

It had been perfect…except at the end of each amazing time with her, there had always been regret in her eyes. As soon as they dressed, she would repeat her warning about how they shouldn't get close. It wouldn't end well. Blah, blah, blah.

He should have believed her.

With a sigh, he headed for his room. He'd almost escaped into the hall when he heard her voice.

"I'll see you in the morning," she called.

His heart seized, and he had to fight to keep from going back to her and begging her not to leave.

She'd said those same words the night she left him.

Chapter Nine

Angel stretched out on the sofa and closed her eyes. She felt safe in Colton's home. The giant dog sneaking up onto the sofa next to her helped with that.

"Don't worry, I won't tell," she whispered, recalling Colton didn't approve of dogs on the furniture. "Just make sure you're off before he gets up."

Pudge adjusted his large body, taking up more than his half of the couch.

Which was fine. She wouldn't be sleeping, anyway. She had too many things to think about. Though…her priorities were a bit out of sorts at the moment.

Instead of focusing on who could have killed Heath, set her up for the murder, and stolen his prototype, she was distracted by how easy it was to be with Colton. She'd assumed it would be awkward between them, but it wasn't as bad as she'd expected.

Of course, they hadn't talked about what happened before. Not just the sex. But the late nights of poker and talking. It had been so easy to tell him how scared she'd felt on her first assignment for Phoenix. He'd told her about his first day at DEA, and how he'd been just as scared. She didn't tell him all the gory details of her past, but she'd felt she could have, if ever she decided she wanted to.

Then one night as they were building giant sundaes at one in the morning, a whipped cream battle transformed into a spark, lighting up the attraction they'd both been trying to ignore.

Abandoning all control, they'd reached for each other, melting into a kiss that had touched her soul. Sticky fingers roamed under clothes, and melted ice cream smeared across the counter when he lifted her up to take her right then and there. Neither cared that they'd knocked over the fudge topping and rainbow sprinkles.

The shower afterward had been a colorful affair.

She smiled at the memories as she lay there in the darkness of his living room. She hadn't eaten ice cream since, knowing it wouldn't satisfy her fully. Knowing it would make her think of him, and she already did that enough without the reminders.

Back then, they'd been playing house. Both of them knew it was short term, but neither had allowed it to ruin their time together. Which made it much more difficult when she'd walked away. She'd thought it was just a casual affair, but she'd been wrong.

He hadn't brought up any of that tonight. Nor had he accused her of being the coward she knew she was.

Just as well. If he wanted to pretend it hadn't happened, she would go along with that plan. She wouldn't be here long enough for it to matter.

As soon as she had a lead, she would leave, and he could go back to his normal life.

Without her.

Chapter Ten

Colton tossed for what felt like the twentieth time in fourteen minutes. He couldn't fall asleep. And who could blame him?

His sleeplessness wasn't because there was a wanted fugitive sleeping under his roof. Or because said fugitive was also sexy as hell. No, his restlessness was caused by his fear that she would sneak out in the middle of the night, and he'd be right back where he was before she showed up on his doorstep.

Alone and bored out of his mind.

Spending the evening at a yawn-fest retirement party hadn't helped. It was too easy to see himself with gray hair, sitting in front of a cake that wished him a happy remainder of his already tedious life.

Was that all there was in store for him? Day after day of monotony, until the day he died?

"God damn," he muttered, and tossed again. There had been a few dark moments when he'd missed his family and the loneliness had been so overwhelming he'd actually wondered if he would have been better off *not* surviving being shot half a dozen times in the chest.

It sometimes seemed as if he was being punished for cheating death.

But for the moment, he had something important to do—keep Angel safe. He almost hadn't recognized the surge of adrenaline in his blood when she'd stepped out of the shadows on his porch. It had been so long since anything had sparked his fight or flight response, he'd worried it didn't work anymore.

Fortunately, his instincts weren't in such bad shape. He'd drawn his Glock pretty damn quick. It had felt good.

Most people wouldn't like finding an intruder on their back porch—even a hot one—but Colton had been yearning for something exciting to happen. He'd been raised for danger and didn't know how to function without it in his life.

For most of his adult years, he'd either been a soldier or a DEA agent. His life had been a constant rush of activity. His brain was conditioned to jump ahead and anticipate his enemy's next move. His body had been trained to be sure and swift.

Now he spent his days with teenagers who didn't think they needed math because they had a calculator on their phone, and he occupied his evenings with more cooking shows than was healthy.

He heard the telltale jingle of his dog's collar and tags moving down the hall toward his room. He knew what would happen next. Sure enough, he felt the dip of the mattress next to him.

"Off," he said firmly but quietly, so as not to wake Angel if she'd managed to fall asleep.

There was a snuffle, then the bed moved again and the jingling moved out of the room. Angel had probably allowed Pudge up on the sofa, so the dog had decided to test his limits.

Not that Colton was complaining. It was nice having Angel here. And despite what he'd said to her earlier, he figured she'd hang around at least long enough for him to pick up the computer she'd ordered after dinner. So he finally let himself drift off to sleep.

It seemed like only a few minutes later when he awoke to the sound of Pudge barking like crazy.

It was still dark.

And someone was definitely outside.

Chapter Eleven

Angel jerked awake at the loud barking.

Amongst the chaos came the sound of muffled voices from the sidewalk. She rolled off the sofa, grabbing her guns on the way, and crouched by the large front window trying to see how many there were.

Colton lived on a quiet street in a peaceful neighborhood. It wasn't the kind of place where people hung out at one in the morning having a chat.

She rolled to the other side of the window, hoping to get a better view.

Nothing.

"Shh," she told Pudge who was still happily fulfilling his duty of ferocious watchdog. "You're going to wake up—"

"What's happening?" Colton asked as he slid down the wall next to her. He pulled the slide back on his Glock and chambered a bullet.

She was momentarily distracted by the hotness of the maneuver, but made herself focus. "I'm not sure. But they're coming for me. You should put your gun away. Just say I forced you to help me."

"Not a chance." His hazel eyes narrowed in offense.

She honestly couldn't tell if it was a moral issue, or the fact that he didn't want anyone to think a hundred-and-twenty-pound female had forced him to do anything.

A thump at the door made Pudge go nuts. He growled and snarled with murderous intent.

"*Mālie*," Colton snapped.

Pudge instantly quieted at the command, but paced frantically.

"You've trained him?"

"Of course."

"What language is that?" It was common in K-9 units to use a different language so only the trainer knew the commands. But she hadn't recognized the one Colton had spoken.

"Hawaiian."

Her jaw dropped. He'd trained his German shepherd to respond to *Hawaiian* commands? Not the textbook German or Austrian for him. Oh, no. Hawaiian.

"What?" he asked, sounding defensive.

"Nothing. Good choice." She pressed her lips together to keep from snickering. She had bigger problems.

Another thump by the window had the dog barking again.

"I'm going to open the door," Colton said.

"I'm sorry. I shouldn't have come." She braced herself against the wall behind the door, hoping he wouldn't do anything stupid on her account.

"Stop. I'm glad you're here. Sit tight."

Angel wasn't good at sitting tight. Normally she took lead. Her being shorter than the other team members gave them all an advantage. Criminals always expected someone taller in a raid than her five feet three inches.

Staying back and cowering against a wall was not her favorite position.

In a rush of movement, Colton opened the door to release Pudge.

"*Hele!*" he yelled to the dog, then pointed at Angel. "Stay."

She wondered if he'd gotten the two orders mixed up. But he moved through the door with his gun raised, and pulled the door shut behind him.

"Damn it!" She peered through the frosted sidelight to make out what was happening in Colton's front yard.

All she could see was chaos, with a lot of shouting and barking.

Damn it! She was going to prison, and Colton would be charged with accessory.

Shit. This was all her fault.

Chapter Twelve

"Kenny Millard?" Colton stared down at the pale boy being held in place by a ninety-pound dog. An egg rolled out of the kid's hand and stopped right next to Colton's bare feet.

He might have put on shoes before launching his attack if *somebody* hadn't eaten them earlier.

"*Hookuu,*" he told Pudge, who stepped back with one last bark.

"Mr. Willis? This is *your* house?"

"It is."

"Is that a—a *gun*? Are you going to shoot me? It was just a few eggs!"

"Who ran off?" Colton demanded. "Was it that Braden kid?"

"Uh…"

"Do not even *try* stonewalling me. You have three seconds to answer, or I call the dog back."

"Y-yeah. It was Braden. This was all his idea."

"Of course it was."

Colton tucked the Glock in his waistband as the lights came on at the house next door. Mr. Simon was a great neighbor. Always kept to himself. But Colton couldn't blame him for investigating the racket. It was the middle of the night, and it probably sounded like World War III had started on Colton's lawn.

"There's a hose on the side of the house," he told Kenny. "Use it to clean up the mess, then go home. Tell your partner I want both of you at school and in my room by seven thirty on Monday morning."

"We don't have school on Monday."

"Seven thirty Monday morning, or I call the cops. It's up to you."

"Fine. We'll be there." Kenny stood on wobbly legs and paused. "Do you always carry a gun?"

Colton grimaced. *Damn it to hell.* If he had to move because of the gun he wasn't supposed to own, Angel would never let him live it down. But after a lifetime of carrying, he'd felt too vulnerable without a weapon. Naked.

"It's just an air pistol," he said. "I thought you were a burglar. Now, go home."

Pudge barked once more to back him up. He patted his dog on the head for a job well done. Then he turned to go back in the house.

He just hoped Angel was still there.

Chapter Thirteen

Angel was opening the back door, ready to run, when Colton came in the front door with Pudge at his heels.

Great. She'd waited too long to make a clean escape. Mostly because she hadn't been able to get her feet to move.

It wasn't fear that had prevented her exit. It was something else she didn't want to think about. The last time she'd felt it had been the night a year ago when she'd left Colton. Like tonight, she'd hesitated and paced the safe house for precious minutes before finally making herself leave.

"Where are you going?" he asked.

"I have to go away. It's too risky to stay."

"Wait just a second." He put his hand up in the way one might gentle a skittish horse. "It was just some kids egging my house. It wasn't the FBI or the police. We're safe."

Angel swallowed and shook her head. "No. I'm going to turn myself in."

"The hell you are," he said, his brows pulled together.

"I'll turn myself in, and this mess will all get straightened out. My boss knows I didn't kill anyone."

It was too dangerous any other way. She should have turned herself in from the start. Now it would look even worse because she ran.

"Good. Do you think they'll let your boss sit on the jury? Do you think they'll let him sit in all twelve seats? You told me what happened; it sounds pretty bad for you. What if you can't prove you didn't do it? What if you end up in jail?"

She puffed out a breath and frowned. He was right.

"I hate putting other people in danger."

"The other people don't mind that much. Do we, Pudge?"

Pudge barked his reply as if he was actually agreeing.

"The last time we were in this situation, you were in charge," he said. "Now it's my turn to give the orders and your turn to listen."

Her lips twitched at the command in his voice. "I don't remember you listening to my orders all that much." She folded her arms across her chest, nodding toward the gun in his pants.

"I listened to the important ones."

She didn't argue. She would have done the same.

"Tomorrow, I'll go pick up the laptop and the other wizardry you've ordered," he said, "and you can do your voodoo to get us a lead."

She liked how he said "us."

"And if I can't?"

"We'll come up with something."

"You're sure about this? I wouldn't mind one bit if you wanted me out of your home." In fact, it would be better if he kicked her out. Then she wouldn't be able to keep making up excuses to stay.

He stepped closer, his head bent down so he was looking her right in the eyes. For a second she thought he might kiss her. She may have swayed toward him in anticipation. Her mind had entered that hazy space when thinking became secondary and urges ruled her actions.

But instead of pressing his lips to hers in the way she'd wanted since she left his place that night a year ago, he turned his head and whispered in her ear.

"This is the most fun I've had since you left." He backed away. "I've been losing my mind from boredom. Please stay."

She nodded as disappointment and desire hummed through her body in equal measure.

Because he only wanted an adrenaline rush, some excitement.

He didn't want *her*.

Chapter Fourteen

God, how he wanted Angel.

Colton had nearly given in and kissed her, but he hadn't. Because it would have been a bad idea. Or at least she seemed to think so. He was all for picking up where they'd left off. He welcomed the electricity between them.

But she clearly chose to ignore it, so he decided to go along with her plan.

For now.

He'd scared her off the last time by asking her to stay with him. He'd put his feelings out there, and they'd been too much for her. He needed to do better this time. Play it cool and act like their attraction was no big deal.

But he didn't want her to leave. Or worse yet—turn herself in.

"Let's just get some sleep, okay?"

"Okay," she agreed, and let her bag slide down her arm to the floor. She was staying. For now.

"We'll figure it out in the morning."

She nodded again as he turned to leave the living room. Pudge whined, looking back and forth between them, obviously struggling with his loyalties.

"You're a good boy. You scared the shit out of that kid." Colton gave his furry friend a pat and a rub behind the ears, and stood. He pointed to the floor, telling the dog to stay with Angel. "See you in the morning."

Once again he left her alone, not sure if he really would see her in the morning. But he didn't have a choice. Short of tying her to a chair, he couldn't make her stay if she didn't want to be there.

He'd just have to trust her.

Even if that hadn't worked out for him so well the last time.

Chapter Fifteen

Angel was still asleep when Colton stopped in the living room on the way to the kitchen early the next morning.

Pudge raised his head from his spot on the end of the sofa, and Colton rolled his eyes. He wouldn't scold him. He'd earned the luxury the night before.

But just that small movement from the dog caused Angel to wake with a start. He remembered sleeping with her in his bed, and the way she always woke up ready for battle. There was being ready...and there was overkill.

He'd asked her once who she thought she was fighting, but she'd never answered. She kept her demons a secret, but he knew they lurked under the surface.

"Shh. It's just me," he whispered, though it was too late to be quiet. "Good morning."

"Morning," she mumbled.

She squinted at the clock and frowned. No doubt she was irritated with herself for sleeping an entire hour straight through. He didn't know how she functioned, but he was pretty sure she'd managed that way for a long time.

"Coffee?" he offered, heading into the kitchen.

"Yes, please."

"Frittata?" He'd been eager to try a new recipe, but it had seemed silly to go to the fuss for one person.

"Is that the egg thing that is basically an omelet that you don't flip?"

"It's a little different. The egg mixture isn't quite the same. It's dense, whereas you want an omelet to be light and fluffy."

"Wow. That's a lot more about eggs than I ever needed to know." When she smiled, he squeezed the handle of the spatula hoping to keep a grip on the utensil as well as himself. "Maybe you should have asked that kid last night if he had any extra eggs."

"That kid is one of my students. I'll be surprised if he doesn't tell everyone in the world I pulled a gun on him."

She frowned. "We may need to move you if there's trouble."

She must have forgotten she didn't have the authority to help relocate him at the moment.

"Let's deal with your problems before we start worrying about mine."

His comment wiped the smile from her face and turned her skin slightly pale. He hadn't meant to snap her back to reality so harshly. Still, she needed to realize the trouble she was in. Last night it was students with eggs, tomorrow night it could be the SWAT team and the FBI. They needed to be prepared for anything.

As soon as they finished breakfast.

Chapter Sixteen

Angel watched Colton at the stove as he made her breakfast. He was damn sexy doing nothing at all, but somehow cooking made him all the more attractive. She especially liked the way his muscles flexed when he whisked the eggs.

A year ago, that would have been enough to launch them into a heated frenzy. Clothing would have been pulled off and tossed haphazardly. He would have picked her up and placed her on the counter while kissing her. They would have groaned together when they joined in an urgent rush.

He would have held back until she cried out her satisfaction, then afterward they would have collapsed back on the counter without a care as to what was displaced in their moment of passion.

But today it was just breakfast. The only action happening on the counter was him plating up their eggs.

He was different than he'd been a year ago. He seemed… content.

Back when he'd first been put in protection, he didn't

know what to expect from his new life. He was focused on one goal—putting Viktor Kulakov behind bars. After spending two years undercover, Colton had evidence on the mobster for trafficking not only drugs, but humans, in and out of the country.

But before Colton could get out, Kulakov had one of his people take Colton down. Six shots to the chest. How he'd survived she still didn't know. She'd seen the scars, four bullets had gone through, and two had to be pulled out.

It was easy to make everyone believe he'd died, mainly because he should have. But he'd survived, and had been ready to testify. Except it didn't work that way.

He had been concerned about his brothers—three older and one younger—and their families. They, along with everyone else, had been told he'd died from his injuries. It was the best way to protect him, as well as his family.

She remembered the day his next oldest brother, John, had seen her at the edge of the cemetery. Rather than run off, she pretended to be visiting a different grave. She should have thought to bring flowers.

He'd greeted her with a smile and told her he was glad she was there.

For a moment, Angel had worried she'd met the man before and he knew who she worked for. All of Colton's brothers worked in law enforcement, out of respect for their father who had died in the line of duty. But she'd never met John before.

He told her she looked like an agent of some sort, and that could only mean one thing—that his brother was still alive and living somewhere else. He'd asked her to tell Colton something. "Tell him I'll see him again sometime."

She hadn't given Colton the message. At the time it had seemed cruel to get his hopes up about reuniting with his brother. It was hard enough to start over. It had to be a lot worse to leave people behind.

She hadn't had that issue when she'd started her own new life.

After breakfast, Colton left for the store armed with a list of things she needed to build her computer system. Once she was connected to the outside world, she hoped to find out who had murdered a good man while he slept, and stolen a priceless piece of technology.

She checked the television, seeing her face occasionally when a talk show ran the story of Heath's death. There was only so much of that she could watch before she started yelling at the TV, so instead, she straightened up Colton's already neat home and played with Pudge.

"Man, this is boring," she told the dog. "How does he stand living like this?"

Pudge didn't have an answer.

She was getting ready to toss the ball for what felt like the eight-hundredth time when Pudge alerted and barked.

"Is Daddy home?" she asked, thinking her words sounded both odd and appealing. Shaking it off, she went to meet Colton in the garage as soon as she heard the door close.

"Did you get everything?" She was actually bouncing with excitement. There was nothing better than getting a new computer. The speed and all that available memory. It was heaven.

"This thing cost thirteen hundred bucks," he complained. "Not to mention all this other stuff. I'm a teacher, Angel, not a billionaire."

She frowned, remembering the billionaire who'd died while she was supposed to be protecting him.

"I'll pay you back," she promised quickly. She should have considered the expense. Unfortunately, she didn't have access to her funds at the moment.

"Sure. Why don't you just write me out a check? I'm sure

no one will be looking at your bank accounts."

She narrowed her eyes on him. "When I get my life back, I'll pay you back for this stuff."

"Yeah, well, not everyone gets their life back," he said softly.

The truth hit her hard. Up until now she hadn't imagined she might need to stay hidden indefinitely. She knew she was innocent, and had assumed it wouldn't take long for the truth to come out. But it was possible she wouldn't ever find any proof.

It was possible she would never be cleared of this crime.

Chapter Seventeen

Seeing Angel's face go pale at his comment made Colton feel like an asshole, but she had to know the reality of the situation. She'd seen it enough in her line of work to know what could happen. Even if she managed to clear her name, she wouldn't be able to go back to work as though nothing had happened.

He didn't know much about the U.S. Marshals, but he knew the DEA didn't like having their agents' faces and names plastered on every television screen across the country. It made undercover work rather difficult.

To make his death realistic, his bank accounts had been distributed to his family as he'd requested in his will, which hadn't left a lot for him. And his teaching salary didn't come close to what he'd made with the DEA.

Still, he shouldn't have snapped at her. It wasn't really about the money.

He realized it wasn't the expense as much as what that shiny new computer meant—it was the path for her to be cleared. He didn't want to be a dick and stand in the way of her freedom. But as soon as it was safe for her to walk down the street without being arrested, she would be gone.

He'd already lived through that and wasn't looking forward to a replay.

She clutched the box to her chest and frowned. "They took my laptop. I'd had a spare, but I left it at home during my last assignment because I didn't want to carry two." She looked away. "I wasn't prepared."

For the first time since she showed up on his back porch, he realized she was blaming herself for this entire situation.

Been there, lived that.

When there was no way to make sense of something, the easiest thing to do was to blame yourself. He'd be damned if he was going to let her do it.

"This is not your fault," he told her firmly. "You could have had ten laptops, and Zeller would still be dead."

"Still, I should have been ready to run. I blew it. Garrett told me to have extra houses completely off the grid in case of something like this. I thought I did, but I didn't bury them well enough. They traced them back to me."

"Who is Garrett?"

"A former teammate. He left the team to go into WITSEC with someone."

So other marshals had gone into the program with someone they loved. But not her. Oh, no. She'd run off while he was sleeping. His anger flashed again.

And yet, it wasn't fair to blame her for wanting her life back. It wasn't right to be angry just because she hadn't wanted him as much as he'd wanted her.

She must have realized where his thoughts had gone because she quickly continued, "I had three places, but they turned out to be useless when I needed them most. When your face is everywhere, you can't even walk into Best Buy and purchase your own computer."

"We can't always think of everything," he said. "We're trained to think on our feet, plan for anything, but in real life there are things we simply can't anticipate."

"I still don't know how they drugged us that night."

"Both of you were drugged?" Colton asked, glad to focus on something else.

"I didn't see defensive wounds on Heath's hands, so he didn't fight."

Colton nodded. "There's some relief in knowing he wasn't aware of what was happening. He wouldn't have been frightened." A small relief, but a relief nonetheless.

"He was completely vulnerable because I missed something," she bit out.

And there it was. Full-on self-recrimination.

Angel wouldn't be able to rest until she'd solved this case. Even if it didn't help her get her old life back, she needed to know what it was she'd missed.

He'd felt the same way with Viktor. Colton had walked into the marina thinking his cover was solid. He'd been with Viktor for two years and didn't suspect the man was on to him, at all.

Colton always got nervous after an information drop or a call in. But it had been six days since he'd reached out to his handler with intel. He'd thought he was in the clear…right up until the moment Viktor nodded at Weller and the man had pulled out a gun and shot him. And apparently kept shooting.

Fortunately, Colton had blacked out.

To this day, he still didn't know what he'd done to tip them off. Maybe it hadn't been anything he'd done. Just as it probably wasn't anything Angel had done.

"I can't image you missed anything," he said soothingly. "You were more than thorough with me. All those little strips of paper you dunked in my water before I was allowed to drink it." He shook his head at the memory.

She dumped all her new gear in the living room and took over the coffee table to set it up. He would have offered to clean off the desk in the office, but he knew she wanted to be out in the living room with a clear view of the driveway.

"Do you mind if I sit over here and do some work? There's only one more week of school left, and I have some things I need to turn in."

"Sure. It's your living room. I'll try to leave a piece for you to live in." She smiled, causing his stomach to do that flipping thing, and reminding his dick it hadn't seen any action since he'd been with her a year ago.

He'd had a few offers, and there were a number of young teachers who appealed, but he couldn't risk it. He couldn't bring an innocent person into this life for more than a dinner here and there.

What if he fell in love, got married, had kids, and then ran into someone who knew Viktor? His options would be to walk away or to uproot his family and take them with him.

No, thanks.

He remembered being a little kid sitting by the window each night, hoping his dad would come home. By the age of twelve, he'd grown out of the constant worry. At age thirteen, his father was killed by an informant who couldn't pick a side.

Fortunately, Colton's three older brothers took on the job of male role model, but Colton didn't want his own children ever to have to go through that. Which was why he had never planned to have children. Or a wife, either, for that matter.

Though, he'd considered marriage with Angel a year ago. He hadn't wanted her to stay with him for the sex alone, though that would have been enough. He'd wanted a partner. An equal. And Angel was on the job. She could protect herself. It would have been different to be married to someone like her.

"Do you hate it?" she asked quietly, dragging him from his thoughts on marriage.

"Hate what?"

"Teaching."

He looked down at the tests in his hands and let out a sigh. "Not really."

She smiled, but pressed her lips together to crush it. "Do you *like* it?" she pushed.

The truth was, he did like it. He liked watching kids reach their potential. He especially liked helping the kids who didn't think they had any potential.

His bitterness toward the profession mostly came from the lonely nights and endless summer it provided. And maybe that his colleagues didn't carry guns.

He grimaced. "I don't like being Dunking Willies."

They laughed together, and he remembered the nights they'd stayed up late playing cards or video games. They'd laughed. Being with her was easy, fun.

"I've missed you," he said without thinking.

To his surprise, she didn't look away or brush it off.

"You would have changed your mind." She sounded so sure. As if maybe she'd thought about it and that truth had kept her from regretting her decision.

"I would have liked to talk to you about it, at least. Waking up to a guy named Justin on my sofa was not the best way to find out how you felt."

"Maybe not. But it was the best thing I could do for you."

He would have argued if he thought he had any hope of convincing her she was dead wrong.

At the time, his life had still been in upheaval, and she had been wild and exciting, but he was sure they would have been able to settle into a happy life together.

It was nice to think so, anyway.

Chapter Eighteen

"Okay, I'm up and running," Angel announced, startling Colton from his tests.

He looked up as she rubbed her palms together gleefully and started typing in a flurry.

He might have asked what she was looking for, but then she might actually tell him, and no doubt he wouldn't understand what the hell she was talking about.

For the next three hours, she sat on the floor in front of the coffee table tapping and clicking and sighing and cursing. Occasionally, she would stretch out a leg or twist her neck from side to side. Even Pudge had grown tired of her company and come to sit by Colton.

He'd finished grading the papers and was looking through a new textbook to be used in next year's curriculum. There had been a huge debate over the books at the teachers' meeting last week.

It seemed silly now that he was sitting in the same room with a woman on the run for murder. Everything came down to perspective.

It was human nature to complain about things, even if those things were nothing in comparison to other people's problems. He was just as guilty of doing that as the next guy.

He'd grown more and more miserable as the end of the school year approached. Knowing he didn't have any plans. But that was nothing compared to Angel's issues.

Despite all the tight places he'd been in, he'd never been on the run from his own side of the law. He admired her courage to go outside the protection of her team to seek justice.

He had every intention of standing by her side for this fight.

For as long as she let him.

Chapter Nineteen

"Maybe I should stay home," Colton said on Monday morning as Angel stretched and went to the kitchen for more coffee.

Not a chance. No way would she allow her presence to disrupt his life more than it already was. She knew it wouldn't be easy to convince him it was safe to leave the house. He wanted to protect her. She understood that perfectly, because she wanted to protect him, too. So she went for a different angle.

"What? And let those little shits with the eggs get away with vandalism? What's next for them? A little B and E? Maybe grand theft? You have to stop it before it starts. You have a chance to cut off crime before the criminal is even fully developed."

Okay, so she was laying it on a little thick. But there was a lot of truth to her words.

Colton just let out a sigh and frowned.

She knew he was worried about her, but she knew he also had another concern. One that was all her fault.

When she'd left like a thief in the night, she'd undermined his trust for her.

"I'll be here when you get back." She repeated her promise, hoping it had a different response this time.

He nodded unconvincingly "I get home around four. I'd planned to make Mexican lasagna for dinner. Would that be okay?"

God bless him, he was so domesticated he actually planned out his meals. She generally ripped open a box of mac and cheese. Occasionally she even had enough time to allow the pasta to cook completely.

"Yeah. That sounds great." It really did.

He paused in front of her, and for a brief moment she thought he might kiss her like every other husband who was leaving for work that morning.

But he just gave her a nod and told the dog to be good and keep watch.

She took her normal spot in the living room, and continued trolling the tech blogs and underground sites, looking for some clue as to who had that prototype.

Technology moved at the speed of light. Whoever had it would want to launch it before someone else developed something similar and took the wind out of their financial sails.

She'd already checked every major player, looking for a new patent or the beginnings of a press release.

Nothing.

If the person who stole it worked for a large company, there would be engineers and programmers already working on it. And those people would be talking about their new toy. They wouldn't be able to help themselves.

Confidentiality agreements might keep them from sharing the details, but they would still be chatting about having the next best thing. Bragging rights on these sites were the main purpose of their existence.

Once she located a person, she could track them to their company and find out the details.

But no one was talking.

Which could only mean the person who stole it didn't have a buyer already lined up.

Who would be so stupid as to try to move a piece of technology that was this hot, *and* connected to a murder? It wasn't as if they could take out an ad.

She had to be missing something.

"Why would someone steal something so valuable if they had no plans to sell it?" she asked Pudge who cocked his head to the side, then licked her knee.

She wondered if Colton talked to the dog as much as she did. Probably not.

Her computer *ding*ed with an incoming email, making her jump. No one on her team would be stupid enough to send her an email. The FBI would be watching their communications, waiting for one of them to reach out.

But it wasn't anyone from Task Force Phoenix. The email was from *redgamer3* at a public email account. She opened it to find three lines in small type.

WELCOME BACK.
IT TOOK YOU LONG ENOUGH.
ARE YOU READY TO PLAY?

"Well, well, Redgamer3. Who might you be?"

Chapter Twenty

Colton hid his disappointment when the two boys showed up. He'd almost hoped Kenny, and his accomplice, Braden, would have bailed, so he could pack up and go back home.

But there they were. Future bench warrants, eager to serve their time so they could move on to their next stellar idea.

"We're really sorry about your house, Mr. Willis," Braden said.

"Just *my* house? Are you sorry about the other houses you hit with eggs?"

"Oh, yeah. For real sorry about that."

Good. *For real sorry.* He refrained from rolling his eyes as he gestured toward the boxes in the middle of the room. The desks had all been moved to one side to make room to work.

"You're going to put those shelves together."

"Sweet. Do we get to use power tools?"

"No. You get to use the scrench that comes with it."

Colton held up the hybrid screwdriver-wrench device and handed it over to Kenny. Braden had already started rooting through the parts and was laying everything out.

This might not take that long, after all.

"Uh, Mr. Willis?" Kenny said while digging through the packing materials.

"Yeah?"

"There aren't any instructions."

"Oh, I know. I have them. Don't worry. If you do it wrong, I'll be sure to let you know, and you can take it apart and start over. It probably won't take you smart lads that many attempts."

They stood gaping for a moment, probably Colton's only moment of pleasure for the day until he got home.

Unless Angel was gone when he got home. He should have bought a telephone to plug in so he could call her. Did they still make telephones that plugged in? He could just imagine the look on the kid's face who'd assisted him through the laptop purchase when he asked for a plug-in phone.

It didn't matter if he had a phone or not. He couldn't keep her there if she decided it was too risky to stay. He just had to hope he'd survive it when she left. Because one thing was for certain. Whether it was today, someday next week, or a month from now, Angel Larson was going to leave him again.

Chapter Twenty-One

"Blast and damn," Angel cursed at the screen. She'd been locked out of a lead and spent an hour getting back in, only to find nothing. "I don't have time for this!"

Redgamer3 was a ghost. He knew all the tricks to keep her from finding out who he—or she—was. She'd traced him to a home improvement company and through two interesting porn sites, only to come back to her own computer. From there she'd backtracked and found the lead that led nowhere.

She stood to stretch her legs and refill her coffee. As she walked into the kitchen she realized Pudge hadn't barked to come back in from his morning walkabout.

He was practically an appendage. She wondered what could have kept him from barking at the door. Unease gripped her as she pulled her gun in case it was a who instead of a what that was keeping him outside.

"Please let it be a squirrel," she repeated like a mantra.

After checking through every window that faced the backyard, she finally opened the door and stepped out onto the porch.

There was Pudge, lying at the bottom of the four steps that led down to the yard. His side was moving up and down rapidly as he panted. It was apparent he was in some kind of distress.

Someone had taken down her dog.

And they were probably coming for her next.

Chapter Twenty-Two

"Shit. Pudge?" she called as she briefly scanned the yard for an attack, then ran to him. This wasn't like him. Nothing would keep him from coming to greet her with a big, sloppy lick.

Instincts told her she needed to secure the yard first. Someone might have done this to lure her out. They could be waiting in the shrubs Colton had strategically planted to give cover along the fence line.

Instead, she set her gun down so she could help her dog.

"Pudge? What's wrong, buddy?" Normally the dog communicated pretty clearly without the use of words, but this time it would have been a lot easier if he could just tell her what hurt. "Oh, God."

His eyes were open but unfocused. His breathing was labored and wheezy. Something was very wrong and she needed to get help.

"I'll be right back," she promised before running off.

Keeping her gun handy, she raced back inside and used

her computer to find a vet nearby. If this was a setup, they were slow to react. No one had jumped her yet. And heaven help them if they did. It was one thing to come after her, but to hurt an innocent animal was uncalled for. She would make them pay.

She'd made a habit of keeping all her things packed so she could run at a moment's notice. She needed to make sure there was no evidence left behind if Colton was suspected of harboring a fugitive. She couldn't let him take the fall.

It was a simple thing to toss her new laptop in the bag and strap it across her body. Getting the dog up was another matter.

She'd named him Pudge because when they had picked him up he was nothing but a pudgy ball of fur. He'd resembled a bear cub and fit in the crook of her arm.

Now at ninety pounds, he weighed almost as much as she did.

"Come on, baby. Up you go."

Using her rescue training, she managed to get him on her shoulders, and used her legs to push herself to a standing position.

"No more sharing my food with you, tubby."

God bless him, he let out a sad little whine of protest. It broke her heart.

"I'm hurrying, buddy. Please hold on, okay? I'm going to get someone to help you."

Following the instructions she'd memorized from the website, she pulled in at Dr. Westcott's office at eight minutes after twelve to see a sign on the door that said they were closed for lunch from noon to one.

Damn.

Pretending she couldn't tell time, she checked the door. It was locked.

The property was multi-purpose. The office was in a small

building, and a sidewalk connected it to a large residence. Hopefully that was where Dr. Westcott took his lunch breaks.

She rang the doorbell then knocked for good measure, all before realizing she hadn't considered any form of disguise.

Too late for that now. An older man opened the door with a frown on his face and the corner of a sandwich in his fingers.

"I'm so sorry, but my dog is dying. Please help him."

The man let out a sigh and nodded. "What kind?"

"German shepherd."

"Okay. Pull around back. It will be easier to get him in. I'll meet you there."

"Please hurry."

"Yeah, yeah. I'm hurrying." Though his response indicated he was put out, his voice was full of concern.

As she got back into the vehicle Colton kept for escape purposes, she realized she couldn't go back to his home after this. She was compromised.

If the vet succeeded, she would drop Pudge off and keep going. It was the only way to keep Colton safe.

The doctor met her by the door, and together they moved the dog into a narrow hall with a number of doors.

"The first room on the left," he instructed and gestured with his chin. "Up on the table."

Once Pudge was situated on the black vinyl, Angel positioned herself between the doctor and the door. Her gun was in the back of her jeans.

"So, what seems to be the problem?" he said more to the dog than to her. "Are you having trouble breathing...?"

"Pudge. His name is Pudge. He's a little over a year old," she said, sharing the information the doctor might need to save the dog.

"His tongue is swollen, and it's obstructing his airway."

"Was he poisoned?" she asked, guilt twisting her

stomach. If this animal was injured in order to get to her she would never forgive herself.

"Why would you assume he was poisoned?" the doctor asked, looking at her. Really looking at her.

Her fingers twitched and she tensed, ready to reach for her gun.

This was it. Her body prepared to run.

Chapter Twenty-Three

"No, no. You have it all wrong. Come on, guys. Think this through. It's a bookshelf. Why on earth would the shelves go vertically?" Colton pointed at the pile of parts at his feet.

"Um. I don't know." Braden turned to Kenny. "Is vertical the up and down one?"

"Yes. Be careful. He might pull the gun on you." Kenny eyed Colton suspiciously.

Damn it.

"I'm ten feet from you. I can hear you talking," Colton reminded the brainiacs.

"Are you carrying the gun now?"

"No." Yes, he was. Since there weren't students in the building today, the metal detectors were off.

"I looked it up and I think it was a Glock," Kenny said. If Colton had punished them with research on firearms he would have been able to leave by now.

"I told you it was an air pistol."

"Nope. See." Kenny proceeded to pull out his phone and

held it out so Colton could see a photo. "The hole in the end of it was a lot bigger than an air pistol. Believe me, I got an up close and personal look at the hole."

It was time to abandon the pretense of an air pistol. Kenny was obsessed.

"It's perfectly legal for someone to keep a firearm for home protection. And had you two bandits been packing more than eggs, I would have been prepared to defend my home from intruders."

"Can you teach us how to shoot it?" Kenny asked.

Part of Colton wanted to say no and go about his business, but the teacher in him—the person who thought maybe these two could turn out to be something better if someone just spent a little time with them—nodded. He could replace their fascination for guns with a healthy respect for firearms.

"Write down your parents' phone numbers on this paper. I'll contact them and make sure it's okay. But it won't be for a few weeks. I have other plans."

Other plans, like helping a fugitive hide from the police while she hunted down the real killer. He could only imagine their faces if he actually said that out loud.

The selfish part of him—the part that wanted to spend more time with Angel—hoped his plans would take more than a few weeks.

Hell, he'd be happy if it took the rest of his life. Except he knew Angel wouldn't want to spend the rest of her life hiding out in his three-bedroom rancher.

"Cool!" Kenny said as he jotted down a number and slid the paper over to Braden.

"If I teach you how to shoot a gun, you'd better use the skill for good. Like saving someone."

"Definitely." Braden shoved Kenny's arm.

"We could become cops. They don't have to go to college." Kenny practically beamed with excitement.

"They can't have a juvenile record, either. So, no more vandalism." Colton pointed out.

"No problem. We promise." Kenny held up four fingers. Obviously he hadn't been a Boy Scout. Shocker.

"You won't be able to become cops if you spend the next four years building this bookcase. Get back to work."

"Can you give us a hint?"

Because Colton wanted them to be done so he could get back to Angel, he conceded and told them where to put the brackets.

When they both nodded with renewed hope, he tucked the instruction sheet away and went back to thinking about Angel and what she might be up to.

He hoped her day was going well.

Chapter Twenty-Four

"I don't think he was poisoned." The doctor looked back to his patient, posing no threat to Angel for the time being. She was still poised by the door. She knew she could outrun him if it came to that, and the gun pressing against her spine ensured she could get away.

If she had to.

"I'm going to guess he tried to take on a bee and lost."

The man moved to a cabinet and removed a yellow box. His movements were sure and slow, but she was jumpy and flinched when he snapped the seal on the flap.

"I'm just going to give him a shot to counteract his body's reaction." He glanced over at her. "Can you come around and talk to him while I inject him. It won't hurt, but I don't want him to be frightened."

This would mean giving up her spot by the only exit. She would be cornered.

But Pudge needed her help.

She let out a breath of determination and moved around

the table.

"It's okay, baby. It's just a shot. It will help you. Don't be scared," she soothed, though she knew dogs could smell fear, and she must reek of it by this point.

Pudge didn't so much as twitch when the shot was administered to the scruff of his neck.

"Now, let's see if there's anything else—"

"Dr. Westcott?" a woman called from the front of the building. "You're back early."

Angel's panic must have been easy to read, because the doctor reacted instantly.

"My assistant. Get in here," he whispered as he held open a closet door and, without thinking, she squeezed in among the boxes.

Not only was she not close to a door, but now she was trapped in a tiny space. What was the doctor doing? Would he write the woman a note telling her to call the police? Would he block the door until they got there?

"Who's this?" the woman asked.

"This is Pudge. He decided to eat a bee. But the bee bit him back. Didn't it, boy?"

"He's gorgeous. Where's his person?" the woman asked.

"She had to run back home. Forgot her wallet."

Shit. She *didn't* have a wallet. She'd left her stash of money and credit cards in her own vehicle. The escape plan had been to take Colton's car to the storage facility to get her own.

She hadn't even thought about money. Her primary concern was to get help. Damn. How was she going to pay this man for his services, and his loyalty?

"Okay. I'll start a file for Pudge. Should I let your one o'clock know there will be a wait?"

"No. I think I'll be done in time."

"Okay."

Angel heard jingling, much as she heard when Pudge left a room, but lighter. The closet door opened and the doctor frowned at her.

"Tell me I won't be sorry for not turning you in when I had the chance," he whispered and raised a furry brow.

Chapter Twenty-Five

"I didn't kill Heath Zeller," Angel assured the vet, looking him right in the eye, hoping to convince him of her innocence.

"Hell, I know that." He grumbled as if she'd insulted him.

"How can you be so sure?"

"This dog trusts you, even when he's scared. Animals know people better than people know people. You can't be all that bad. Plus, you rushed him in here not caring that I might have called the police." His voice was still low, so as not to alert his assistant.

"He's not really my dog, but I had to help. No matter what happened."

The vet nodded once, went to the door, and stepped out in the hall. "Rose? Can you go pick up a package at the post office? The green card is on my desk. I was going to do it at lunch, but I got tied up."

"Sure thing, Dr. Westcott. Can you cover the phones?"

"Yes. I'll be fine until you get back. Thanks."

The front door opened and closed, and the doctor came

back into the exam room.

Pudge was breathing easier by now. The medicine was working. He whined and Angel rubbed his neck to comfort him.

"It's okay, boy," she soothed.

The doctor petted him, then pried his mouth open, which Pudge didn't care for.

"My, what big teethies you have," the doctor joked, as if Angel was any other pet owner instead of a wanted murderer.

"I'm going to need you to hold him down. I see the stinger in his tongue."

"Pudge," she complained. "Why were you eating bees?"

She leaned on his shoulder and rubbed his chin as the doctor made quick work of grabbing his tongue. Using tweezers, he yanked the stinger out of Pudge's tongue.

"There you go," Dr. Westcott announced.

"I have a problem." Angel bit her bottom lip.

"Nationwide manhunt is a little more than a problem, I'd say."

"No. The thing you said about me forgetting my wallet."

He chuckled.

She grimaced. "Maybe you should have turned me in for the reward money to cover the bill."

"Nah. It's okay. One thing I've learned over the years is that everything works out."

She hoped that was true. If so, this man would win a billion dollars in the lottery and the people responsible for Heath's death would get hit by a meteor. She frowned at that last thought. No. Death by meteor was too good for them.

"Thank you," she said, knowing the words weren't enough to convey her gratitude.

He nodded.

"So, who do you think set you up?" he asked casually.

"I'm not sure yet. I'm still working on it."

"I guess it's kind of hard to conduct an investigation from behind bars."

"Yes. That's why I'm trying to stay on this side of those bars."

"Well, your friend here is good to go. Good luck to you." He patted Pudge and helped him down from the table.

"Thank you for everything." She'd never be able to thank him enough. Not only had he saved Pudge's life, but he'd saved her, as well.

She paused at the door wanting to tell him the truth.

"I really didn't kill Heath Zeller, but I have killed other people."

The man shook his head. "So have I. It's not the same thing. That's us doing our jobs."

She realized this was not just a veterinarian, but a veteran as well.

She nodded in understanding and respect, then patted her leg for Pudge to follow her out of the building.

While she wanted to trust the doctor, she also knew people changed their minds. Especially when rewards were involved.

It wasn't safe to go back to Colton's house.

Chapter Twenty-Six

"You two have ten minutes, then I'm leaving and you'll have to come back tomorrow," Colton threatened Kenny and Braden later that afternoon during their third try at the bookcases.

The boys groaned their displeasure.

"I gave you the instructions two hours ago and you still can't figure it out," he added so they understood how disappointed he was.

He'd thought his little lesson might spark some love of engineering, or at the very least, prepare them to be men—who never read instructions. But no. Ten minutes in, they'd already broken the scrench and lost three screws.

"I think we got it this time, Mr. Willis." The boys stood to the side, glowing with pride. Braden even held out his hands presenting their work.

"Good. Now move them over to the wall and put that pile of books on them."

"Any particular order?" Kenny asked.

"No." He didn't want to wait around while these two

mastered the alphabet. He just wanted to get home to Angel.

As he tossed his things in his bag, eager to leave, he was stopped by a loud *crack* and the sound of books falling to the floor.

"I told you that wasn't the way it went," Kenny challenged his partner in crime.

"I'll see you tomorrow morning. Seven thirty," Colton said as he rubbed his temples and sighed.

He was still muttering curses regarding the mental capacity of the neighbor boys when he pulled into the garage and got out of the car.

He would solve their problems tomorrow. For the rest of the evening, he would enjoy every moment he had with his guest.

The first sign something was wrong was the silence when he walked into the kitchen. Pudge wasn't eagerly greeting him, tail wagging and dancing in a circle to go out.

"Hello?" he called as he moved into the living room.

It looked like the same living room he'd been walking into for the last year. There was no laptop on the coffee table, bracketed by guns.

No beautiful woman sitting on the floor tapping away, completely oblivious to her surroundings.

"Oh, no."

He went out into the backyard and rushed to the gate. Across the alley, he opened the garage and went in. The space was damp and cool, but mostly it was empty.

His woman was gone. His dog was gone. And his 2004 Corolla was gone.

His life had become disturbingly similar to a country song.

Chapter Twenty-Seven

Running surveillance in a suburban neighborhood was difficult enough. Doing it with a rambunctious German shepherd who was still ramped up on epinephrine was a different kind of challenge. It bordered impossible.

Angel hid out, waiting for a few hours after Colton got home to make sure Dr. Westcott kept his word about not calling the cops. It would have been easy enough for him to write down the plate number as she drove away. The doctor had seemed sincere, but this was Colton's life, and she wouldn't take any chances. Especially not with a stranger.

Even so, she hated being suspicious of everyone and everything. This was no way to live—on the run and on her own.

Except, now she wasn't on her own. Colton was there to help. As much as she hated putting him in danger, she couldn't fight the urge to come back and see him again.

Maybe it was guilt over the way she'd left him without a word the last time...but she didn't think that was it. She needed him. And not just to give her shelter from a world that was hunting her.

It was time she was honest—if only with herself—about the real reason she'd come here.

She sighed, and petted the dog who had his head hanging out the open window.

"Do you want to go see Daddy?"

Once again, the reference tightened something in Angel's chest. She had never given a thought to having children. Her life, paired with her past, made it impossible. But every once in a while, a tiny thought would tug at her, and for a brief moment she found she wished she could have it—a normal family.

People to love her.

She had her team. Task Force Phoenix was her family. They'd taken her in and given her a life. But they weren't hers.

"God, I think I'm in big trouble," she told Pudge.

She didn't see anyone watching the house, and no suspicious vehicles had driven by repeatedly. When she felt confident it was safe, she pulled into the alley and parked next to the gate.

Pudge ran like a shot to the back door as soon as she let him through the gate. She was only halfway across the yard when the back door opened and man and dog greeted each other properly.

He was watching her steadily as she approached the back porch.

"I thought you left," he said, his voice steady, his face expressionless.

She wanted to kiss him. Kiss away the pain she could see haunting his hazel eyes. The pain *she* had caused.

Instead, she stayed a few feet back.

"And stole your dog?" Her brows creased.

"We both know he's more your dog than mine."

How great it had been the day they'd gone to pick up the puppy. For that moment, he had been *theirs*. Not his or hers.

"I told you I wouldn't leave." She expected him to throw the truth back in her face. That she'd said that same thing before, and hadn't kept her word.

"You took all your stuff." Even now his voice wasn't accusatory. Just stating a fact.

"We had an emergency. I wasn't sure if I would be able to come back." She still wasn't sure.

"Come tell me about it while we eat. I'm starving."

So was she.

Damn, it was good to be home.

Chapter Twenty-Eight

Colton didn't like that Angel had put herself in danger of being caught, but given the circumstances, he knew he would have done the same thing. And he was awfully glad she'd saved his dog.

"If you think it's not safe for me to stay, I can go. I watched the house to see if any cops went by. I didn't see anything suspicious, but that doesn't mean I'm in the clear. It's your call."

It wasn't his call. At least it wasn't his brain's call. His heart had already made the decision.

"Stay. If anything happens, we'll face it together. I think we would have seen something by now if the vet had called the police. They wouldn't wait around giving you time to flee."

This was true, but not the reason he wanted her to stay. Coming home to an empty house this afternoon had nearly ended him. He didn't want to be alone. He'd face whatever happened from this decision, as long as she was there when he got home tomorrow.

When they were done discussing the attack of the bumblebee, she asked about his day.

"Seriously? You expect me to tell you about my day after that story? I can't compete with that." His days of having exciting stories to share were over. Now he lived a mundane, boring life. His dad would call it an anybody job—his term for a job anyone could do. Being a cop was a somebody job, meaning you had to be somebody to do it. Somebody special.

Lately, Colton had begun to feel like nobody, special or otherwise.

Angel rolled her eyes. "Is that what we're doing? Competing? I kind of thought it was called sharing."

His own eyes went wide. She wanted to *share* something with him? This was big. Bigger than big. He cleared his throat, wanting for anything to share with her, wishing there was something more exciting to tell than the bookcase collapse.

"It was just a normal day." He couldn't help but frown.

"I don't know what a normal day is." She shrugged. "I've never had one. So I'd like to hear about yours."

"Okay." He shook his head, and told her about his day.

Eight minutes later, he wrapped up the story with the part where it all collapsed. She laughed and his heart yearned for something different.

For the last year, he'd missed her. Like crazy. He wished she would have stayed in his life, but back then it had just been loneliness. Now he saw what life could actually be like with her. Sharing stories about their day. No matter how mundane those stories were.

She assisted him with dinner, and he realized how much fun it was to cook with someone else. Especially when that someone was Angel.

It wasn't just about sex and a good time. It was all the parts that made up a life. He wanted all of them with her.

"Thank you for coming back," he said quietly, meaning it to the tips of his toes.

She nodded, but didn't say anything in return.

"You almost didn't?" he guessed. He was certain that had been the plan.

"I shouldn't have come back. The longer I stay here, the more I'm putting you at risk."

"Shouldn't that be my decision to make?"

She shrugged, but it was clear she didn't agree. Pudge had rested his chin on her leg at the sad sound of her voice.

"Did you train him to do that?" she asked.

"What? The puppy dog eyes? No. He came with those. Standard equipment."

They laughed, and the tense moment was over. She was here for now. Colton would enjoy the time he had with her. Even if he didn't know how much time he had.

"Before Pudge munched down a helping of bumblebee cordon bleu, did you find anything on the internet?"

"Actually, I had a lead, but lost it."

"I wouldn't be upset if it takes at least two more days. The school year is almost over."

"No problem, Colton. We can put off our secret agent mission long enough for you to hand out report cards."

"Thank you for being so accommodating." He winked, and the smile she gave him in return hinted at more than just friendship. Lust gripped him by the throat as well as the balls.

Chapter Twenty-Nine

Despite being squeezed on the sofa with a giant dog crushing her feet, Angel felt pretty happy. It had been a good day.

She'd saved Pudge. She'd had her faith in humanity restored, and she was having the best time with Colton. They'd been flirting during dinner, and she'd hoped he might make a move, but when he didn't, she realized that was for the best.

They didn't have a future together. Even if she wasn't being hunted by the law, she had a job that was far from normal. What husband would appreciate his wife pretending to be the girlfriend of a technology mogul?

One who used to live that life and would understand, her brain supplied unhelpfully.

Some might say she was playing house again. And she knew it was true, but playing house was as close as she would ever get to the real thing, so why not enjoy it while it lasted?

Once the inconvenience of being wanted for murder was over, she would be going back to Task Force Phoenix, and

Colton could go back to helping the neighbor kids repay their debts to society.

She smiled at the story he'd told. While he complained about being bored, she knew he was a good teacher. The kind that touched kids' lives and made a difference, even if he didn't realize it.

It was just as noble a cause as defending world leaders from terrorists, or technology moguls from espionage.

She pushed that last thought aside, knowing it only brought heartache and guilt. She couldn't think of anything she could have done differently to save Heath Zeller. She didn't know where she'd gone wrong, but she had failed.

She got up, feeling restless and in need of something else to think about. She wasn't strong enough to hold the bad things at bay on her own.

It shouldn't have been a surprise to find herself standing by Colton's bed. It wasn't the first time she'd come into his room to watch him sleep. Surely, it would be considered some kind of disorder, but she felt at peace in his room.

In sleep he looked younger. The hard lines that made him look so sexy when he was awake were softened.

Even when he was at rest, she noticed the definition in his arms in the light from the window. He was a large man, but in sleep he didn't seem so daunting.

He looked...vulnerable.

Vulnerability was one of the things that kept her from getting a full night's rest. She'd never been a heavy sleeper. Her psycho brother had liked to surprise her in the middle of the night. Once she'd woken to a pillow covering her face. He'd held her like that until she passed out.

When she'd awoken later, she wasn't sure it had really happened. Except there were new bruises on her arms where he'd sat on her.

She wasn't kidding about the psycho part. That part of

her life was over. But it had left its scars on her ability to sleep soundly.

Sleep was for people who felt safe enough from reality, and from the dreams that came for them. Her dreams all too often offered nothing but torment, even now. She was better off avoiding them whenever possible.

She smiled down at the man who had starred in the rare but delicious sex dreams she'd had. She wished she could crawl into his bed and touch his bare chest. She knew under the sheet she would find boxer briefs. He preferred to sleep naked, but hadn't in years, in favor of being ready to run at any minute.

It was sad they had to live this way. Always on watch, always ready to run.

God, she was tired of running.

She paced like a ghost in his home until the dawn came.

When he came out to leave for work, she played the part of the dutiful wife wishing her husband a good day at work. When his car was gone, she let out a sigh, and completed the recurring task of removing her fingerprints from his home.

Just in case.

Chapter Thirty

It only took an hour for Kenny and Braden to correct the mistake on the bookshelf and put it together correctly. Colton was glad, because seriously, he couldn't spend another whole day in their company.

Using the phone in the school office, he called his cell phone, which he'd left at home for Angel.

"How's it going?" he asked.

"Good. The only thing Pudge ate today was part of a Pringles can."

While that didn't sound great, at least it didn't have a stinger, nor would he have to replace his shoes.

"He's eaten those before," Colton said wryly. "It should be okay."

She laughed, and he wished he could go home and be with her.

"I'll finish up and be home by three."

"Okay. See you then."

They sounded like any other married couple making

plans for the evening. Except, they weren't married. Hell, they weren't even a couple.

He shook off the disappointment and walked back into the classroom. The bookcases were against the wall holding books.

"Wow. You did it." He blinked in surprise. That hadn't taken long, at all.

"We kind of cheated," Kenny confessed.

"Cheated? How so?" Colton had only been gone for ten minutes at the most. It wasn't like they'd had time to bring in professionals to finish the task.

"I told you it didn't count as cheating." Braden shoved his partner in the shoulder.

"We looked up the instructions online and watched a YouTube video."

"Oh." Colton didn't know how to respond to this. Still, it wasn't as if they wouldn't have access to instructional videos out in the real world. "That was resourceful. And now you're finished, so it worked out for all of us."

"Don't forget you said you'd take us shooting, right?" Kenny asked for the second time today.

"I haven't forgotten, but as I said, it will be a few weeks. I have other plans for now."

He just wanted the day to be over. He almost wished he would have let them egg his house and move on. He only had to make it through a half day of classes tomorrow and he would be free.

It was odd how eager he was for something he'd originally been dreading. What a difference a woman could make.

Speaking of women, Danielle walked in with that smile he'd been ignoring for months. The kind that promised there were other things available. All he needed to do was ask.

"Some of us are heading over to Benny's after work. Do you want to come?" That last sentence might have sounded like a hint, except he didn't think Danielle even realized what she'd said. Christ, he'd been hanging around high school boys for too long. Everything was a silly innuendo.

"Uh, I'm going to have to pass. I have plans tonight."

"Oh." She seemed surprised by this, and rightfully so. Normally, he was the one who coordinated a trip to Benny's just so he could spend his evening with other humans.

As it was, he was counting down the seconds until he could run by the grocery store and get home to Angel. He was making her chicken cacciatore. And he needed to get a bottle of—

"Are we still on for Chris and Leslie's wedding?" Danielle asked.

It took him a few seconds to remember what she was talking about. "Oh. Uh, sure. I'm meeting you there, right?" He felt like a complete asshole, making a date with another woman—that wasn't really even a date—when the woman he wanted but also wasn't dating was waiting for him at home.

However, the wedding was a month away, and Angel planned to have her mystery solved by then. Where would that leave him? She would be gone, and he would still be here, trying to make a life out of what he'd been given.

Danielle tried for more. "I could pick you up, if you don't know where it is."

But he didn't have more to give. Even if there was no Angel, he wouldn't have agreed to make this a real date.

He couldn't risk it. Not when dates could potentially lead to something else he couldn't do—fall in love with someone who would never truly know him.

"That's okay. I'll drive myself. In case I need to leave early to let my dog out."

"Oh. Okay." There was a flash of disappointment, but she recovered quickly.

That was why he had taken her up on the offer in the first

place. Danielle wasn't needy or desperate. She was a friendly woman with a nice smile. And that was all he would be able to handle, especially after Angel was gone and his heart was left in shreds.

"I'll see you later." He nodded and hurried to his vehicle before he agreed to more things he wasn't capable of.

He raced through the grocery store like a contestant on one of those shopping spree game shows. He knew it wasn't normal to live every day racing against the clock. Knowing every second counted. But for all he knew, she could already be gone by the time he got home. He could already be too late.

He slowed as he approached his house, his heart pounding at the sight of a black sedan parked in the driveway.

What the hell?

He felt the same adrenaline rush that took over when he was in deep cover and needed to act the part. As his heart pumped erratically on the inside, he forced himself to remain cool and collected on the outside.

Since the garage door was blocked, he pulled in next to the other car and got out.

A man stepped out of the driver's side of the sedan. Definitely government agent. He had the look. Dark gray suit and sunglasses.

Colton glanced at the house where his dog was barking from inside, but he knew instinctively Pudge was the only one inside.

Angel was gone.

Chapter Thirty-One

The visitor was thin, and shorter than Colton. Not a threat, unless he had backup nearby, or a gun. Colton swallowed at that last thought. Getting shot was a bitch. It had been a difficult recovery, especially with the added agony of knowing his old life was over.

"Hi, there," Colton greeted the man with a smile that matched the neighborhood in which they stood. He opened the back door of his truck and unloaded the bags.

"Do you need some help?" the man offered with a return smile.

"Nah. I got it. The lazy man's load." Colton would much rather struggle to carry everything at once than make another trip. Second trips were for pussies. "What can I do for you?"

"Do you have a moment? I have some questions."

"Okay. Is your child one of my students?" he asked, knowing that wasn't the case. "Because I already turned in the grades."

"No. I'm Special Agent Markel. I'm looking for someone."

Markel held out his ID and Colton shifted the bags to hold the wallet closer for inspection. FBI, as expected.

"All right. Come inside, let me put these down." He walked into his home with complete confidence that there wouldn't be any trace of Angel. There wouldn't even be so much as a fingerprint. She was that good.

Pudge barked and growled at their guest when Colton opened the door.

"*Mālie*," Colton ordered and Pudge ran to the back door. This was normal protocol for his dog, but he wondered if Pudge wasn't drawn to the backyard because Angel was hiding out there, rather than an urge to relieve himself.

No, she wouldn't stay so close. She wouldn't take that risk.

Moving to the kitchen, he dropped the bags on the counter.

"Do you have to go out?" he asked Pudge, getting a single bark in response. "Good boy." He scratched him around the neck and let him out. "Mind if I put the cold stuff away?"

"Go ahead." Special Agent Markel had walked into the kitchen, and was taking in everything while acting as though he wasn't.

"So, who are you looking for?" Colton asked. It had been a while since he'd needed to play a part. He slipped right into character, all innocence and curiosity.

"Surely, you recognized the woman on the news as the deputy marshal from your protection detail last year."

Colton nodded and put the milk in the fridge door. "I did. Sorry, I wasn't sure if you knew who I really am." He smiled. "It's supposed to be a secret."

The man nodded. "Don't worry. Your identity is safe. We thought maybe she'd turn up by now, but we've been forced to reach out to a wider circle of people she might contact."

"To be honest, I'm not surprised she hasn't turned up.

She seemed to know how to hide. She taught me a lot. I've been here almost a year now, and no one has suspected a thing." He closed the refrigerator and looked at the FBI agent. "Am I in danger? I mean, she was off my team before I was assigned to this location. She wouldn't even know where I am, right?"

"I'm just being thorough, which means I've heard some talk about why Angel was taken off your team before the trial."

"What kind of talk?" This should be good.

"There were rumors that she wanted off your team because the two of you had become intimate."

Colton laughed. "We can't be the first two people who took advantage of the whole bodyguard situation, right?" He laughed again. "She was able to keep sex separate from her job. And trust me, that was all I was to her. A job." At least that part was true.

"Are you saying you haven't had any contact with her since she was reassigned?"

Colton shook his head. "Nothing until she showed up on my TV screen." He looked the man right in the eye as he stretched the truth. It wasn't until after the news report they'd had contact. When it seemed the agent bought it, Colton decided to do a little fishing. "I get what the San Francisco PD might think, but the FBI knows she didn't do this, right?"

Markel cocked his head to the side. "What makes you think that?"

"She's many things—tough, feisty, and a cheater at cards—but she's not a cold-blooded killer."

Markel pulled out the folder he had tucked under his arm and opened it.

He pushed two photos across the counter to Colton.

"I assure you, Mr. Willis, she *is* capable of such a thing."

Colton picked up the photos. They were old. Not from

the recent murder. The same scene taken from two different angles. Two people in bed. One was a woman, and he assumed the other was a man, but there was too much blood to be sure.

"Angel's parents. She stabbed her father sixty-two times and her mother eighty-seven, after slicing their throats in exactly the same way Heath Zeller's throat was cut."

Colton couldn't swallow, though he kept trying. The horror on those pictures was sickening. Blood everywhere, arterial spray and off-fall spattered the walls.

Markel pulled another photo from the folder, and Colton's heart stopped. It was Angel—younger—covered in blood and staring off at nothing. Markel slid the picture to the side to show a mugshot of the same girl.

This couldn't be. Not his Angel.

"How did she ever become an U.S. deputy marshal if she'd done something like this?" Colton's brain supplied the question at the same time his heart reminded him how damaged he knew Angel was. He'd seen the scars on her body.

Had her parents been abusive and she'd simply protected herself? Eighty-seven wounds seemed extreme for defense, but she could have blacked out.

He tried to remember if she'd ever mentioned her parents, and didn't think she had. She hadn't shared much about her old life.

In fact, he didn't know much about her, at all.

This might explain why.

"Her teachers said she was always shy and closed off," Markel said. "She rarely made eye contact with anyone. No friends. As a teenager, she had a few brushes with the law. Shoplifting, fake IDs. Minor stuff. Nothing to worry about."

Markel tapped the photo, to draw Colton's attention back to the tragedy. "She was eighteen when she killed her parents in their sleep. Just like Heath Zeller. She was tried as an adult, but was found not guilty by reason of insanity. She didn't remember the incident. She said she did it in her sleep."

How many times had Angel wandered into his bedroom the last few nights while he'd been sleeping? At least twice he'd heard her, including just last night. How many times had he not even noticed?

The agent pulled out another photo. This one was of Angel laughing with an older man who had his arm around her.

"Supervisory Deputy Marshal Josiah Thorne knew her father, and used his pull to get her into a test program he was initiating. Have you heard of Task Force Phoenix?"

Colton shook his head, but he did remember hearing someone refer to her team by that name.

"It was a test project at first. Thorne recruited people brought into WITSEC who had more to offer than just sitting around taking it easy." The agent glanced around his house and Colton stood up straighter. "Mess-ups who wanted to turn over a new leaf. Rise from the ashes, and all that shit." The man shook his head as if the thought of wanting to better oneself was ridiculous. "She tested well, and even passed her psych eval."

When Markel pulled out the next photo Colton almost didn't look. But it was just another photo of Angel in the arms of a man. Both with white-blond hair. They may have passed for siblings if he hadn't been looking at her in an intimate way with his hand low on her hip. It was the embrace of familiarity between lovers.

"Her first partner, Lucas Stone. As you can see, they were more than just partners. Until he fell off a bridge. She said he jumped, but there was blood found at the scene."

At this, Markel flipped to another photo. The edge of a bridge, with blood—a lot of it—on the barrier. Angel was standing to the side, her expression blank.

Colton didn't know how much more of this he could take, but the man continued.

"Even after this, she remained on the team. She was known to be vicious when threatened, and unable to form attachments to others. It made her a perfect deputy marshal for WITSEC. Until she killed again."

Colton knew the part about being vicious and unable to form attachments was true.

But was Angel really a killer?

Chapter Thirty-Two

Colton couldn't fall asleep. It was almost one, and he needed to be at school in the morning, but he couldn't stop thinking about Angel.

After Special Agent Markel left, Colton had checked the hiding place under his closet, as well as the backyard. The vehicle in the shed was still there, so she'd left on foot, and taken her things, including the computer.

He might have gone looking for her, but he worried Markel might follow him. Not that he'd given the agent reason to doubt him.

Colton had played his part well, mainly because the sick expression at seeing those photos had been genuine. As for the story, he wasn't sure what to believe.

He'd known men who went home every night to their wife and kids, but spent their day moving heroin into the country. They told jokes and were sociable. Guys you'd want to be friends with, and have a beer with on Friday nights. No one would know what they were capable of.

It stood to reason he didn't know what Angel was capable of.

But it didn't matter now.

Angel was gone.

And he couldn't do anything about it.

But the part of the puzzle that kept him from falling asleep was...if she ended up killing someone else, it would be his fault. He knew how easy it was to make people believe whatever one wanted. He'd spent eight years doing just that.

Angel was sexy, with a curvy body that could arouse a monk. And her smile could make a man overlook the fact she was a lethal adversary. Had his dick kept him from stopping a murderer on the loose?

He glared down in the direction of his dick, wishing he was smarter than that part of his anatomy. Apparently, that wasn't the case. It never had been, not with her.

Exhausted from the day, he finally started to slip toward the edge of sleep when he heard the familiar jingle of Pudge's tags. Then he felt the bed move with the weight.

"Get down," he ordered, not happy with his dog. Even if he had been blinded to her true nature, Pudge should have known better.

The dog licked his hand.

The hand that was hanging over the side of the bed. The *other* side.

His heart began to pound, he could hear the blood rushing through his temples. It wasn't Pudge who had just gotten into his bed.

It was Angel.

Chapter Thirty-Three

Angel felt Colton's body tense when he realized she was there.

Not that she should be there.

She'd taken off. She should have kept going.

But before he'd left for work that morning, he'd said the same thing he always said. "If you're not here when I get back, good luck and take care of yourself."

He'd made it sound as if she would be leaving because she had no choice, but she'd seen the doubt in his eyes. He expected her to leave him like she had the last time.

Maybe it was because she didn't want to let down another man in her life, or maybe it was that she was selfish and wanted to stay here with him. Whatever the reason, she couldn't make herself go. She'd turned around and came back.

His response to her being in his bed was not what she'd expected. She'd hoped he'd pull her close and kiss her. Maybe those kisses would even lead to more.

It seemed she'd abandoned the plan to keep things

professional at the same time she realized she couldn't leave.

She remembered how amazing they'd been together. Now that she had admitted her need for him, she was ready to let him know how much she wanted him. But he didn't seem to be in the same place.

He was still tense.

"You came back." His voice barely moved the darkness.

"Yes."

There was some shifting, then the light came on. He looked her over.

She hadn't been brave enough to get into bed naked, so she was wearing a tank top and sweats. But his gaze seemed to go straight to her hands.

Was he expecting her to have something? A cup of coffee? A gun?

He let out a breath and looked at her. It wasn't a breath of relief that she was back. He didn't look happy to see her. He looked…frightened.

"What is it?" she asked. He was a seasoned agent. It would take a lot to get him this worked up. Maybe he'd had a bad dream.

"Why did you kill your parents?"

She nearly fell off the bed at his question. Whoever their visitor had been, he'd planted doubt in Colton. Big doubt.

It was a familiar tactic. If you wanted someone to give up the other person, you had to make them a suspect. She hadn't thought it would work so well on Colton. But then, she already knew he didn't trust her. And for good reason.

She'd acted as though she'd cared for him. She'd said things to make him believe she was in the same place he was. And then she'd left while he was sleeping.

"He told you I killed them," she whispered.

The only answer was a stony look while his eyes searched her face for the truth.

"You believed him." It wasn't an accusation, just a sad statement of fact.

"I don't know what to believe. I know if you did it, there was a good reason. I hope there was a good reason."

"Can I show you something?"

He nodded and she slid off the bed. She hurried to the living room to get the computer, and walked back as it booted up. Pudge followed her the whole way.

She crossed her legs and rested the laptop on her knees as she pulled up the browser and typed in the headline she knew by heart.

CASSANDRA LARSON, SOLE SURVIVOR OF HEINOUS ATTACK.

"Your real name is Cassandra?" he asked. She nodded as she tilted the screen toward him so he could read the appalling story of her past. "It was your brother?"

His whole body seemed to relax at the knowledge as she nodded in confirmation.

"You were hurt." His eyes flared with concern, even though it was obvious she was fine now. Physically, at least.

She pulled the strap of her shirt down so he could see the worst of her injuries—the scar at her left collarbone. The one he was already familiar with from their lovemaking, though she'd never told him the truth about how she'd gotten it. Had the wound been a bit higher, she wouldn't have been the sole survivor of the attack.

"Tell me what I'm not reading here," he said, finishing the article, and she found that for the first time in her life she wanted someone to know what had happened to her. What had really happened.

And she wanted it to be Colton.

Chapter Thirty-Four

Colton waited as Angel closed the computer and shifted to get comfortable. Pudge jumped up on the bed by her side, and Colton didn't have the heart to chase him down this time. He could imagine this tale would be gruesome, and didn't mind that his dog wanted to offer her support.

"You've seen my scars before," she started.

Yes. When they'd been naked. They'd touched and kissed each other's scars with reverence and acceptance in those nights of passion. Neither of them had asked questions, knowing they didn't want that darkness brought into those moments.

"I don't ever remember a time when I didn't have scars on my body. My brother, Nicholas, was five years older than me. He'd always been *rough*. At least that was the word my parents used. Looking back, I realize they were in denial of what their son really was."

Without thinking, Colton reached out and took her hand. He had brothers. They'd often been rough. They'd hurt each other. But Colton could tell this was different.

"They were good parents. They always made sure we had the things we needed. We went on great vacations. They loved us. We should have been the perfect family, and I'm sure a lot of people thought we were. But there was a darkness none of us talked about. My brother." She rubbed her forehead and looked at Colton. "Please don't think they were bad."

This seemed important to her so he nodded. "Okay," he agreed.

Though he'd already jumped to the opposite conclusion. Clearly, they hadn't protected Angel when she'd needed them. In his mind, that was what parents were supposed to do. No matter the threat. But he knew that wasn't always the case. Not by a long shot.

Bad things happened all the time.

"As I got older, I realized it wasn't normal for me to be terrified of being alone with my own brother. My friends didn't have those issues. Their siblings were more protective or annoying than anything. I never had friends stay over at my home. I was worried about their safety."

Pudge wiggled closer and rested his head on her thigh. He must have sensed her inner pain. She used her free hand to pet him.

"By my senior year of high school, I was looking forward to getting out of the house. I had two months of school left. I only had to survive the summer and I'd be leaving for college. I never planned to come back. Nicholas had gotten worse. He hid in his room a lot, but when he came out, the darkness in him manifested in strange ways. He'd take my things and break them. Things I'd loved. Gifts from my parents. I didn't dare say anything, or he would go into a rage and accuse us of hating him."

She let out a breath, and Colton tensed, knowing she'd arrived at that worst part.

"I'm not sure why I woke up. It was probably a sound,

though I don't remember it. Maybe it was because the house had grown cold. I don't know. But I was suddenly wide awake and knew something was wrong."

She released his hand and wrapped it around her. Her skin was covered in goose bumps. He sat up and pulled her into his arms. Offering his warmth. But knowing the chill came from inside where he couldn't reach.

"When I listened, I realized there *was* a sound. Barely there. Muted. I didn't know what it was, but I was compelled to go look."

She shook her head. "I must have known it came from my parents' room on the other side of the house, but I don't remember why now. I went down the hall and found their door open almost halfway. None of us slept with our doors open. That would be a silent invitation for Nicholas to enter."

She swallowed and leaned into Colton. He bit his cheek to keep from saying anything. He didn't want her to stop talking.

"There was light coming in from the street, and all I saw was blood. Blood everywhere. My brother was kneeling over my mother, stabbing her. The sound I'd heard had been the knife sliding against her ribs and my brother's heavy breaths from the exertion."

"Oh, God," he said, unable to help himself, holding her tight. He'd seen the photos, but now he felt the fear behind them.

"I ran to my room and got the cell phone I'd gotten for my birthday. I called 911 and looked for a place to hide. I'd never been able to hide from him before. I knew he would look under the bed, or in my closet. So I went across the hall into his room and hid in the back of his closet. I'd never gone into his room before. I wasn't even sure if his closet was big enough, but I worked my way inside and hid under some clothing."

"That was smart. You have good instincts," he praised her stupidly. He knew the end of the story. He knew her brother found her.

Colton almost wished she would end the story there. He didn't know if he could handle the rest. Even having her here, safe in his arms, didn't stop his need to protect her from the past.

"I heard him in my room. When I wasn't there, he called for me to come out. He said—" Her breath caught for a moment before she went on. "He said he wasn't going to hurt me." She surprised him with a small, humorless laugh. "All he'd ever done was hurt me. But I don't think he understood."

She shook her head as if she'd just figured that out.

"It didn't take him long to come looking for me in his own room. He opened the closet, and when he shut the door I thought I was safe. But only a few seconds later, he opened it again and dragged me out."

Colton jumped, but covered it by running his hand down her back.

"He was babbling something about how I didn't love him enough, and how our parents hadn't loved him enough. I tried to tell him I did love him. But I didn't convince him."

"There's no reasoning with a sociopath." Colton exhaled and felt her shrug.

"He was exhausted. He could barely hold the knife straight. His muscles were trembling with fatigue. He was covered in so much blood it dripped off the hem of his T-shirt onto my pajamas. Because he was so weak, I was able to fight him. I even made him drop the knife. But he was a twenty-three-year-old man and I was even smaller than I am now."

Colton looked at her in his arms. He'd always known she was small, but he'd never once considered her weak. With the training she'd gotten in the marshals, she would have had a chance against a grown man, but back then she was just a frightened girl, fighting for her life.

"I knew what was going to happen. I won't say my life flashed before my eyes or anything, but I do remember thinking, 'This is it? I made it this far just for this to happen?' Then the knife came down into my neck."

Pudge whined as if he understood, and rooted his head along her leg.

"The blade hit my collarbone and deflected down instead of up. It got stuck in my shoulder blade, and he didn't have the strength to pull it out. Not with the handle and his hand being so slippery. He went to his desk to find another knife, and that's when the police moved in. Nicholas laughed when they told him to freeze. Instead, he held the knife up higher and rushed them. They shot him before he took two steps."

"And you were finally free," Colton said, glad to have it over.

But she shook her head and let out a breath.

"No. I'll never be free."

Chapter Thirty-Five

Angel felt so much better getting the story out. Thorne was the only other person she'd told the details of that night. Even then, she'd kept it short, and didn't tell him how terrified she'd been.

In the comfort of Colton's arms, she felt safe to let it all out.

"I'm so sorry about your parents," he whispered.

"Thanks."

He reached over and turned off the light, then flipped the covers up over her. A silent invitation for her to stay, thank God.

She let out a breath and closed her eyes, wanting desperately to be with him. She was suddenly dead tired, and thought she might actually be able to sleep for once.

"Thank you for coming back," he said.

"Thank you for letting me."

"You always have a home with me."

The word struck her with the force of a bullet...but one

filled with good things instead of pain and death.

A home.

She hadn't thought of anywhere as home since that night her life had been destroyed by her brother. But being with Colton *did* feel like home. Even better, it was a home where she finally felt safe.

She'd never had that before.

A few minutes later, his breathing steadied into a comforting rhythm, and she felt herself being pulled under with him.

When she awoke, the sun was coming in through the curtains and Colton was gone. Pudge was still snuggled up against her back, his hot doggy breath stirring her hair.

Given a choice, she would have picked the other male to have stayed. Although Pudge wouldn't have been able to make her breakfast, if she was right about the sounds and smells coming from the kitchen.

Starving, she went to investigate, and found Colton at the stove, shirtless.

She wanted nothing more than to walk up behind him, wrap her arms around his waist, and rest her cheek on the bare skin of his strong back. But she didn't.

Last night she'd slept with him, but it had been very different than before. He'd offered her support. He hadn't suggested anything more.

To touch him would start something they wouldn't be able to finish. It had taken all her strength to leave him a year ago. She didn't know if she could do it again.

Even if there was no other choice.

Chapter Thirty-Six

Colton's hands were stirring pancake batter, but his mind was working on something else. He was trying to figure out how he could help Angel heal from her scars.

Not the physical ones. He knew her body had healed long ago. But her heart was still broken for her family. He knew she'd loved her parents, but there was something in the way she'd talked about her brother. She'd loved him, too. Despite everything he'd done to her, he'd been her brother. Sibling bonds ran deep.

Colton's own brothers had done things to him that had seemed unforgiveable at the time, but he loved and missed every one of them.

She'd been betrayed in the worst way. She'd loved her brother who was incapable of loving her back the way she deserved. And there was nothing Colton could do to help her.

In light of her confession about her parents, he hadn't been able to question her about her dead partner. It was obvious Markel had twisted the truth to get Colton to turn on Angel. No doubt, the story about the partner was just as untrue as what he'd told her about her parents.

He decided to let it go. It wasn't important. He knew Angel wouldn't have killed anyone unless it was warranted.

"Last day of school?" Angel asked, startling him as he was throwing pancakes on a plate.

"Yep. Half day. All the kids come in, do nothing, and leave again. It's a complete waste of half a day." They kept their conversation light as they sat down to eat, but it drifted off into silence.

When Pudge barked to come in, they both jumped.

Colton stopped his furry friend at the door. "Uh-uh. No dead animals in the house. Take the poor, innocent squirrel back outside." He closed the door and sat down at the table. "I don't know how to help. I feel powerless," he admitted in a rush. So much for letting their middle-of-the-night confessions go.

"Maybe we could look into a doggie intervention." She had intentionally misunderstood.

His lips twitched at her joke and he met her eyes. Silently begging her to tell him what she needed.

With a sigh she gave in. "Thank you for wanting to help, but I'm okay. Really, I am. It helped to tell you what happened. I didn't realize how much I was still keeping in. Thanks for listening."

Listening didn't feel like enough, but he'd give her whatever she needed. He now understood why she didn't sleep well. No doubt she was always listening—expecting—some danger to step into her room when she was most vulnerable.

It had felt good to have her safe in his arms, but he couldn't do anything to help her, short of what he was already doing by listening, and providing a place to hide. Being this helpless went against his male need to fix everything.

After making sure the dog didn't bring in a gift, he told

Pudge to take over the watch and Colton headed out to his truck. He and Angel said an awkward goodbye and waved.

Should he have kissed her?

He shook it off, and drove on.

He'd put on a brave face before leaving for work, but the truth was, he was afraid to go. Something felt off, and he was worried she might get skittish and run. She'd shared a lot with him the night before, and sharing was not Angel's specialty.

He was just turning onto Spruce Street when he felt a prickle along the back of his neck. Not the ordinary unease of leaving Angel alone, but like something from his past life as a DEA agent.

In the rearview mirror, he noted a white sedan two cars back. It wasn't out of the ordinary—white sedans were a dime a dozen—but this one in particular caught his attention. A piece of the windshield stripping was pulled up and the rubber bounced around like the antennae of an insect against the roof.

He'd seen it go past the house this morning when he'd let Pudge out to retrieve the newspaper at the end of the driveway.

Instincts kicked in, and he turned right into an alley without signaling. The woman in the mini-van behind him hit the horn and flipped him off.

The sedan paused, but continued on without turning.

Colton let out a sigh of relief. He was being ridiculous. Why would anyone be following him? Surely, there was more than one white vehicle in the world with the windshield stripping coming loose. It was common.

Due to his detour, he was late getting to class. Most of his students were already seated and looking at him in confusion.

"Late night, Mr. Willis?"

He didn't respond, but it had been a late night. And now it was obvious he looked as bad as he felt. The reason for his delusional behavior on the drive to work could have been because he was exhausted.

"Uh, Mr. Willis? You okay, dude?"

Colton glared at Richie in the front row. "Didn't we talk about how you're not supposed use the term dude when conversing with your elders?"

"Yeah, but it's the last day." Richie squinted at him.

"Rules still apply on the last day. And all summer. And for the rest of your life."

"But eventually I will be older than everyone, and I will be their elder. Can I call people dude then?"

Smart-ass.

"No. Not then, either."

The rest of the class laughed as Colton told Richie to sit up straight.

There was a time when Colton had been the smart-ass, funny kid. Though, he'd always referred to his teachers by their name, or sir or ma'am. His father had taught him respect for his elders.

Hopefully this lesson—however brief—would stick with Richie.

"Okay, everyone. Pull out a piece of paper." This command was met with collective whining.

"Are we having a quiz? I thought the grades were already in."

"Relax, Madeline. We're not having a quiz. But we're here, and we're going to learn something."

Group groan. At least they knew how to work as a team.

"I didn't bring any paper because it was the last day."

"Would someone please give Marcus a piece of paper?" The boy opened his mouth. "And a pencil."

When everyone had their tools in front of them, Colton gave them their assignment. "I want you to list all the real-world things people do every day that require math. And the person who has the most things on their list wins something."

Pencils started flying. And then Richie the Smart-ass raised his hand with that impish grin that had half the tenth-grade girls following him through the halls.

"Yes?"

"Can I use divvying up a six-pack of beer among four friends?"

"Of course." And he'd be sure to share *that* with his parents.

"Cool."

As graphite scratched across paper, Colton walked between the desks checking over their progress.

"You can't list every item in the grocery store as a separate line, Bryn."

"But—"

"No."

At the last row, he stopped to look out the window at the gorgeous day. The day he was missing with Angel. The sunlight glinted off a windshield across the street.

The loose weather stripping flapped in the light breeze.

Chapter Thirty-Seven

Angel was getting nowhere fast. She hadn't been able to track the email message from Redgamer3, and after an entire day of worming her way into blogs and personal email, not to mention the deepest corners of the Darknet, she still didn't have a clue who had the stolen prototype. Or who had killed Heath to get it.

Apparently, whoever took Zeller's technology was in no hurry to sell it.

It made no sense.

No one was talking. Except about how she had offed Heath in a jealous rage. Naturally, they were still talking about that.

She even had a nickname now. *The Mantis*. Because the female praying mantis killed its mate during sex.

"Very clever, asswipe," she muttered. "Maybe you should stop spending so much time watching Animal Planet in your mother's basement."

Great, she'd resorted to stereotyping.

She rested her forehead on her keyboard, praying to the gods of technology to give her a clue.

Her computer chimed with a new message from Redgamer3.

I HAVEN'T HEARD FROM YOU.

DOES THIS MEAN YOU DON'T WANT THE PROTOTYPE BACK?

I THOUGHT YOU'D BE MORE FUN.

She ground her teeth. "Okay, asshole. We're on."

She hadn't planned to interact with Redgamer3, but after hitting a wall on her searches, she had little to lose. She checked to make sure her location was invisible, and responded.

I THINK YOU MUST HAVE THE WRONG PERSON. I DON'T KNOW WHAT YOU'RE TALKING ABOUT.

Best not to show her cards too soon.

The answer came back immediately.

COME ON, MANTIS.

SURELY YOU REMEMBER.

THE DEAD MAN IN YOUR BED?

She thought out her reply before typing. If this was the real killer—and she felt maybe he was actually legit—she wouldn't want to mess up an opportunity to pull him out where she could get to him.

HOW DID YOU GET MY EMAIL? HAVE WE MET?

The answer came back immediately.

I DON'T THINK THESE ARE THE QUESTIONS YOU WANT ANSWERED.
WHAT YOU REALLY WANT TO KNOW IS...
HOW DID I DO IT?

"Christ." She sat back against the sofa and covered her mouth in surprise. This person knew her. Or at least it seemed they did. She read the three lines again, noting that all of his correspondence so far had appeared in three lines.

Maybe that was important, but she put it aside for now so she could focus on what they'd written, and how to respond.

HOW'D YOU DO WHAT?

While she wouldn't be able to use an email to get out of a murder rap, she could see what the killer might reveal.

THIS IS NOT AS MUCH FUN AS I THOUGHT IT WOULD BE.
YOUR NEW ROOMMATE.
HAS MADE YOU TAME.

At the sound of the garage door opening, she picked up her gun and went to the window to make sure Colton was alone. Was he the roommate Redgamer3 was talking about?

Was he watching her now?

Pudge barked his happy welcome, and Angel followed him to meet Colton in the kitchen, still carrying her gun.

She took a breath to calm her tattered nerves. Redgamer3 was not here. He wouldn't have been able to track her to a physical location.

She was sure of it. Colton didn't need something else to worry about, so she wasn't going to say anything. If she told him about the emails, he would want to help, and he couldn't. Whoever killed Heath was dangerous as hell, and she would make damn sure they never came in contact with Colton.

She relaxed slightly, glad he was home where she could make sure he stayed safe.

As soon as he walked into the kitchen his gaze searched for her anxiously.

"What is it?" she asked, her heart racing again. Had Redgamer3 contacted him?

No. Colton would have called. She needed to calm down.

"I'm glad you're still here," he said.

Ah. Okay. Back to that.

She'd done this. She'd made him think she was ready to bolt at any second.

The worst part was, she wasn't sure she wouldn't. She wanted to think of herself as a better person now. As someone who would stay and face her fears of commitment rather than running away.

But she wasn't sure.

Last night, he'd held her. It had felt nice, but she'd be lying if she said she didn't wish it had been more.

A lot more.

She couldn't blame him for not wanting to go down that path with her again. He'd opened up his heart and asked her to stay with him, and she hadn't even had the decency to face him when she turned him down. She'd run off like a coward in the night.

"I'm sorry," she said out loud at the same moment he opened his mouth to speak.

His eyes widened as he cocked his head. "For what?"

This was her chance to backpedal. She could make up something else...or she could be honest and face this thing between them.

She opened her mouth, not sure which was about to come out.

Chapter Thirty-Eight

Colton was waiting for Angel to explain the reason for her apology when Pudge rushed past him toward the back door, growling. The fur on the back of his neck rose in a way Colton knew meant bad news.

He hadn't gotten a chance to tell Angel about the car. Maybe he would have told her…or maybe he would have kept it to himself so as not to worry her.

"Please tell me he sees a bunny," she said with hope in her voice.

"That's not his bunny noise."

"Can't a girl catch a break?" She sounded more annoyed than scared, but he shouldn't have expected anything else. Angel was always calm and in control of the situation. "I watched the house until the guy with Markel left. I didn't give them any reason to be suspicious."

He decided to confess because it was important she knew what he knew. "Are you sure? Because I think someone was following me this morning."

"What did you do?"

"I shook them."

"So they know that you know you were being tailed?" As convoluted as her question was, he understood.

He grimaced. "When someone is following you, your instinct is to lose them."

"I'm not accusing you of messing up. Although I wouldn't blame you since you've been out of the game for over a year."

He didn't need a free pass. He hadn't messed up. "I assure you, I didn't wreck your cover."

"I didn't say you did—" She was interrupted by Pudge as he put his paws on the door, barking savagely.

"They're coming. Go hide," he ordered, knowing she wouldn't like that.

"I don't want to hide." She pulled her gun and chambered a round.

Normally he found that sexy, but this time fear rattled his spine. He could lose her. Whoever was waiting on the other side of the door would take her away. Either in cuffs or a bag.

If the person in his backyard was law enforcement, he didn't want anyone to get hurt. After all, they were just doing their job. They didn't know she was innocent.

"Wait a second," he said, thinking of another option. One that might actually get her to stand down rather than going with a more aggressive option. "The neighbor lady makes the best apple dumplings I've ever had, and she always makes enough for me. I don't want to have to move because of a shootout in my backyard."

"Someone contacted me," she said. "Via email."

Surprised, he waited for her to continue. He could tell she didn't want to tell him. "Who?"

"I think it was the killer. They're playing a game. I don't think they can really know where I am."

"But they said they did?"

"Yeah." She sighed and nodded.

Pudge was still barking viciously.

"Angel, you can't shoot someone in my backyard because you think it *might* be the killer."

"Fine. I assume you have one of those nifty Hawaiian words for *attack*?" She nodded toward the dog who was desperate to get out.

"Yes."

He moved to the door and grasped the knob. While he didn't want to hurt his neighbor, a kid messing around with eggs, or a cop doing his duty, he also didn't want to put Pudge at a disadvantage if someone was coming to finish off the loose end they'd left at Heath Zeller's apartment. If Pudge wasn't allowed to attack, he could be hurt, or worse.

Colton opened the door and gave the command. Pudge leaped over the railing and tore off down the length of the yard. When he ran under a bush, Colton thought maybe he had been wrong about the bunny, but then he heard a man shouting for help.

After a number of incoherent—and painful—sounds, the man shouted, "I'm with Thorne."

"Shit," Angel said as she pushed past Colton, yelling, "Stop! Pudge, don't hurt him!"

As if that was going to work.

Chapter Thirty-Nine

Angel was impressed by the way Pudge released U.S. Deputy
Marshal Dane Ryan as soon as Colton called him. She patted
the dog on the head. He'd done his job well. Even if he'd
mangled a friend instead of an intruder. That wasn't his fault.

"What the hell is wrong with you?" she snapped at Dane.

"At the moment what is wrong with me is that I have
holes in my leg," he muttered angrily.

"Is that the same leg—"

"Where Samantha shot me? Yes. Yes, it is."

"Oh, hell. I'm sorry. It's just you're not our first visitor."
She frowned down at the blood soaking through his pants.
This was bad.

The poor guy had been ordered to take the gun away
from Samantha Hutchinson during an op to bring her in.
The woman had been scared, and who could blame her?
Four U.S. marshals and a father she'd thought long dead
had surrounded her, all armed to the teeth. When Dane
had followed Supervisor Thorne's order to disarm her, Sam

had shot Dane in the leg. It had all turned out well in the end…except for Dane ending up in the hospital and physical therapy.

He'd just been released back to work, though he still had a slight limp. Pudge probably hadn't helped with his rehabilitation.

"Markel was here already?" Dane asked, and gasped as Angel pulled him to his feet.

"Yes," she confirmed, and added sardonically, "Thanks for the heads up."

"We weren't sure you were here. Your *fax* was a bit vague."

"Hello," Colton said, leaning down to inspect the damage to Dane's leg. "For the record, she was planning to come out guns a-blazing."

"Colton, this is Deputy Marshal Dane Ryan, Dane— Colton, er, Duncan."

"Nice to meet you." Dane held up a bloody hand in a gesture that said he wasn't able to shake.

"Right. Let's get inside and fix you up. You're going to be fine," she said, trying not to wince at the amount of blood already covering his jeans.

"Will you stitch me up?" he asked.

"Sure thing." She'd stitched him up the last time he was injured. And another time when he got shot in the shoulder during a raid. And that time he was pushed off a boat and his arm caught on a hook.

She'd stitched up everyone in her team at one time or another. They all liked her work. It was what family did for one another. Well, theirs, anyway.

As Colton helped guide Dane into the bathroom, the doorbell rang, throwing Pudge for another loop.

Angel looked out the window to see a white sedan in the driveway and Josiah Thorne waiting on the front porch. She opened the door to let him in, staying back so no one could see her.

When she shut the door, her boss looked her over for a moment, then pulled her into a hug. It wasn't the first time he'd hugged her, but it had been a while.

"I'm glad you're okay, kid."

Kid. He'd been calling her that since she was an eighteen-year-old...kid. She knew he wasn't insulting her. To him, it was a term of endearment. And since he was the closest thing she had to a father, she let it go.

"Are they watching you?" she guessed.

"Yeah. Markel is trying to use this story to oust me and shut down Task Force Phoenix. He says I should have known you were unstable. I told him to kiss my ass."

Angel smirked as she showed him to a chair.

"Ouch, God dammit!" Dane shouted from down the hall.

"He didn't get shot again, did he?" Thorne only seemed slightly concerned. He cared—she was pretty sure. He just had a cold demeanor.

"No. Guard dog," she explained as said dog came up and put his big head on Thorne's leg for a scratch.

"This dog? He's just a big sweetie." Thorne rubbed him behind the ears, clearly seeing no threat. Not even when Pudge's mouth fell open and his dopey tongue slid out over those impressively pointy teeth.

"You know Dane. Such a baby." She laughed.

"I heard that," Dane called from the bathroom. "Are you going to stitch this up or let me bleed to death slowly?"

"I'll be right there!" she called before turning back to her boss. "Can I get you something to drink?"

"I'd love a beer. The flight was a bitch."

"Dog bite in here! Blood loss!" Dane complained as Colton walked out laughing.

"Colton, this is Supervisory Deputy United States

Marshal Josiah Thorne." Wow, what a mouthful.

"Colton, nice to meet you."

"Nice to meet you, too. I've heard a lot about you."

"Don't tell him that, he'll think I like him," Angel stage-whispered to Colton as she went to the kitchen to get them both a beer. Colton sat across from Thorne, and the two of them started talking about the dog as if they were great friends.

After delivering the beers, she grabbed a bottle of whiskey and headed to the bathroom to take care of her patient.

Chapter Forty

"How's she holding up?" Thorne asked as soon as Angel was out of hearing range.

Colton could tell the query was out of concern rather than questioning her sanity. "She's sound. She's not sleeping, but I don't think that's anything new."

"No. It's been a very long time since she's slept through the night."

How would this man know, except if—

"The two of you...?" Colton's eyes went wide. Thorne was old enough to be her father. Though, he did have all his hair. He also had that distinguished look about him that some women liked.

"God, no." Thorne shook his head. "Her father was like a brother to me before I joined the Agency and then moved to the Marshals. When he was killed, I tried to look out for her when I could."

"Bringing her into Task Force Phoenix?" Colton asked.

The man's head snapped up. "She told you about that?"

"Yes. And I know what happened with her parents, too," Colton added.

Thorne snorted in what sounded like surprise.

"She didn't have much choice but to tell me. Markel showed up here with photos. He told me she had killed them, and was pretty damn convincing about it, too. Obviously trying to get me to give her up."

Colton was embarrassed that he'd even considered the story to be true. While he wouldn't have given her up, he had been more than nervous when she'd turned up in his bed.

"Weasely little rat," Thorne said in disgust.

"I get that he'd want to have his name attached to solving this case, but he made it seem...personal."

"I started Task Force Phoenix for people who needed a fresh start or were starting over. Angel was twenty-one and in jail for identity theft. Markel had gotten dismissed from a police department for forgetting where evidence was supposed to go. He thought I should take him on, but I passed him over for Angel. I guess he's bitter about my choice. I've never regretted my decision. I guess he's trying to take both of us down in one fell swoop."

"You think he killed Heath Zeller?" Colton's hand instinctively fisted. Markel had been so close.

"No. He wouldn't have been able to get past Angel."

"She's very thorough." And yet, someone had gotten past her.

"She's the best at her job. And—"

"God damn! Son of a bitch! Mother fucker!" Dane yelled from the bathroom, making Thorne wince before he finished his sentence.

"—at causing a lot of pain."

Colton couldn't argue with that. He knew when she left it would cause a lot of pain for him.

Chapter Forty-One

"This is going to hurt," Angel warned Dane with a frown.

"Oh, good. Thanks for telling me. I thought it was going to feel like kittens—God damn! Son of a bitch! Mother fucker!"

"Nope. Not like kittens." She hid her laughter as she blotted the excess antiseptic from the wounds. "Just a few more times to make sure the bite marks are cleaned out."

"I thought they say dogs' mouths are cleaner than ours."

"True, but that doesn't mean theirs are clean, it just means ours are worse."

"Oh. They should mention that part."

She tilted her head at him. "They lick themselves, Dane. Do you want that in your wounds?"

"No. Go ahead. Could you blow on it?" Dane's color was looking a little better, but he was still shaky. He'd lost a lot of blood.

"No. I'm not blowing on it." She may have rolled her eyes.

"Remember the time that guy ripped a chunk of your

hair out? I blew on it for you."

"Blowing on it makes it worse. The oxygen makes it evaporate even faster, which is what causes the burn." She couldn't believe she was having this conversation with an adult.

"Never mind. Your scientific dissertation is more painful than the cleaning."

After the next round of cursing, which included a few bad names for her future unborn offspring as well as her deceased mother, she gave it one more dousing of antiseptic and set the bottle on the sink to hand him the other bottle. The one containing a different kind of alcohol.

"Do you think this is a good idea?" he asked as she was threading the needle.

"What? You don't like red? There isn't any black. It's this or green."

"Red's fine. I'm talking about you being here."

"What? You don't trust Colton?" That was ridiculous.

"I don't trust you with Colton."

She rolled her eyes and pierced his skin with the needle. He sucked air through his teeth and let it out slowly. She paused as he took another swig of the whiskey. A much bigger swig.

"What's that supposed to mean?" she asked as she bent her head to continue her work. The important thing was to keep the stitches small so they didn't scar. Not that it would matter—not with a giant scar just three inches above it.

"I remember you being on his watch and ditching it at a moment's notice. Justin barely got there before you ran off to go help with another case."

She shrugged. "So?"

"So you're emotionally attached to this guy, and being emotionally attached makes people sloppy."

"I thought that was tequila," she joked, but it didn't work.

He gave her the Serious Dane Ryan look. They'd been good friends since he first joined the team four years ago. He'd been her new partner after things with her old partner, Lucas Stone, went south.

Though, south was a bit of an understatement. What had really happened was she'd trusted someone she shouldn't have because she'd become emotionally attached to him.

Christ, she was making Dane's case for him.

"If you get caught by law enforcement, you're screwed." Dane winced when the thread caught. "We need more time to prove this murder isn't on you."

"I'm not going to get caught." At least she hoped not.

"When push comes to shove, we never leave the people we love."

"Are you saying you're in love with me?" she asked. Dane had never left her when she'd needed him. She batted her eyes at him and stuck out her bottom lip.

"I love you like a bratty little know-it-all sister. If this guy hurts you or causes you to get caught, I *will* end him." Dane winced as she jabbed him again.

"Ah. You're going to end the guy with the attack dog?" She smiled up at him like the bratty little sister he accused her of being.

"Stop chatting. You're only on the first bite mark." He took another large sip from the bottle.

She concentrated on sewing up all four wounds, then sighed at her work. "I think your modeling career is over, but they'll hold. Keep an eye on them for infection."

"I will. Thanks." He pulled up his pants and scowled at Pudge, who had taken a spot outside the bathroom door. "I hate you."

"That's not nice. He's still a puppy."

To help sell it, Pudge rested his chin on his front paws and looked up at Dane with those big brown eyes.

"Is that how it happened? You fell for the eyes and didn't see the fangs?"

She knew Dane wasn't talking about the dog anymore. "Ha ha."

"Make sure you don't get bit."

Right.

Unfortunately, it was much too late for that.

Chapter Forty-Two

"You were following me today," Colton stated, having glanced out his front window to see a familiar white car.

"How did you know?" Thorne asked conversationally.

Colton pointed out the window and smiled. "It has a distinctive problem with the weather stripping on the windshield. You're driving around looking like an angler fish."

Thorne laughed at his joke. "Don't worry. We were just making sure no one else was following you before we made contact. If she's caught, I won't be able to help her if I'm implicated as well."

"Why did you come personally? Why not just send someone?" Colton asked.

Surely, there would have been a way for her boss to communicate without anyone knowing. They were U.S. Marshals. Their main job was keeping people hidden. They would have to know how to do that without showing up at someone's doorstep.

Thorne glanced down the hall and lowered his voice. "I wanted to make sure she was okay."

"Isn't she always okay?"

She always seemed cool and calm under any circumstance. But he knew it wasn't always the case. Colton knew her well enough to see when something was bothering her, no matter how much she tried to hide it.

"No. Not always."

Apparently he wasn't the only one who could see when she was faking.

Colton knew she was taking Heath Zeller's death hard. He saw the guilt in her eyes when she spoke of what happened. And so far, she hadn't told him any of the details. That was a sign she wasn't dealing with it.

Maybe this man would know how to help.

"She feels responsible," Colton said. "But what could she have done? She said she was drugged." No one would have been able to keep Zeller safe if they were unconscious.

"I *was* drugged," Angel said as she helped support a pale-looking Dane out to the living room.

"Will you live?" Thorne asked his other deputy. Dane's answer was a glare as he slumped into a chair by the window and peered through the curtains.

Thorne turned back toward Angel. That was when Colton realized this man truly cared about her. He might not know how to show it, but Colton saw it in the older man's gaze—concern, worry, and pride.

The same things he'd seen in his own father's eyes when Dad had looked at him and his brothers.

"Have you figured out how they did it?" Thorne asked, his brows rising expectantly.

She bit her bottom lip for a second before shaking her head. Obviously not wanting to give up, but too curious not to hear her boss's theory. "No. I've been playing it over in my head. We didn't drink anything that wasn't tested. I made dinner myself."

"Toothpaste." Thorne's lips pulled up in a smug, lopsided grin.

"Toothpaste!" She palmed her forehead. "I should have thought of that."

"Whoever it was knew you would be thorough."

"They also know how to contact me by email," she said reluctantly.

Dane shifted in his seat by the window. "You've tracked the message?"

"I've tried."

This statement had Thorne and Dane exchange a look of surprise.

"You've not been able to come up with an identity? Or an IP address, at least?"

"No. Nothing. Whoever it is has some powerful tools. They're using a nucleus and a sentry. Normally, it wouldn't be a problem, but this Redgamer3 has a pretty cool setup. It's just swinging back around into itself. I'm literally chasing my own tail. I'd be impressed…if he wasn't such a diabolical monster."

"Hmm." Thorne frowned, and his hands folded in his lap.

"Do you have a guess who it is?" she asked him, leaning closer with excitement in her eyes.

Again Colton was reminded of his own father by their exchange. The way Detective Jack Williamson used to sit around the table with his five boys and his wife and share selected details of a case he was working.

He would give them enough clues he'd already uncovered so they could come up with the answers on their own. If there were answers. Unfortunately, some of those cases were never solved. And some nights, his father didn't want to talk about his cases.

Those nights when his cases hit too close to home. Kids and families.

Every one of Jack's sons had followed him into the force in one form or the other. Colton knew his father expected them to serve in some way. It had been engrained in them all since birth. During those dinners, he'd set their course.

When he died, each of the Williamson sons had vowed to pick up where their father left off. Helping others.

Colton looked over at Angel, and knew he'd let her into his home because she needed help. But the reason he was so desperate for her to stay was something else entirely.

Each day they spent together would make it harder when she left, but he would take what he could get and remember it always.

Angel's posture shifted, moving closer to Thorne. She resembled a child waiting for someone to get to the exciting part of the story. "You must have an idea, or you wouldn't have shown up here with that smug-ass grin on your face."

Thorne nodded. "I have a lead. I'll remind you, *my* face is not the one all over the news, so I'm not sure why I should be the one exerting myself to find the killer. Maybe you should put in a little more effort instead of lazing about."

Angel laughed, and Dane let out a huff of disinterest. Even Colton knew the man was bluffing. He cared about Angel, and was probably missing sleep himself to get her out of this mess. Josiah Thorne might want his deputies to think he was a tough old bastard, but it wasn't working.

Angel rubbed her palms together. "All right, then. Spill it."

Chapter Forty-Three

Like Angel, Colton also moved to the edge of his seat in anticipation as Thorne paused, then let out a dramatic sigh before finally answering.

"Fine. Heath has a younger brother who has his own struggling tech company," he said.

Angel shook her head. "I know that. But I checked him out. Noah was no threat. He doesn't have two nickels to rub together. What kind of hitman would take a job from a guy who can barely pay the electric bill?" she said with a look of irritation.

"The kind of hitman who knew he wouldn't get paid, and who'd planned to keep the prototype for himself from the beginning."

Angel looked over at Colton, then back to Thorne. "Noah was double-crossed? You know this how?"

"People are saying the reaction to his brother's grisly death wasn't entirely shock and sadness. There's apparently been some throwing of chairs and yelling behind his office door."

"Could be he was cut out of the will or life insurance," Colton offered.

But Thorne was already shaking his head. "He knew he was never in. It's no secret the Zeller boys were not brotherly."

Angel looked thoughtful. "Heath told me his brother stole one of his ideas when they were in college. He said it was an important lesson to learn. It was why he always kept his latest creations with him at all times, and didn't talk about them until they were ready to launch."

"It's pretty bad his own brother would want him dead." Colton thought about how close he was with his own brothers, and how devastated they must have been when he'd been killed. Or so they thought.

Then he looked up to see Angel staring at the floor, and realized his mistake. Shit. Her brother hadn't just wanted her dead. He'd actually tried to kill her himself.

"I didn't mean—"

"It's nothing." She held up her hand to stop his apology. A muscle worked in her jaw. "I think we need to look closer at the brother. I, of all people, know what brothers are capable of. And being in tech himself, he would have access to the best blocking capabilities. If I know where the email originated, it will help me make the link."

She looked so small sitting on the loveseat all by herself.

Maybe it wasn't the right time. Maybe she wouldn't appreciate the gesture in front of her boss and co-worker, but he couldn't help himself. He sat beside her and pulled her close, holding her tight.

To his surprise, she let him.

Chapter Forty-Four

"I'm so stupid," Angel complained as she scrolled through Noah Zeller's business emails. "Why didn't I think to look closer?"

She'd checked him out in the first days after she acquired a computer, but saw nothing but the normal emails of a business operation. However, since last Friday, he'd been sending quite a lot of them regarding a missing shipment.

He wasn't Redgamer3—at least not according to any account she had found—but he was involved somehow. And she was going to find out how.

Hacking into his phone proved more of a challenge, but soon she was seeing his texts in real time. Every few hours, Noah was writing to someone named Jim, asking when he was going to deliver his product. Quite the indecipherable code.

"He sounds desperate," Colton said as he read over her shoulder.

After their little moment on the sofa, Thorne and Dane

had left. Not before giving her an encrypted phone so they could keep in touch.

Angel should have been embarrassed that she'd let Colton comfort her. But she'd liked having his arms around her. She felt safe. For years she'd been taking care of herself, but with Colton she felt like she didn't have to do everything alone. She was still a bit raw, having told him her gruesome tale. All those feelings had been churned up, and she couldn't help but feel vulnerable.

Her talk with Dane still echoed in her head though. She knew from personal experience what happened when she allowed her emotions to make the decisions. She'd once thought she was in love with her first partner. But it turned out to be a huge mistake.

Not only had she missed the important clues that he was unstable, but she'd realized too late she couldn't have loved him. Because she didn't know him at all. Not only did he have a dark secret, but he'd even created another identity.

In the days after she'd killed him, she realized he had tricked her but she had not been paying attention. She'd been too naive and star-struck because the sexy marshal had taken her under his wing to show her the ropes.

When she'd pulled the trigger she'd known there was no other way to stop him. Lucas Stone had never truly existed. He was nothing but a reminder of what happened when she let her heart get involved.

As Colton set down a cup of tea next to her laptop, she knew it was far too late to stop her feelings for him. Her heart had brought her to his doorstep, and it was the reason she was still sitting in his living room.

She needed to find this Jim person, or better yet, Redgamer3, so she could move on. If she could just solve this case quickly so she could go back to work, she might have a chance of saving both Colton and herself from the pain that awaited them.

Turning back to her screen, she laughed wryly. "Noah actually thought Jim was going to deliver a billion-dollar piece of hardware after he'd done all the dirty work. Apparently, Noah didn't get any of the smart genes." She shook her head.

It was better to joke than to think too hard about how similar the situation was to her own. While she knew Noah wasn't the actual killer, it seemed likely he had hired the person who was responsible for Heath's death. He'd essentially killed his own brother, even if he hadn't been in the room with the knife.

"Can you find this Jim, or find out if he's Redgamer3?" Colton asked, hope and excitement in his voice. He'd mentioned how being a math teacher wasn't all that exciting. She hadn't realized how bored he must be.

"Not yet. Jim never emailed him back. Not once. I only see the message exit from Noah's system. I don't see it hitting a mailbox on the other end."

"So no one ever read them?"

"I can't be sure." She rubbed her temples. She was trying too hard. When she got in too deep, she couldn't see anything. She needed a distraction.

She looked at the man sitting next to her. His hazel eyes moved as he scanned the screen looking for some way to help her. His lips… God, she remembered those lips. Soft, yet firm and filled with naughty promises.

He'd kept all those promises.

It would be easy to lean into him, and let him take her away for a few minutes—no, hours. But she knew her story had only two possible endings—jail or back to her old life—and neither one of them would be fair to Colton.

She shoved down her lusty thoughts and brought up a different browser to finish something else she'd been working on when she couldn't sleep.

"I have a surprise for you," she said a few minutes later when she was finished. She turned the screen toward Colton, and heard his gasp of surprise.

"Is that—?"

"Yep. Your nephew." She watched the smile spread across his face as he sat down next to her to stare at the photo. "Looks like he's grown a lot in the last year."

"I'll say. He's walking." Colton pointed at the video as if she wasn't looking. She was. "Where did you get this?"

"I hacked into your sister-in-law's Facebook page. Here, you can scroll through the photos." She moved the screen closer to him as she stood to go. She wanted to give him some privacy while he looked at the photos of the family life he was no longer a part of.

She hadn't been sure whether or not it would be cruel to share the pictures, but she'd thought it over from his perspective, and decided he would want to see them.

She pointed at Pudge on the way out of the kitchen. "No more barking at strangers. If anyone else shows up, just eat them."

Pudge barked in approval, and followed her outside where she threw a ball for him for fifteen minutes.

When she came back in, Colton was standing by a window with his back to her. She heard a sniff and saw him wipe his face with his arm. He didn't turn toward her, though she knew he'd heard her come in with her jingling companion.

For a tough guy, Colton Williamson had a soft, gooey center.

She sat down at the computer to get back to work, and noticed something on the page. "What the hell?"

"What's wrong?" Colton asked, his voice hoarse.

"Your sister-in-law, Robin, is friends with you on Facebook. Did you have an account before the shooting?" It didn't seem likely, what with the dial-up and all.

He gave her a doubtful look. He wouldn't have spent any time on a computer unless it was absolutely necessary.

"Right." She clicked to go to the profile, and there was a photo of Colton with his brother, John. They looked like twins, but John was two years older than Colton. The cover photo was a muscle car.

"Any idea what the password would be?" she asked. "I can hack it, but that will take time."

Colton studied the page and shrugged. "Try seventy-three Mach One. That's what the car is. We bought it together and fixed it up."

After a few variations, Angel hit on the one that worked, and opened the page.

"I'm in."

"What is it?" Colton leaned over her to see his page.

"It looks like a memorial, of sorts. It's a bunch of people sharing stories about you. And…" She tilted her head, taking in a younger, leaner Colton. He was probably about twenty. "Photos. Wow." She flipped through proof that Colton had never suffered with adolescent awkwardness.

He squeezed in next to her. The side of his body pressed up against hers.

She'd already slept beside him, and allowed him to hold her. Sitting this close wasn't going to change the path they were heading down.

He laughed and shared some of the stories as she continued to scroll through the comments.

"I miss these people," he said quietly.

"It's obvious they miss you. I'm sorry it worked out like this. Viktor Kulakov is still out there. Until they come up with a charge sticky enough to put him away for life, you are in danger. There is no statute of limitations on murder." And without hard proof, the prosecutor was afraid the case would be dismissed. Viktor had lots of associates to pin things on if he came under suspicion. They only had Colton's testimony, and the prosecutor wasn't willing to show his cards.

"Weird, John never posted anything. He must not have an account," Colton said.

"He does. He was also in Robin's friends list." Angel bit her lip, deciding whether or not she should share the story about meeting John at Colton's funeral.

Rather than let the man think his brother had abandoned him, she let out a breath and faced the truth.

"He probably didn't post anything because he knows you're alive."

Chapter Forty-Five

"*What?*" Colton choked, eyes wide. This had already been a crazy day. Now to find out his brother knew he was alive?

Angel winced before she went on. "I wasn't sure if you would want to know. It doesn't change anything, but I probably should have told you before."

"You told him I was alive?"

"Of course not," she said defensively. "He saw me hanging out at the cemetery during your funeral."

"You went to the cemetery? What are you, a walking cliché?" To a detective as sharp as John, a strange government official lurking around would be nearly the same as straight out telling him something was up.

"At the time, I didn't know you yet. You were still in the hospital and pretty messed up. But, yeah. I went to your funeral, because it seemed like the right thing to do. I wanted to make sure I knew you a little bit, because if you didn't make it, I would be the only person at your second funeral."

He swallowed, slightly irritated that she'd been able to

see his family when he couldn't.

"I was also watching to see if Viktor or his people showed up. He sent someone to your other funeral. The one for your cover—Robbie Vanderhook. I wanted to make sure he wasn't on to the real you. I was also gauging the crowd to see if your friends and family seemed to be buying the story."

"The story of my death, you mean? Did you check to make sure the tears were real?" he snapped. He didn't mean to be rude, but it hurt that his family had been put through this.

"No. But I can tell when someone's acting and when it's real. Blotchy skin, red eyes, runny nose."

If he needed a list of what it looked like to deal with gut-wrenching heartache, he could have easily looked in the mirror. Seeing photos of his family moving on while he was here alone had just about killed him.

"And did you see anyone who didn't look the proper level of devastated?" He hated to think of the pain he'd caused his family. Even if he'd had no choice. He knew every one of them would have understood, but it still pained him that he'd hurt them.

"No. They were all plenty devastated," she said sadly. "But after the service was over, John came up and smiled at me. He said he was glad to see me."

"Let me guess. You were wearing black pants and white shirt, the official uniform for a U.S. deputy marshal at a funeral."

"You know, most people are too distraught to notice what other people are wearing at a funeral."

"Did you confirm I was alive?" He didn't know which answer he was hoping for. To give John hope wouldn't be fair, but to confirm Colton was still alive but they would be unable to share their lives with one another wouldn't have been easy for John, either.

"No. I couldn't. Besides, at that time I wasn't sure how much longer you'd be alive. I definitely didn't want to get his hopes up just to let them down again if you'd really died. But it didn't matter. He didn't need confirmation from me. It was as if he just *knew*."

Colton understood what she meant. Though John was two years older than him, the two of them had been like twins. Colton had been the best man when John married Robin. They'd asked Colton to be Tyler's godfather when the kid was only a few days old. He'd mumbled his answer with his best Brando impersonation.

Colton missed a lot of things about his old life. Taking down drug dealers, carrying a gun, and shoes without tassels, to name a few. But the thing he missed most was hanging out on a Saturday afternoon in his brother's backyard. They'd sit in the shade with a beer and reminisce about how much trouble they'd gotten into when they were younger. And plan adventures for the future.

"Oh, no," Angel whispered, yanking him from his memories.

"What is it?" He looked at the screen, scouring it for bad news. He didn't know how much more he could take.

"You have a private message."

Chapter Forty-Six

Angel wasn't surprised to see John's photo pop up on the message app. *After* explaining to Colton what a message app was. She'd met John briefly and knew how much he and Colton looked alike.

The message wasn't very long, and she read it before realizing it wasn't her business.

HEY! I SET THIS ACCOUNT UP IN CASE YOU MIGHT READ IT SOMEDAY. I HAVE A FEELING YOU'RE NOT DEAD, SO IT COULD HAPPEN. IF IT TURNS OUT I'M WRONG AND YOU REALLY ARE GONE, THEN I'D RATHER JUST PRETEND YOU'RE READING THIS. IT MIGHT BE STUPID TO HOPE, BUT I DON'T KNOW HOW TO HANDLE THIS WITHOUT HOPE. I MISS YOU, MAN. I KNOW I'VE GOT THREE OTHER BROTHERS, BUT NONE OF THEM ARE YOU. ROBIN'S PREGNANT AGAIN. IF IT'S A BOY WE'RE NAMING HIM AFTER YOU. PLEASE DON'T BE DEAD.

She heard a sniff and looked over at Colton, expecting

him to be laughing at that last remark. But he wasn't laughing. His eyes were wet, and though the tears hadn't breeched, it was close.

"I'll give you a moment alone," she said before moving to step away.

His large arm snaked around her waist and pulled her back, his face pressed against her stomach.

"The last thing I need is another goddamned moment alone. I'm fucking sick of being alone. Please just…"

She wrapped her arms around him, allowing her fingers to stroke through his hair in what she hoped was a comforting way. It had been so long since anyone had needed her for anything emotional, she had to think about what to do. It didn't come naturally anymore. That thought bothered her.

What had she become? She wasn't heartless—she felt his pain acutely—but she didn't know what to say to make it better. And she desperately wanted to make it better for him.

She wasn't sure if he'd cried. If he did, it was silent, the way most men did. Instead of releasing her, he pulled her into his lap.

"Thank you," he said against her hair.

"I'm so sorry. I wish there was some way…" There were no words to finish the rest of that sentence.

If there was some way she could go back in time to that afternoon when he was shot, she would have protected him. She hadn't even known his name at that point, but she would have done her job to keep him safe.

She moved to hold him closer, but he turned his head and pressed his lips against hers. It wasn't soft or brief. It was intense and all consuming, as if he'd been using all his strength to hold it back, and couldn't keep it contained for another second.

She felt the same way. She held him close, their kiss going deeper. He moaned as his hands grasped her ass and settled her onto the hard ridge in his jeans.

Up until now, she'd believed she was capable of keeping things friendly. Yes, she'd been as attracted to him as always, but she'd been in control.

There was no control now.

She whimpered when he pulled away far enough to remove her shirt. The small distance between them was too much. The time they'd been apart had been too long.

Why had she left? At the time, it had made sense, but now— Now she'd do anything in her power to stay with this man.

They were moving. Actually, he was moving and she was hanging onto him. He'd picked her up and was carrying her down the hall. He only faltered a second as he shouldered open the door to his bedroom.

They'd slept together before. But this was more than just lust or holding someone to offer comfort. This was everything—all of those feelings and more, combined. This was taking and giving in a frenzy of need. The need to be closer.

"Angel?"

"Yes," she answered his unspoken question, wondering if either of them would have had the strength to stop, even if they'd wanted to.

But she, for one, had no intention of stopping.

Chapter Forty-Seven

Angel was vaguely aware that this wasn't a good idea. But she didn't care. The only thing that mattered was being closer to Colton, in every possible way.

She barely had the patience to get out of her pants. Even as she yanked them off, her need to be with him was intense. It hadn't been like this before. Time had made her needy.

She wanted him naked, and it seemed the fastest way to make that happen was to get naked herself. Rather than take the time to undress each other, they went the more efficient route and ripped off their own garments.

"God." He swallowed as he paused to look at her. "I thought I'd remembered how beautiful you are. I thought my fantasies were pretty close, but they weren't this good."

She might have said thank you, or she might have told him to stop talking and focus on undressing, but she didn't get the chance. He was kissing her again, and her thoughts scattered off into pleasure.

He didn't play around. No doubt, he could tell how

desperate she was. He touched her. His fingers slid inside her, and they both moaned. He continued to stroke her, and while it felt incredible, she wanted more.

She needed him.

All of him.

She let out a whine of frustration, and he chuckled into her open mouth.

They were on the bed, though she wasn't quite sure how she'd gotten there… Right, he'd carried her. She was happily dazed. When he reached out to open the drawer of the nightstand, she nearly shouted in joy. She squirmed against the fingers of his other hand in anticipation.

"Oh, no," he whispered after a brief pause.

"Oh, no, what?" She was instantly alert and listening for danger. Even sex couldn't turn off her instincts entirely.

"These are expired."

Angel took the familiar box from him to study the date herself. Surely, he was reading it wrong. Condoms didn't expire. At least, not when owned by a man in his sexual prime.

"Is this the same box you had when we were together last year?" she asked in confusion.

He shrugged, then nodded. "There were still some left, and I haven't been with anyone since you."

"Seriously?"

They stared at one another, out of breath.

"Yeah. I don't want to have to lie to someone. And I doubt I'd be able to handle someone screaming out the name *Duncan* without laughing. And since I can't tell anyone who I really am, I was holding off until I figured it out. They don't tell you how to deal with these kinds of things when you go into protection."

She bit her lip, and confessed, "I haven't been with anyone since you, either."

What did it matter if he knew she hadn't found anyone

she wanted to be with? Or that she still thought of him, and wished she could have stayed.

"I didn't ask," he said with that sexy grin she loved.

"But you wondered."

"A little." He held up the box as the smile slid from his face. "What do we do about this?"

She studied the date again and frowned. "They're only two months out of date. I'm sure there's a buffer."

"You're *sure*, or you *think* there is?" He tilted his head, hope in his eyes.

"They would have to leave a buffer in case someone didn't even bother to check the date. They wouldn't want to get sued."

"I'd sure like to be using the condom, rather than talking about it." He brushed a hand over his hair and winced.

"Me, too. Let's just go for it." She couldn't believe those words had come out of her mouth. She was always the epitome of safety. She knew a baby would end her career, and normally she wouldn't ever take that kind of risk.

But this was Colton.

And deep down, a part of her knew the odds of getting her career back were slim.

"And if something happens?" He raised a brow, surprise clear in his eyes.

"We'll figure it out."

Good grief. She *never* took this kind of chance with her future. She was always in control of her life—ever since she was twenty-one and gained control of her crazy life, that is.

It was the reason she'd left Colton a year ago without a word. Because she'd been losing control, and had been far too tempted to stay with him when he'd asked.

"If this goes bad, I'll be the one reminding you it was your idea," he said as he ripped one of the condoms from the strip.

"Sure, sure. Come on." She made the hurry up motion then bit his neck in that spot by his ear that made him groan. The sound of the condom wrapper ripping was followed by a delicious pressure as he entered her in one thrust.

She may not have known it when she was fleeing San Francisco, but this was one of the reasons she'd come here. She'd wanted this feeling again, and only this man would do.

Chapter Forty-Eight

Colton knew better.

He *knew* it was a bad idea to fall for Angel again. She'd nearly destroyed him the last time. He could almost remember that icy feeling in the pit of his stomach when he'd walked out that morning and found Justin on his sofa and Angel gone. No note, no nothing. As if she'd never been there.

As if she hadn't left a giant fucking hole in his heart.

He *also* knew he was lonely, and wasn't making the best decisions at the moment. Yes, she was hot, which—again—didn't help with his decision-making abilities.

He *damn well* knew not to pin their future on a condom that had expired two months ago.

He wanted her, but some control remained. Had he wanted to, he could have stopped. If she'd balked, he could have satisfied her in another way until he could make a run to the drugstore.

But he didn't stop, and the reason scared him almost as much as Viktor Kulakov did.

He couldn't even put the thought to words. All he knew was, he was going for it. He'd risk the condom because, honestly, it didn't feel like that much of a risk.

It wasn't as if he could compel her to stay, even if they made a kid together. But the idea of having a baby with Angel, well, it didn't scare the hell out of him, as it should have.

Surely, this was just his base instincts coming through. The need to procreate was in every man's genes. It wasn't that he was desperate to tie himself to this particular woman. This woman who refused to get attached to anyone. This woman who had been broken and alone for so long he didn't know if he would ever be able to put all her pieces together again.

But she had everything he could ever want. She was tough and smart. And God, she knew how to move when she was under him. She tilted her hips up on his down stroke, and nearly ended him when she nipped at the skin where his neck met his shoulder.

He might have asked her to slow down, but he could tell she was ruthlessly chasing an orgasm, and he wanted to help her catch it. He went deeper, and she gasped before tensing in that beautiful way that meant she was going over.

When her muscles spasmed around him, he allowed his own release a few strokes later. He held his position until she'd ridden the last wave, then relaxed on top of her, shifting his weight slightly so he wouldn't crush her.

"Colton." His name was a whisper on her lips, which about broke his heart. It wasn't just that he hadn't heard his real name in a while, but he hadn't heard it like this—dripping with satisfaction.

They stayed joined together until their breathing slowed, then he rolled to his side and pulled her next to him. Maybe if he held her tight, she wouldn't be able to leave him.

Her head lifted as she stared at him, her chin on his chest.

"The condom seems to have held," she reported.

He had been afraid to look. On this side of desire, he could see exactly how stupid he'd been. Now was not the best time for them to bring a child into the world. She was wanted for murder. If they couldn't clear her, or keep her hidden, she would go away for a very long time.

And he had a phony name and was living a fake life.

"Look, I..." She paused, and he took the opportunity to stop her.

"If you're thinking of saying anything that even slightly resembles regret, just keep it to yourself. I survived sex with The Mantis. Give me a few moments to bask in the victory." He chuckled until she elbowed him in the ribs. "Come on. It's a kickass name. Maybe you should have a cape."

"I don't want to talk about capes."

He let out a breath and closed his eyes. He knew what she was going to say, and he couldn't take it. "I'm riding a wave of bliss over here, and I don't want you ruining it," he cut her off before she could destroy him with her doubts.

"I wasn't going to ruin anything. I'm on my own bliss wave, so there," she snapped and even stuck out her tongue.

She put her head back down on his chest and he counted the seconds—fourteen—before she lifted her head again to look at him.

"We shouldn't have done this."

And like that, his wave of bliss turned into a tsunami of pain.

"That's it," he said as he reached over to grab up the box. "There are two left, and we're using them right now." The first one had worked just fine. He wasn't about to let a box of condoms go to waste.

Maybe he was playing the odds, but he was going to make love to her until she stopped doubting that they could actually work.

Chapter Forty-Nine

Angel didn't actually think two more times was a realistic goal, but Colton proved her wrong. She'd never been so happy to be mistaken.

Yes, she still had doubts this was the best idea. Certainly, a mental health professional would side with her, that starting a relationship during a life crisis was ill advised. Especially if said life crisis involved going away to prison or running from the law for the rest of one's life.

"All I'm saying"—she took a dearly needed breath after round three—"is that you have to agree our timing is off." Was she out of shape? Apparently, her training didn't prepare her for sex marathons.

For their third time, she did all the work. Riding him to the finish. If it had been a race, they would have tied.

"Babe, our timing was perfect," he said with a crooked grin on his handsome face. Despite his smile, there was still sadness lurking in his eyes. Sadness she'd caused.

"You know that's not what I meant," she said.

"Yeah." He pulled her close and nuzzled her neck. "Let's sleep. Things will be better in the morning."

She doubted that. In her experience, the worst things were revealed when she woke up. It was why she didn't sleep.

"Rest," he whispered. "I'm going to go let Pudge out. He and I will keep watch."

She was exhausted. Maybe she could actually sleep for a few hours.

When she awoke, it was still dark and Colton was pressed against her back. Pudge was lying across her feet at the bottom the bed. No doubt, he'd jumped up there after Colton fell asleep.

Unable to sleep any longer, but not willing to move, she listened to Colton's even breathing against her shoulder. His hands twitched occasionally, making her wonder what he might have been dreaming of.

She was starting to drift off again, when his twitches became more aggravated and he murmured in distress. She moved away, ready to wake him from his nightmare.

Suddenly, he jumped up and said her name.

"I'm here. I'm fine. Right here, see?" She reached over to turn on the light to make sure he could see.

He winced and blinked, but put his arms around her and pulled her back down next to him.

"I'm sorry about that," he murmured against her hair when he had caught his breath.

"Do you want to tell me what it was about?"

"The same thing it's always about."

"Viktor?" she guessed.

She felt him nod.

"There's a lot of cover to keep Viktor from finding my brothers and my mom. But…"

She nodded, glad the DEA had done a good job of protecting him before he'd taken on the Kulakov job.

She'd read his file. Make that, files.

The one where he was Robbie Vanderhook, an ex-marine from Boston who had trouble with authority and had gotten into an issue with the law. That was the one fed to Viktor to get Colton into his circle.

After the shooting, when Viktor's men were rooting around to make sure Colton—Robbie—was really dead, they were told the truth. Or the next version of it, anyway. Detective Robert Gates was an undercover officer. His wife had died a few years ago and he'd been a mess. He'd taken the Kulakov job because he had nothing to lose. No other family. Not even a dog. He'd been shot six times in the chest and died of his injuries.

It was Robert Gates's funeral that had been attended by Frank "Butch" Seaver, one of Viktor's men. Angel had watched the man from behind her dark glasses, wondering if he'd been the one to pull the trigger six times before leaving Colton to die on the floor in an empty marina.

The backstory and the funeral had been enough to satisfy Viktor. There hadn't been a need to look any deeper. Of course, if he had, there were other layers of protection between Viktor and Colton's real life. And his family.

New identities for his four brothers, their wives, girlfriends, children, and his mother would have been a nightmare. Thus the reason for the extra coverage on his true identity.

Colton had survived, kept his family safe, and managed to stay clear of Viktor.

Now she was here, putting all of his efforts in danger. If she was caught here, he would be implicated and his face would be plastered all over television along with hers. It wouldn't take long for Viktor to see it and start digging again.

She slipped out of bed while Colton slept, and felt the guilt wash over her, as it had every night since she showed up at his door.

The longer she stayed, the more danger he was in.

Damn it. She shouldn't have come here.

Chapter Fifty

Colton was used to getting up alone. He didn't even panic when he reached across the cool sheets and found the bed was empty. He remained calm when he walked out to the living room and found it empty as well. Her laptop was gone and so was her bag.

"Where's Angel?" he asked Pudge when the dog slinked off the sofa to come greet him. Colton had decided to let the rules about the furniture slide, and followed Pudge to the back door.

Only when she wasn't on the back porch did Colton's heart begin to race. Was there some danger? Or had she simply left?

He spotted movement down by the willow and relaxed. She was sitting on a bench, her laptop next to her, but she was looking up at the sky, the sun shining on her face and glinting in her inky black hair.

She was beautiful, and she was still here.

His heart filled with hope, despite his mind's attempts to

protect himself.

Pudge ran up to greet her, and she smiled and rubbed him behind the ears.

"You're outside," Colton said as he walked closer.

"I needed some fresh air and sunshine. If the feds swoop in and take me because I am out here, then so be it. It was worth it."

It was a perfect morning. It was still cool, but the sun made it comfortable. The sky was cloudless and bright blue.

"Did you think I left?" she asked as she raised her hand to block the sun from her eyes.

He decided to be honest. With a shrug he nodded. "Not at first, but then when you weren't in your usual spot, I became...concerned."

"Concerned." She raised her brow, then frowned. "What you should be concerned about is that I'm still here putting you in danger."

This again. He rolled his eyes and sat next to her, making her move her laptop out of the way.

"I'm glad you're here." It was the truth, and not just because of the amazing sex, but for the sorely missed excitement she'd brought back into his life. "I'm going to go get us some breakfast. Do you have a request?"

She shook her head and opened her mouth to protest, but he cut her off.

"You'd better be here when I get back, or I'm eating your cinnamon roll." He pointed at her to emphasize his words as he turned to go back to the house.

He knew the tough guy routine wouldn't work, but he made himself get in the truck and head into town to pick up breakfast. He'd seen something in her eyes that made it a little easier to leave.

Whatever it was he thought he'd seen, he knew she'd still be there when he got back. Some kind of affection? Or maybe she was just hungry.

While he didn't race to the café, he might have picked up the pace on the way back.

She was back in her usual place at the coffee table when he returned.

"What are you doing?" he asked as he dropped the bags with the breakfast pastries and a new box of condoms on the counter. "You have a devious smile. That's either really good or really bad."

"I'm tired of waiting for this Jim person to make a move—assuming he's the one with the stolen hardware. And I haven't found a link to Redgamer3. So I've decided to take matters into my own hands."

Oh, hell. That didn't sound good.

"How so?"

"I'm pushing him into a corner."

"Ah." He poured a cup of coffee, carrying it over to top hers off. He put their breakfast on plates and went to sit with her, knowing she was too busy to come to the table to eat.

"Tell me about this corner. And please use real people words."

"I've been using Noah's email to contact other tech firms, telling them what his brother developed, and how it was stolen. And if anyone buys it and tries to use it, they will be an accessory to murder."

"Have you ever tried meditation to help you sleep?" he asked instead of addressing her announcement. The woman was wound too tight.

"I'm trapping the killer."

He watched as she sucked sticky sweetness from her thumb. His cock twitched, and for a moment, he forgot what they were talking about.

"He won't be able to sell the prototype, which means it will be worthless to him. He'll have two options. Sell it to

Noah, or kill Noah to shut him up. Either way, he'll make a move, and I can grab him."

That brought Colton back from his lust-induced state. "You mean *we* can grab him."

"No. Not we. *Me*. Alone."

Colton laughed until he realized she wasn't joking. "You honestly think you were going to tell me this plan and I was going to say, what? Good luck? Hope it works out? Are we going to exchange Christmas cards?"

"You can't get involved." This was said with dead seriousness. She actually thought she could make him stay behind while she faced a murderer alone. Fuck the whole woman equality thing. He knew she was strong and capable. This wasn't about him thinking she couldn't handle herself, or him having a caveman complex.

This was about protecting himself as much as her. If something happened to her, he wouldn't survive it. He couldn't sit there while she faced this alone.

He couldn't.

But he also knew he wouldn't be able to force her to relent if she was adamant in her decision. He'd have to reason with her.

And if that didn't work, he'd beg.

"Wait a second. Originally, the plan was that I would help."

She put up a hand to stop him. "I know. But you're safe here, Colton. I can't risk you getting hurt or having your cover exposed to help me."

"Hold up." He put his hands up in a stop gesture like hers. "Last year when you were protecting me, you insisted on walking in front of me every damn time we left a building. You were willing to risk your life for mine. But I'm not allowed the same courtesy? I'm not even allowed to help you?"

"That's right. It's my job."

He could see by the way she set her hand on her hip, she actually thought this would work. It didn't. Not even close. His plan to reason with her went to hell as anger took over.

"This is ridiculous. You don't even have a fucking job anymore. You're a fugitive. Your only job is to hide out and not get arrested for murdering someone."

"But—" She wasn't going to stop arguing. He would have to come up with a new plan.

Giving up on words, he kissed her hard, hoping to communicate on a different level how important she was to him. When she was well and thoroughly kissed, he pulled away and looked down into her icy blue eyes, waiting for her to say something that would really make him lose his temper.

To his surprise, she smiled. "You could have just said you'd like to come along," she said.

"That's it." He picked her up and tossed her over his shoulder. Grabbing the bag with the condoms along the way, he took her back to the bedroom where he made love to her until she could only gasp and moan and not tell him he wasn't coming with her.

He wouldn't let her leave him behind again.

Not this time.

Chapter Fifty-One

Angel was so spent she could barely move. The muscles in her legs—as well as other places—were still trembling. When Colton wanted to prove a point, he did a pretty thorough job of it.

She might have protested when he'd picked her up caveman style and taken her back to his bed, except that's where she'd wanted to go, and he had longer legs and walked faster.

Then he'd stripped her down, kissing her with a desperation she knew was more than just sexual need. She'd scared him, and he was laying claim to her body, her heart, as well as her plan to catch a killer.

When he slid into her, all her good intentions fell away. She couldn't leave him. She wanted him too much.

How could she walk away? Why didn't she have the strength to do the right thing?

She hadn't been able to do it this morning. She knew it wouldn't get any easier the longer she stayed with him. Even if it was for his own good. She was too selfish to leave. It didn't help that he didn't want her to go.

Her thoughts broke into distracted fragments as pleasure ripped through her body. A surge of ecstasy wiped away any lingering doubts for the time being. There was no murder investigation or worries about her future. There was only this man, right now, in her arms.

She gasped for air as he rolled to her side, his hand resting on her stomach in a possessive way she liked far too much.

Eventually, their temporary bliss transitioned into reality. She let her head fall to the side so she could look at him as he kissed her shoulder.

"We need to stop," she said. It would be more difficult to make sense of their situation if they ended up in bed every time she didn't agree with him.

"I bought the twenty-four-count box."

"Damn."

She couldn't seem to help herself when it came to him. All her training and self-control went to hell whenever he kissed her.

And somehow, it was even better than it had been a year ago. Maybe because she'd had a year to think about how great they were together. A year of missing him.

"Promise me you'll stick around long enough to use up the box," he whispered as he looked up at her with those stormy eyes.

She wanted nothing more but to make that promise and a million more. To wrap her arms around him and never let go.

"You know I can't promise anything. The SWAT team could be on the roof right now getting ready to rush in and take me off in cuffs," she said, making light of the tense moment.

"They're not on the roof. Pudge would be barking."

"Maybe they came up with some kind of spray that keeps

dogs from smelling them." She wasn't willing to give up yet.

"Wouldn't we hear them up there? Four two-hundred-pound men just strolling around on the roof?"

"Okay. So maybe they're not on the roof. Maybe they're in one of those armored cars and they're headed up the street, ready to crash into your house."

His brow rose. "It seems excessive for just you."

"But I'm The Mantis."

They laughed together and she realized she had never felt happier in her life. She felt at home here with him, even if she didn't have a solid understanding of what home was supposed to feel like.

"Am I allowed to call you—"

"No. Only I can use that name."

Silence fell when the laughing died down. "Promise me you won't leave unless you have to." This was a different request, entirely. One she couldn't hide from.

She kissed his neck before moving to his chin, then his lips. Soon enough, he was moving on top of her, his request forgotten for the moment.

God, she wanted to promise to stay. Her life with him was so peaceful.

Until Pudge started barking.

"Hell. If that's the SWAT team, I'm going to be really pissed off." He rolled off the bed and tossed her a shirt. "Go hide."

She tilted her head to listen. No footsteps on the roof. She hurried to the front windows to look out. The man in the SUV was almost to the front door when she recognized him.

"Oh my God!" she gasped.

Chapter Fifty-Two

Colton didn't know what was going on, but Angel opened the front door and practically threw herself at their visitor before dragging him inside.

Not only was it not a great idea for her to be exposed to people driving by, Colton didn't like the way she smiled at the man while wearing nothing more than one of his T-shirts and her panties. She'd just jumped out his bed after making love, and now she was excited to see this guy.

Except Colton knew the man. Deputy Marshal Justin Marks. His handler.

Justin was the deputy who'd taken over for Angel after she left his detail.

"*Angel?* What the hell are *you* doing here?" the man asked, looking between her and Colton in total confusion. Then he took in her ensemble and sniffed with a frown. "Never mind. Don't answer that."

Now she was the one who looked confused. "But if you didn't know I was here, why did you come?" she asked, her words slowing as if putting it together as she spoke.

She turned in Colton's direction at the same time Justin looked at him.

Colton's blood ran cold at the worried expression on both their faces.

Justin let out a breath before dropping the bomb. "I'm here to speak to Colton. It's about Viktor Kulakov."

Chapter Fifty-Three

When Justin was seated, and Angel had changed into real clothes, she sat next to Colton and took his hand, ready to support him as he'd done for her so many times through her ordeal.

"He knows?" Colton asked. Two words that needed no explanation. She and Justin both knew what he was asking.

"DEA hasn't been able to get another agent into his circle as deep as you were. Viktor's been very cautious. They did have another agent in at a much lower level. He's been there since before you were taken out."

It wasn't unusual to have an overlap. It wasn't even that strange that Colton wouldn't have known about the other agent. It would be easier to play his part if he wasn't looking out for someone else.

"Is the other agent still in?" Angel asked.

"No. His body was found a few days ago. From the looks of it, he'd been tortured."

The only reason Justin would be sitting on Colton's sofa

telling them this story was if this story had something to do with Colton. She tensed in preparation for bad news.

She wanted to reach for her laptop and look up the file herself. She still had access into the federal network. Through a roundabout way.

"Did the other agent know me?" Colton asked.

"He didn't know who you were, but he might have known you were planning to testify." Justin clamped his jaw. "People can't keep their fucking mouths shut, and people end up hurt."

"And Viktor knows the only way I'd be able to testify was if I hadn't been killed when Weller shot me."

"Correct."

"So Viktor knows Colton's alive." She was the one to say it out loud. They all knew, of course, but it needed spoken.

"There's been some activity in your cover file," Justin said, then turned his gaze to Angel. "The DEA did a damn good job of encrypting those files. Kulakov doesn't have anyone good enough to get through. But he's been looking. Maybe you'll want to—"

"Yes. I'll make sure they're impenetrable." She reached for her laptop. This was too important to wait.

"My family," Colton whispered as his face went pale. She reached out and squeezed his hand.

"I'll make sure your real information is locked up. We can pile on more layers of protection if we need to. We'll keep your family safe." She would make damn sure of it.

"The DEA is also working on it." Justin turned to Colton. "I just wanted to make sure you are aware of what's going on. I didn't want any link from our office to your new identity, which is why I came in person." He looked over at Angel again. "I don't need to tell either one of you how important it is for you to keep a low profile right now."

Meaning, if Colton's face was spread across the news as

her accomplice, he wouldn't make it to any trial.

"If my profile gets any lower, I really will be dead," Colton grumbled.

"We have multiple plans in place. If we think he's too close to figuring out your real identity, we can have every one of your family members to safety within an hour."

No doubt Justin thought an hour was impressively quick, but Angel knew a lot could happen to a person in an hour. From the frown on Colton's face, it was clear he didn't think an hour was good enough, either.

"They'll keep putting up more walls of protection as fast as he tears them down. I know moving your family isn't ideal, but if it's the only way, we won't hesitate to do whatever's necessary to protect them."

Colton nodded and let out a breath. "Thank you."

Angel had already launched her bore program to locate any fragments of information regarding Colton's real identity. It would take a little while to run.

Justin stood to leave. "I'll stay in touch. If it looks like he's on your trail, we're ready to move you again, too. Stay alert."

"We've been on alert for the last few weeks," Colton said.

Justin glanced over at Angel with a look of annoyance. "Right." He pointed to the back door. "Angel? Can I talk to you for a moment in private?"

"Yeah." She bit her lip as she followed him out to the backyard. She had a pretty good idea what he was going to say, and she had no defense. Justin was a huge guy. The only way she'd ever been able to best him physically was when she'd figured out he was ticklish.

He spun on her as soon as they were out of the house. "What are you *thinking*?"

"I needed a place to stay, with someone I could trust." This was reasonable, but she knew Justin—being Colton's handler—wouldn't care about what she needed. His job was to make sure Colton didn't get exposed.

"And there wasn't anyone else that fit that description? You had to come here and wreck this guy's life *again*?" He crossed his arms over his immense chest and stared down at her.

Ouch.

"I'm not wrecking his life," she snapped, though she knew that was a lie. She'd known it since the night she first showed up on his back porch.

But she didn't need Justin's attitude.

"You weren't there, remember?" he said. "*I* was. I was the one sleeping on his sofa the morning he came out expecting to find you. The morning after you ran off and didn't even leave the guy a fucking note. *I'm* the one who saw that, and couldn't do a damn thing. I don't like to get sucked into the emotional shit, but that guy was broken when you left."

She swallowed, and opened her mouth to say something, but what was there to say? It was all true. She'd hurt Colton in the worst way, and she was in a situation to do it again, at any moment.

"You and I don't get to have this, Angel." He ran his hand over his buzzed hair. "We knew when we signed up we were giving up our families, and a chance at a normal life. I tried to have both, but it doesn't work. Not for those of us in Phoenix."

Justin had taken on the role of big brother for the entire team. He was always giving them advice and sharing his wisdom. It might have been annoying if it wasn't so heartfelt and sincere. And usually right on target.

"When I signed up, I didn't have a family to give up," she said. "But now..." She didn't know how to finish that sentence.

"There is no good way out of this for Colton. Whether

you get picked up, or you go back home, he's still stuck here without you."

"I know. He knows it, too. He's not expecting—"

"Bullshit." Justin walked in a small circle and waved a hand at her. "You think I don't know what is going on? I've had my share of T-shirt-and-panties mornings. Hell, you are getting way too close."

"I'm not. I'm—"

Oh, hell. She was. She couldn't lie to Justin. Or to herself.

She let out a breath. "Do you know how many times I've almost died, Justin? A lot. There've been times when I've been alone, wondering why I'm still there. Feeling like maybe none of it was worth it."

She stepped away when Justin reached for her. She wasn't done yet.

"When I'm with Colton, I think maybe *this* is why. And I feel really glad that I lived through all the shit just so I could have a few moments with him. Maybe it's not fair. And you're probably right—I am too close, and it's going to hurt like hell for both of us when the time comes for me to move on. But you know what? It's a hell of a lot better to have a few moment of happiness than to constantly wonder why I even bother to survive."

Justin let out a sigh and gave her a grim look. "I just don't want you to hurt anymore. You've already been through enough. The thing with Lucas—"

"This is not like Lucas. I'd lost myself in him. It wasn't healthy. It's different with Colton. I'm still me, just better. Happier."

"I wish this could work out for both of you," Justin said sadly, and she saw in his eyes he didn't think it was possible.

"Thank you. But sometimes the good things are worth the hurt." She hoped this was one of those times she survived.

"I'll trust you. You know what you're doing. Just keep his

face off the news."

She nodded. "I will."

The smirk on Justin's lips was fair warning. "Just think what the press would say if they knew The Mantis really did kill one of her lovers."

She smacked him in the arm—it was like hitting a wall. "Lucas Stone wasn't my lover when I killed him. He wasn't the person I knew."

At. All.

"I know. I'm sorry." Justin pulled her into a hug so tight she thought her ribs touched in the center. "He tricked us all."

They walked back in the house silently. Justin pulled her into another bone-crushing hug, then gave some last-minute instructions on reaching out if there was any trouble.

"I'll walk you out," Colton offered as Justin moved for the door.

Angel took a spot next to Pudge, and they both watched as the two men stepped out into the driveway to talk about her.

Chapter Fifty-Four

"What's Task Force Phoenix doing to find Heath Zeller's real killer?" Colton asked as soon as he and Justin were alone. As much as he wanted Angel to stay with him, he didn't want it to have to be like this. With both of them hiding and not knowing what danger lurked around the next corner.

Virtual prisoners in his home.

He wanted Kulakov behind bars. And he wanted Angel to stay with him because she chose to, not because she didn't have any other options.

"We're not officially working the case, since there is no case. Everyone is convinced it was Angel who killed him, so they don't want to waste resources on chasing down a phantom suspect. But we're all working on it off the books."

"But you all have other cases to work, too?" Colton suspected.

"Yeah." Justin let out a sigh. "We have to make it look legit."

"So, what do you have so far?"

"Not much of anything. We know Noah wasn't the killer. He has an alibi. He may have set up the hit, but we don't have proof yet."

That's what Colton had figured, but hearing it out loud made his head hurt.

"Look at it this way. It gives you two some more time together," Justin said with a sad smile before he slid into the driver's seat, and put the car in reverse. "Take care of yourself. Contact me immediately if anything seems off." With a wave, Justin drove away.

As much as Colton liked having more time with Angel, he wished it wasn't this way. She was there because she was trapped. For now. He didn't like the uncertainty that she could be gone at any minute. They really needed to have a talk before he got in any deeper. He needed an answer to the question he'd asked just before the untimely interruption.

When he went back into the house, Angel wasn't in the living room. He called her name, and she answered from the bedroom...where he found her lying in his bed, naked.

"Where were we?" she asked as she reached for him.

God help him, but he went willingly into her arms.

Chapter Fifty-Five

It didn't go unnoticed by Colton that Angel had used sex to distract him from his worries…and that he had let her. There were now only twenty-one condoms in the box.

Before Justin showed up, Colton had asked her to stay again. He knew damn well he was setting himself up to get another no from her. And he didn't know if he would survive it.

She was asleep when he came back from the bathroom. He climbed in behind her and wrapped an arm around her waist. She fit perfectly against him.

She fit perfectly into his life.

Why couldn't she understand how great they could be, and give in to it? Why couldn't she love him as much as he loved her?

His body tensed with that revelation. He should have realized that was what he was feeling. *Love*. Hadn't he watched his brothers, one by one, shift their lives to focus on that one person who fulfilled them?

Except, in each case, the recipient of their affection felt the same way and didn't run off in the middle of the night in terror of commitment.

He let out a sigh and pulled her closer, enjoying the moment while he had it. He knew asking for promises from Angel wouldn't work. He'd have to convince her it was worth taking a shot with him.

He must have fallen asleep, because he was pulled from his dreams by the sound of Angel whimpering next to him. She thrashed around, and her arms came up protectively, shielding her from some unseen attacker.

In an effort to save her, as she'd saved him from his own subconscious, he shook her awake.

Fists flying, she gulped in air and sat up. It was a good thing his reaction time was still up to speed or he might have gotten a broken nose.

"You're okay, you're safe. It's Colton. I've got you," he said firmly, dodging her blows.

She froze, then slumped against him and let out a sigh of relief. They were both haunted by their pasts. How much he wished they could both find some peace.

"I could have been killed," she whispered.

He frowned, but wanted to help if he could. That meant narrowing it down.

"Which time?" he asked.

And she burst into tears.

Chapter Fifty-Six

Angel didn't know why she was crying. She *hated* crying. It served no real purpose, and rarely did it ever make her feel better. Still, it was impossible to stop, so she simply gave in and allowed the sobs to rack her body and destroy her temporary peace.

Colton turned on the light and pulled her close.

"It's okay," he soothed. His strong arms held her so tightly it was difficult to breathe, but she didn't want him to let go. He was safe. "Tell me about it."

She'd had to go through a lot of analysis before she joined Task Force Phoenix. Her past, paired with her previous life of crime, put her at the top of the list for some kind of mental disorder.

After being shot on the job by her own partner, not to mention then killing him, she'd been forced to attend her four required meetings with the shrink before she could be released back to duty.

But none of those sessions prepared her to talk about

what haunted her now. She knew instinctively it would help to talk about it, though. And Colton was here. Willing.

She pulled away so she could look at him. "Why didn't he kill me, too?" she asked.

Colton licked his bottom lip and brushed a tear from her cheek. "I don't know all the details, but from what you've said it sounded like the cops showed up and stopped him before he had the chance."

She shook her head. She hadn't been clear regarding who *he* was. Colton assumed she'd meant her brother.

She could see why he'd misunderstood.

And yes, that question had plagued her thoughts since the night she sat curled up in a blanket at the police station while the detective worked out what had happened to her parents. She'd been questioned, and she'd told them what she'd seen, and how her brother had attacked her. Her voice, though quiet, had been strong. At the time, it had seemed as though someone else was talking. Like a stranger was relaying a story. A horribly gruesome story. Not *her* story.

While the coffee had been hot enough to burn her tongue, it didn't stop her body from shaking, or warm her from her emotionally frozen hell.

All these years later, it still didn't feel like the story belonged to her. She kept it apart from her. Something she would deal with another time.

Someday.

But...not today.

Not ready to plunge into that black hole, she shifted the conversation to a different situation.

"No. I didn't mean my brother. I meant the person who drugged me and killed Heath. This Jim, or Redgamer3, whoever he is. He was there. He touched me to move me into position. He could have done anything he wanted." She shivered. "He could have killed me, too. Why didn't he?"

Colton's brows creased, then he shook his head. "I'm guessing he wanted somebody to pin it on."

"But no one has been able to track him. He was able to get away with it. Why leave a loose end?" It didn't make any sense.

Those emails taunted her. Did he leave her alive so he could play with her? Was she nothing but a mouse being toyed with by the cat?

"The police are using all their resources to find *you*. They're not looking for anyone else. It's the perfect plan to get away with murder."

She nodded, but didn't feel any better.

He let out a breath and pulled her back against him. "Is that what's really bothering you?" he asked, his voice soft.

She tensed with fear. Not the kind she felt on an almost normal basis—the fear that kept her one step ahead of a criminal—but a more personal fear.

He knew her. Too well.

He knew when she was lying. Even to herself.

Chapter Fifty-Seven

Angel knew it was time to face her demons. If she ever wanted to get past this, she knew she needed to deal with it. And Colton was here. He cared. He'd help her pick up the pieces when she broke apart.

"I— No." She wasn't just upset about her failure to protect Heath. Not by a long shot. Her heartbeat kicked up painfully.

She tucked her head under his chin and traced trembling fingers along his bare chest. She could feel his heartbeat thumping under her fingertips, and felt his chest rise and fall as he took in air and let it out. Life.

As she trailed back up her fingers brushed over the raised skin of a scar. One of six similar marks. Proof that he, too, had faced death and walked away. She knew from his file that two of the bullets hit organs, while the other four missed vital targets.

If anyone understood what she was feeling, it was Colton.

"You've seen my scars," she started.

"Yes. I think they're beautiful. They're proof that you

lived through something horrific. They're symbols of your strength."

"If my brother had come to my room first, I wouldn't be here." Her breath caught in her throat. She'd always known this, but saying the words out loud made it real.

Colton nodded slowly. "In a criminology course, they might say it was because you were the lesser threat. Nicholas would have started with your father because he knew he could overpower you and your mother."

"You think it comes down to strategy?" she asked.

Colton shrugged and twisted his lips to the side as he thought it over. "In my experience there are two kinds of criminals. There are the kind who plan things out, and know what they're doing. They choose it. And then there are the people who can't help themselves. There is no strategy, there is just an empty soul and madness."

She nodded in agreement.

"For that last group, I don't think there is a way to rationalize their behavior. We'll never know for sure why they do something, because we're trying to make sense out of something that is senseless."

"This scar." She pulled up her shirt to show a circular scar much like the ones on his chest. Hers was right under her ribs. "I was shot by my partner. When I got hit, I lay there wondering if anyone would find me in time."

Colton's eyes widened. "I would like to get my hands on him." His voice was low and threatening.

"You can't. I shot him back. He's dead. But I should have died then, too. Just a few inches and the bullet would have hit something vital. Like when I was with Heath. He was murdered right next to me, yet the killer murdered him and left me unharmed."

Colton blew out a breath and brushed her hair back from her face. "You sound upset that you survived. Most people would feel lucky."

She didn't really want to go into that whole mess with Lucas. So she diverted the subject a little. "I guess I just feel there must be something...good...I'm supposed to do with my life. I've escaped death so many times, this can't be it."

He nodded, and she could tell he understood.

"I've wondered the same thing," he said. "And then something happens, I make some difference, and I think, was that it? Was *that* the thing I'm meant to do?"

"Like what?" she asked, momentarily forgetting about her own situation.

"Like rescuing damsels who are wanted by the law, for one."

This was a joke, she could tell.

Then he turned serious. "In January, one of my students came in after class and told me he was failing almost every subject. His parents were going through a rough divorce, and seemed to be focused on hurting each other instead of making sure their son was handling things okay."

"Poor kid."

"He asked if he could have an extra credit assignment to get his grade back up. He told me the other teachers had all given him reports to write or projects to do. It seemed asinine to give a student *more* work to do when he was already struggling. How would that help?"

"Good point."

"I asked him to come in the next day and I would come up with something. When he showed up I got out my guitar and held it out to him."

"Wait. You play the guitar?" She sat up to look at him. She'd had no idea.

"Not well. I just started last year. But it gives me something to do in the evenings."

She felt the familiar guilt. Had she stayed with him,

maybe they would have found something fun to do together. Maybe she would have learned to play the drums and they could have gone on tour.

"Anyway, we took turns playing the chords from the book I brought. Then we put them together and played a little song. It wasn't bad, and he seemed more relaxed when we were finished."

"Music can be very therapeutic," she observed.

Many times when she was having trouble with her thoughts, she'd turn on some hard music and play it as loud as she could without disturbing her neighbors. Feeling the bass pound through her body made her feel alive.

"We did this almost every night for a month, and his math grade came up on its own. I checked with the other teachers and he was doing better in their classes, as well."

"He just needed someone to take the time," she said, feeling ridiculously proud of Colton for being so sensitive to the child's needs.

"I told him I was proud of him, and he told me that the day he came into my room to get his extra credit assignment he was at the end of his rope. He had been planning to go home and end his life. He told me he'd felt like he was drowning and wasn't able to breathe. He didn't see any other way out."

Angel felt tears in her eyes again as Colton swallowed down his obvious emotion.

"Maybe that's why I didn't die when Viktor ordered Weller to shoot me and leave me for dead. If I wasn't here, would that kid have gone through with it? Who knows? Maybe he'll do something amazing someday."

"You're still saving lives, even as a teacher," she said and smiled.

He pulled away to look down at her. "I guess so. I didn't think of it like that."

"You don't need a gun and a badge to help someone." He

was helping her now by offering her a place to hide. And his strong arms to hold her.

"The truth is, I do like teaching. I like the way the students all start off looking at me like I'm crazy, then one by one their eyes light up when they understand what I'm talking about. I can tell the one or two who just don't get it, and I reword the concept until I see that light come on."

She gazed at him with even more respect than she'd already had for him. "You have a purpose. That's what's important."

"I guess. But if you think this means I'm backing down when it comes time to chase down this bastard with you, you're wrong."

She would find a way to keep him safe when the time came. Justin told him to keep a low profile. That wouldn't be possible if he got caught up in her plans and ended up on the news as an accomplice to The Mantis.

But for now, she didn't want to argue.

"I wish I didn't need to fight my way out of this situation," she admitted. She was so tired of fighting. Tired of running from things that scared her.

Including the man lying next to her.

He looked over at her, curiosity in his eyes. "What?"

"I sometimes wonder what it would be like to just fade off into the shadows and live off the grid. Or better yet, clear my name and start a completely new life. A normal, quiet life where the biggest challenge of the day is grocery shopping or getting someone to a soccer game."

"You're serious?" he asked, almost warily. He was watching her face intently.

Was she?

She'd just been talking and it had come out all on its own. But now that she gave the idea more room…

It felt right.

She wanted a normal life—whatever that might consist of—and she wanted kids. A family. A real family that didn't hide what was really going on. That didn't have secrets they never spoke of.

All it would take was fading into the shadows, or clearing her name.

Unfortunately, she didn't have a clue how to make either of those things happen.

Chapter Fifty-Eight

Colton was blown away by Angel's revelation. Finding out she'd killed her partner and survived a childhood with a demon psychopath hadn't surprised him as much as this last admission.

Angel—tough as nails, take no prisoners—Larson wanted…*a family*?

Sure, she hadn't come out and said that, exactly. But the soccer game comment hinted at such.

Could it be they were standing on opposite ends of the spectrum? She wanted what he had, a quiet life, and he wanted what she had, action and adventure?

Okay, maybe he didn't want what she had right at the moment, but what she would have once she was cleared of murder and could go back to work as a deputy marshal.

And somewhere in the middle of all that, they wanted each other. Or at least he wanted her.

"You could have that, you know." He brushed her hair back from her face so he could look at her more clearly. Her cheeks were pink. If he didn't know better, he'd think she was blushing.

Was the independent woman in his arms feeling embarrassed that she wanted something as mundane as a family life?

"I have to clear this up first," she said, quickly brushing it off.

"I'm coming with you," he reminded her.

"We'll see."

It wasn't a straight out no. He was wearing her down. He knew she would try to shake him when the time came, but he was prepared. He would be there when she faced this asshole. Whether she wanted him there or not.

And then, when she was free…

He was surprised to realize that the mundane life didn't seem so bad if she was in it with him.

Hmm. Maybe it *wasn't* the danger and adrenaline he craved. There were different kinds of action and excitement. Like the kind he felt with her. She made him feel alive even doing the simplest, everyday things.

He cleared his throat, a little stunned by *that* revelation.

"Maybe we can work together to clear your name," he suggested carefully, "then we could both work on that other thing together. The part with the groceries and the soccer games."

Nothing.

"Or maybe you had someone else in mind for that job…?" he hinted.

Nothing.

"Angel?"

He noticed her head felt heavier on his chest and felt her steady breathing against his skin.

She was asleep.

Well, damn. She'd completely missed his proposal…of

sorts.

He laughed at himself and turned off the light. "I think your purpose in life—why you survived everything—is to drive me fucking mad," he whispered into her hair before he kissed her and followed her to sleep.

When he awoke, she was gone. And that familiar fear washed over him.

They'd talked about some pretty heavy issues in the middle of the night after her nightmare. What if she couldn't handle it? Again.

What if she ran? Again.

Throwing off the covers, he rushed out into the living room. And found her sitting cross legged at the coffee table in front of her computer.

His dog's head was resting on her knee. Everything was normal.

"You okay?" she asked, worry in her eyes as she reached for the gun sitting next to her laptop.

"Yeah, yeah. I'm fine. I just—" He shook his head. "Never mind. Is there coffee?"

Chapter Fifty-Nine

Angel knew Colton's reaction wasn't from an intense need for caffeine. He'd practically run out into the living room like there was a fire.

His quickness to cover it up meant it was her. He was still afraid she was going to run off in the middle of the night as she'd done before.

She wished she could convince him that wasn't going to happen. The problem was, she wasn't sure it *wouldn't* happen. The truth was, she *had* thought of running this morning—as she had nearly every morning.

Especially after last night. When she'd told him she might want to settle down and have a family.

What had she been *thinking*?

Why would a man who was bored to tears in suburbia want to settle down and have a family with The Mantis—who didn't know the first thing about being in a healthy family? He needed something more.

He needed action and excitement.

He needed a job. With Thorne.

Colton would be a perfect candidate for Task Force Phoenix. He had all the necessary skills, and he wanted to give back. He might have been recruited when he entered WITSEC if he hadn't been in the ICU at the time.

That was something she might be able to arrange. He was going out of his way to help her. The least she could do was ask Thorne to give Colton a job when this was over.

She thought about how that might work. The two of them on the same team. She worked well with Dane, Justin, and Donovan. Even Garrett, on the off times when he'd needed a partner for a job. While she didn't want them to get hurt, she wasn't petrified with fear when they were in danger. They had her back and she had theirs. That was how it worked.

But if she was planning something even remotely dangerous with Colton, it would be different. She would want to keep him close.

Protected.

God, if he could hear what she was thinking. He'd throw her over his shoulder and carry her straight back to his bed.

Hmm. Not a bad idea…

Chapter Sixty

This is the life, Colton thought to himself as he sipped lemonade while sitting on his back porch. It was a beautiful day, the sun was shining, and there was a breeze that kept it from being too hot.

Between sips he would toss a tennis ball to the end of his yard so Pudge could chase after it like it was the first time they were playing this game rather than the thousandth.

Colton smiled. The best part was the woman sitting next to him. He'd talked her into taking a break from the computer to relax. When he wasn't throwing the ball for the dog, his hand rested happily in hers.

Ever since she'd mentioned how she might want a normal life, he'd been thinking about it. Imagining how it would be.

Wanting it.

Of course, in his fantasies they wouldn't have two Glocks sitting on the small table between their chairs. For now, this was how it had to be. Always on alert and ready for anything.

But maybe one day, they would be watching Pudge play

with a small child, and the only thing on the table would be the bouquet of flowers they'd picked together that morning.

He let out a breath at the thought just as Pudge started barking. His ball was stuck under the small shed at the end of the property.

Bark, bark meant come and free my best friend.

With a sigh of annoyance, Colton stood to make the voyage. He'd only taken a few steps off the porch when the gate at the side yard opened.

Before he could identify the visitor, Angel's reflexes kicked in and her gun was up and cocked on the boy.

"Holy shit!" Kenny put both hands in the air as Colton took a step closer, holding his hands up in a stand-down motion.

"What's going on?" Colton asked the neighbor kid, giving Angel an *are-you-serious?* look as she put the gun down and tried to act normal.

The kid glanced between them nervously. "I just wanted to ask you about shooting the gun. You said to give you a few weeks, but you never called."

Colton's shoulders notched down. "Jeez, kid. Why don't you ring the doorbell like a normal person?"

Kenny's wide eyes were still glued to the gun by Angel's side, even though it was no longer pointed at him. "I thought if I rang the doorbell you wouldn't answer. I figured you'd pretend you weren't home."

That was exactly what he would have done. Damn it.

Kenny spared a glance for Colton, but then went right back to staring at Angel. Colton wasn't sure if it was because the boy recognized her, or because she was wearing short shorts and a tank top and Kenny was seventeen.

Pudge came up to investigate, and Kenny petted the dog. "Thanks for not having him attack me this time."

"He didn't attack you last time. Trust me. He can do far

worse than hold you down." *Just ask Dane about the four holes in his leg.*

Angel still hadn't moved or said anything. It looked as if she wasn't sure how to handle the situation. He didn't blame her. He wasn't quite sure what to do, either.

"Look. Now's not the best time. Give me a few more weeks," Colton said.

Kenny shook his head and held out his cell phone. "Nuh-uh. I know how this works. My mom does it to me all the time. Later never comes."

"I promise, I really will call your mother to set something up, but as you can see, I have a guest."

"And your guest could probably show me how to shoot as well as you can." He nodded toward the gun in Angel's grip.

Despite it hanging by her side, she was still holding it as though that was a totally natural thing to do.

"I need to do this." Kenny looked back at Colton, and for once he didn't look like a goofy kid. He looked like a man. "I need to see if I'm any good at it before I fill out an application for the police academy. If this is just one more thing I can't do right, then I need to know before I sign up."

Colton brushed a hand over his hair. He really wanted to help his student, but—

"Either you call my mother to set it up, or I'll call the police and tell them you're shacked up with The Mantis."

"Shit," Colton whispered with a grimace. It seemed he'd drastically underestimated the kid. "I really wish you hadn't called her that."

Chapter Sixty-One

"Are you going to kill me now to keep me quiet?" Kenny asked with even wider eyes. "Braden knows I was coming over here today." Kenny's voice shook a little as the bravado dropped off.

Angel was still holding the gun, but taking out a seventeen-year-old seemed a little drastic to ensure her freedom. Plus, Colton probably wouldn't appreciate her shooting one of his students.

"We're not going to kill you," Colton said, then looked at her as if to make sure.

"We can take him out shooting," she offered, barely resisting rolling her eyes. "How bad could it be?"

Colton gave her a stricken look. "He broke a scrench."

"That was Braden," Kenny protested. "And I would've had that bookcase together right the first time if I hadn't listened to him."

Clearly, the kid had already mastered the art of hostage negotiation. He'd bested two trained federal agents to get his way. He couldn't be *that* dim witted.

Colton pulled his phone from his pocket. "What's your mother's number? I'll call and see if she gives you permission to shoot a gun. But if she doesn't, that's the end of it. And you can't tell anyone about—" He pointed toward Angel.

"Your girlfriend the killer?" Kenny filled in the blank.

Great. A comedian, too.

"She didn't kill anyone." Colton said, his voice flat and serious.

"I figured as much. She's too hot to be a murderer."

Right, because attractive people never killed anyone. A memory of Lucas Stone flashed through her mind. White-blond hair and warm brown eyes. Handsome as a movie star.

Maybe police academy was a good idea for this kid. He'd get an enlightening there like nowhere else. But strangely, she actually thought he might end up making a damn fine cop.

"Come on," she said with a wink toward Kenny. "Let's go shoot something."

This would be fun.

Chapter Sixty-Two

After Colton carefully spelled out all the dangers of target shooting, Kenny's mother still gave her permission to take him to the range. Now they were all loaded up in Colton's truck. His student was in the back seat with Pudge, while Angel sat in the passenger seat...wearing a disguise.

Or what she called a disguise. Colton called it a hat and a pair of sunglasses.

She'd simply pursed her lips when he'd pointed out the obvious.

Kenny was no help. He'd told her no one would know it was her because they only showed her face on television, and in real life guys would be looking at her— He'd gestured toward his chest, and Colton had knocked the boy in the back of the head while Angel just laughed.

The kid did have a point. Seeing her curves and other features *was* distracting.

No one else was at the outdoor range at eleven o'clock on a Tuesday morning, so they got out of the truck and set up their stuff.

Colton walked out to set up the targets with Pudge, while Angel went over all the parts of the gun in detail with the kid. They took it apart a few times, until Kenny could identify all the pieces and put it together himself.

They went over gun safety, and explained that a gun was never a solution to a problem.

When it was time to shoot, Colton instructed Kenny on the proper way to hold the pistol, and how to squeeze the trigger rather than jerk it back.

Only three shots later, he had one on the paper. Six more shots got it in the center.

"You're a natural," Angel told him, earning a big smile from Kenny.

"I am? Really? I'm not normally good at anything."

Kenny was a mediocre student, but he could have been better if he'd actually tried.

Still, Colton could see how important this moment was for the kid. And he was playing a pivotal role in how Kenny's life might turn out. Sure, it would be up to the boy to make it happen, but Colton had set things in motion. He hoped the kid would do well for himself.

"Kenny, I think you'd make a good cop. Though, you know, being a cop isn't just about shooting a target."

"Because I might be forced to shoot a real person."

"You might. But they would train you so you know when you shoot to stop versus shoot to kill."

"Have you ever had to shoot to kill?" Kenny asked, his gaze bouncing between both of them intently.

Colton and Angel both nodded slowly. "Unfortunately, yes."

"Have you ever been shot?"

Colton briefly considered evading the question, but decided Kenny deserved the truth. So he gave the same reluctant reply.

Kenny's eyes narrowed. "You're not really a teacher, are you?"

For all his trouble with the bookcase, Kenny was proving to be a pretty sharp detective.

But before Colton could open his mouth to answer, Angel took over. "He *is* a teacher. He's a very good teacher. That's just not *all* he is. Do you understand?"

Kenny nodded, and his mouth pulled up in a smirk. "I knew I was right." He pointed a finger at Colton and nodded again in satisfaction at his rightness. "Don't worry. I won't tell anyone anything about either of you."

"Thanks. We're both trusting you with a pretty big secret," she said calmly.

Colton was impressed she wasn't upset at being identified. She probably knew he was prepared to discredit the boy if he went to the police. Kenny wasn't a huge threat when his teacher could bring up the egg incident and convince the police he was just causing trouble in retaliation for his punishment.

"It's okay. I won't let you down," Kenny assured them, looking ready for the next challenge.

Colton nodded and handed over another clip of ammunition. And realized his life still had a purpose and meaning, even if he wasn't a DEA agent any longer.

Chapter Sixty-Three

A week later, they were still waiting impatiently for Jim to respond to Noah's requests. Angel monitored Noah's emails daily, but so far it was only condolences for the death of his brother, with hints of offence that Noah would even assume the sender was involved.

Noah was probably a mess, thinking everyone suspected him. She had hidden her sent messages in a different place than his email files so he wouldn't know why everyone was emailing him out of the blue. The little weasel deserved a little panic.

Surely by now, this Jim person was feeling the squeeze. One by one, every viable software company had been shut out from his possible offer of the stolen technology. He was only left with one possibility now—Noah. Jim should be getting desperate enough to make a move on Noah, one way or the other.

She'd also sent taunting emails to Redgamer3, but had gotten no reply. And she still hadn't been able to find him.

On the Viktor Kulakov front, the good news was that Colton's cover came up solid. He was safe from the ruthless drug lord and his goons.

For now.

There was nothing for them to do but wait. And not very patiently.

She was going stir crazy. Last week's trip to the shooting range had been her only venture outside the house and yard in ages.

Thankfully, the nights were anything but boring. They were almost through the box of condoms, and she had no intention of leaving any time soon. Time for a new box.

"Oh, hell," Colton said while sitting at the kitchen table with a pile of mail.

She glanced up from her laptop. "What is it?"

"I forgot I'm going to a wedding this Saturday. One of the teachers I work with is getting married. I already RSVP'd I would go."

"Then you should go, so it doesn't seem suspicious. Maybe you could sneak out a piece of cake for me."

"I could make you cake if you want." He wrapped his arms around her and tugged her down onto his lap.

She grinned. "I really only want the icing."

"Even better, we could have a lot of fun with icing." He licked her neck, making her laugh. U.S. deputy marshals weren't supposed to turn to mush when a man kissed their necks.

She waggled her eyebrows and stood up to halt the distraction of his tongue. "I'll keep that in mind."

"I'd rather stay here with you," he said.

Once again he was willing to put his life on hold to stay with her. She couldn't continue to be selfish. "It might seem odd if you don't show up. You're usually dependable. People might think it's suspicious."

"Normal people don't think things like that are suspicious," he reminded her.

He was right. Normal people were oblivious. They turned up on the news claiming they had no idea their neighbor was a serial killer. Regular folks were always shocked to find out their co-worker had body parts in his freezer.

The general population mainly assumed everyone was good until proven otherwise, and someone shoved a camera in their face to tell them how wrong they'd been.

She knew better. She knew what darkness lurked in people's homes. How a normal family could easily include a psychopath.

She suppressed a shiver. Colton needed to go to this wedding to keep up appearances, but she really didn't want to be left behind, alone with her thoughts.

"I'll go with you as your date," she said brightly, without really considering the implications.

He frowned. "No way. It's not safe."

"I'll make sure it's safe."

She would have to dress up, even more than usual because she'd need to be in disguise. A real disguise, not just a hat and glasses. She'd had to dress up when she was "dating" Heath, and hated the thick makeup and heels. But at this point, she would do just about anything to get out of the house.

"There's a lot of overlap at weddings. *I* shouldn't even have agreed. What if the bride's cousin is married to the girl I took to prom?"

"Then why did you agree?" she asked.

He was right, of course. But the rules were starting to blur. They needed something fun to do while waiting for Jim to take the bait. She'd even almost suggested they take Kenny shooting again as a distraction.

Colton glanced away and bit his lip.

She'd expected him to tell her he was lonely and wanted

to be with people, but...there was something else going on here. He looked...guilty.

Then it hit her.

"Do you already have a date for this wedding?" The words blurted out, sounding accusatory.

Damn it! She had no right to be jealous, or to expect any level of exclusivity. She'd made it clear she had nothing to offer him long term, and he was trying to make a new life for himself.

"No. Not a date. Just another teacher. I told her I would meet her there." Another look of guilt.

Angel was torn between relief and confusion. "You didn't offer to pick her up?"

"It's not a real date." He spread his hands as if his excuse made sense.

She knew Colton planned things better than this. "But if you wanted to hook up afterward, she would have to follow you in her own vehicle."

He held out his hands. "That's why I didn't offer to pick her up. I wanted to make sure we wouldn't be hooking up."

"Why?" He'd obviously made these plans before she came back, so her feelings hadn't been a factor. Not that they should be now, either.

"As the person I'm sleeping with, you're not supposed to encourage me to hook up with other people," he snapped.

"I'm not encouraging," she said, baffled. "I'm just wondering why you didn't take advantage of the opportunity."

There was something going on here. Something she instinctively knew ran deep with him. What the hell?

There was a long moment of silence, as if he was trying to come up with an answer—any answer but the truth.

Finally, he let out a gust of breath and said, "Because I'm still hung up on you, and Danielle is not you." The second it was out of his mouth, his expression said he wished he could suck it back in. Then with a defiant lift of his chin, he leveled a look at her. "You burned me, Angel, and I'm not over it."

And there it was.

His admission almost broke her heart.

She stood and stepped back from him. And the truth just burst out of her. "I'm so sorry. I shouldn't have left like I did. But...I didn't think I could go if you were awake. You would have said something to make me stay, and I would have, and it wouldn't have been good."

It felt good to let it all out, finally. To tell him how torn up she'd been to leave him.

He shook his head sadly. "You're wrong. It could have been very good."

Could it?

From the first moment he'd ever kissed her, she'd felt safe and balanced when they were together. Sure, there were the normal butterflies of excitement. But it was the safety in his arms she treasured most.

In her career, she was trained to protect herself from all types of threats, but she had never felt truly safe unless Colton was with her. Back then, and especially now.

It had taken a long time before she'd realized what that feeling was.

Even now, she refused even to think the word, let alone say it out loud.

Only after recognizing how she felt about him did she realize that, in her entire life, she'd never experienced the sense of safety she felt with him. Growing up with a brother who was volatile and dangerous meant she had never been able to let her guard down. It meant she had never been free to care about anyone. Not the way she cared about Colton now.

After her family was taken, she had been thrown from one dangerous situation to the next. Even with her team, she worried she wouldn't be truly accepted if she didn't toe the line, meet their expectations.

The biggest of those expectations was loyalty to the team. Leaving Task Force Phoenix to run off and live with Colton had not been an option. Not back then, not now. If things didn't work out, she wouldn't be able to go back to her job.

Colton thought things would have been good between them, and maybe they would have. Maybe it would have worked out. Maybe it could still work out.

But there was no guarantee.

"You would grow bored with me. I'm not that exciting. I can sit for hours in front of a computer and not even notice the outside world."

"I've seen how you get. I understand that. I'm not looking for someone to entertain me. I want someone to share my life with. Not every second of every day. Just knowing you're there would be good enough."

She understood what he meant. It was the reason she'd run before. Because what he described made perfect sense to her, and she wanted it more than anything. But the whole idea terrified her—of letting herself fall in love and be happy.

Because something always happened when she gave in to that kind of happiness. Something ugly, and violent.

"I can't be that person. I'm sorry," she whispered.

How she wished she knew how to be that person.

He came up behind her and wrapped his warm body around her. She shivered away the chill of their conversation.

"I didn't mean to push. I just…" He pressed a kiss to the top of her head. She felt her hair stir from his deep breath. "Would it be safe for you to come to the wedding? I'd love it if you could go with me, but I don't want to risk you getting caught."

She was glad to let the heavy moment go. For now. Though, she knew it was far from over. At some point she would have to leave again.

And she just didn't know how she would do it.

She straightened, and plastered on a smile. "When I'm done with the makeup, you won't even recognize me." She was determined to squeeze in every single possible minute of happiness with him while she still had the chance.

"Then I'll call my friend and tell him I'm plus one."

She knew those memories would have to last through a lifetime of loneliness.

Chapter Sixty-Four

Packages arrived in an endless stream over the next few days, and one of the bedrooms had been taken over by Angel's project.

Colton could hardly wait to see the results as he paced in the living room the day of the wedding. One might have thought he was the anxious groom instead of merely a guest.

One of the packages that had arrived was the couple's wedding gift. He thanked Angel profusely for thinking about it, because he'd forgotten. He'd had a lot of other things on his mind.

The jingling of Pudge's collar alerted Colton that she was coming. The dog rarely left her side. It was fine, because it meant Pudge would protect her even if he wasn't around to give the command.

He was prepared to be shocked. She'd told him he wouldn't recognize her, so he knew her appearance would be a drastic change from the woman he took to his bed each night.

But he was more than shocked. He was downright stunned by her altered manifestation. In the photos of her on the arm of Heath Zeller, posing as his girlfriend Aubrey

Daniels, she'd been stylish, sophisticated, and sexy. Colton had expected something similar now.

The brunette in front of him looked like a Bohemian goddess. The short, flowy dress hung off one shoulder, the other side high enough to cover the scar at her collarbone. Strappy sandals created the illusion of her being taller than she was. Her normally straight black hair was curly, and the softer brown locks flowed down her back. A thin braid held it back from her face.

Probably the biggest difference was her eyes. Normally a piercing light blue that cut straight to his heart, they were now the color of warm chocolate. It wasn't unpleasant, it just wasn't...her.

She spun for him and he noticed a tattoo on her shoulder. Though her body was covered in markings, she didn't have any tattoos. Her scars were proof enough to the world that she was tough. Those scars were mostly covered now by the long, billowy sleeves of her patterned dress.

He didn't know how to react.

After staring for a few seconds longer, he settled on, "If I didn't like you so much the other way, I could really like this." At least it was honest.

It must have been the correct thing to say, because she smiled and came closer to kiss him.

"It's weird," he said with a frown. "I feel like I'm cheating on you...with you." He kissed her again, thinking of *his* Angel while his eyes were closed.

"Would you think I was Angel Larson, wanted murderer, if you saw me?"

"No. You'll do." With the gift in one arm, he offered her the other. "Shall we?"

Part of him felt the normal excitement of going on a date with a beautiful woman.

The other part of him prayed they weren't walking into danger.

Chapter Sixty-Five

As they were seated in the church, Angel felt the weight of everyone's gaze on her and fought the urge to cringe away. In this situation, the scrutiny wasn't because she was a wanted fugitive. It was because in their eyes she had wronged their friend, Duncan.

Her cover was Cassie Benton, Colton's ex-girlfriend from Baltimore. When he'd taken the teaching job in Oregon, she'd refused to come with him. But she'd flown out for a few weeks to see if they could make it work.

She knew from experience the best cover stories had some truth woven into them, and she felt a twinge of regret knowing this story held more than *some* truth. The only part that wasn't real was that they were from Baltimore. And her name.

As the ceremony began, everyone moved their focus to the bride walking down the aisle toward her impatient groom. Colton's fingers squeezed tighter around Angel's hand and she gripped him back.

That simple gesture was as clear as a full-out conversation. He wanted this. He wanted to be married. To know he had someone, and that someone was his alone, and forever.

She had to admit, she wanted that, too. But even if she were able to overcome her own deep-seated fears, she didn't know how they would survive the day-to-day rhythm of a mundane life. While normal was all she'd ever wanted, it wouldn't be enough for him. She knew he needed more.

Time and again, he'd told her he was bored being a math teacher. That he needed more excitement. He'd shared how much he missed his old life.

How could he willingly want to saddle himself with a woman like her? Someone afraid to let her guard down for fear of losing the very thing she loved most? Someone whose idea of paradise was mac and cheese and a bottle of wine in front of a roaring fire. Someone whose greatest wish was to be boring and mundane, and...normal.

Hell, she didn't even know how to be normal. So much of her life had been spent pretending. Pretending her brother wasn't dangerous. Pretending her home was safe. Pretending she was tough and capable. Pretending she didn't mind being alone.

Pretending she didn't want a life with Colton.

As the bride and groom said their vows, Angel felt the sting of tears in her eyes and a tightness in her throat. She hadn't thought to bring a tissue since she'd never been overcome by her emotions before. She hadn't even known she *had* those kinds of emotions.

She used her fingers to dab away the unshed tears, careful not to smear her mascara or dislodge a contact. It wouldn't do to spend the rest of the wedding looking like a Siberian husky.

Finally, the ceremony was over, and people began to move out of the church to await the newlyweds' departure to the reception. The sun from the perfect day beat down on them and Colton smiled at her with some emotion in his eyes.

"You okay?" he asked.

"I'm fine," she lied, and put on her smile. Pretending, once again.

He hugged her close, and murmured, "Sure, you are."

The man had the most uncanny ability to see through her pretenses, and she treasured him even more for it.

She hugged him back, and felt her heart break in a million pieces.

She wished with all her being there was a way to make this work between them.

But she just didn't see how.

Chapter Sixty-Six

At the reception, Colton was seated next to Angel at the table with the rest of his colleagues, including Danielle, the woman he had planned to meet at the event. He'd called her a few days ago to explain the situation.

Although he and Danielle hadn't planned an official date, he didn't want to be a jerk by just showing up with another woman. Danielle had told him on the phone it was no problem, and even wished Cassie and him the best toward repairing their relationship.

Only now, it was obvious he had misread the situation.

Danielle was staring at them, no doubt looking for some chink in Angel's armor. Colton wasn't too worried—he knew all the cracks and fissures intimately—but it wasn't good to have someone looking at her so intently.

They might see past the disguise.

Angel was smiling and laughing, and having a great time chatting with his friends. Though *friends* was not really the word for people he'd never given the chance to really know him.

She'd even managed to wrangle a reluctant Danielle into conversation.

While Angel's "remember that time" stories worked to ensure the rest of the table knew how much she valued their past, it was apparent they caused Danielle pain.

Damn. He'd completely messed this up and would need to fix it.

After the meal and the traditional cake sharing, bouquet toss, and garter throwing, it was time for the dancing portion of the evening. He patted Angel on the leg, noticing her dress had pulled up and he was touching bare skin. He'd have to come back to her bare skin in a moment. Right now he had something else he needed to take care of.

"Danielle, would you care to dance?" he asked her.

After handling her surprise and glancing at Angel for her reaction, Danielle nodded and stood.

There was an awkward moment on the dance floor while he found a place to put his hands, then they started moving in a circle. This never would have worked, even if Angel hadn't come back. He felt no real attraction to this woman.

"I owe you an apology," he said.

"For what?" She tried to brush it off, but he could see she knew exactly what he meant.

"When we made plans to meet here, I thought it would be as friends who didn't want to go to the trouble of finding a date for the event. But I think maybe you thought it was something else."

"I didn't think anything, Duncan."

So, she wanted to play games. He nodded. "Okay. Well, I'm still going to apologize. If for no other reason, than we had plans, and I had to change them at the last minute."

"It's really fine. I mean the two of you obviously belong together. I hope it works out."

That last sentence stung like a lash, and not just because he could tell she didn't really mean it.

He hoped it worked out too, but he knew from past experience that having hope was a dangerous thing. He remembered vividly how much it hurt, even months after Angel left, still hoping she'd come back.

He'd thought he'd known better this time, he'd thought he was prepared. But here he was, doing it all over again.

Hoping.

Chapter Sixty-Seven

Angel was glad Colton had asked Danielle to dance. It was clear the woman wanted more than friendship from him. She hadn't outright glared, but Angel had felt her intense stares of ill-wish—one step below glaring on the list of responses to jealousy.

Unfortunately, Angel felt more than a bit jealous of the other woman, as well. Even when their dance had ended and Colton was now leading Angel to the dance floor with a big smile, she felt incredibly envious of what the other woman had.

Freedom. Peace. Choices.

A future.

Danielle could go wherever she wanted, do whatever she wanted, be herself. Something Angel had rarely been able to do. The other woman probably got up every morning after a restful sleep, secure in the knowledge she would survive the day.

And when Angel was gone, Danielle would have the

possibility of a future with Colton.

"Did you fix things?" she asked.

He smiled and shook his head. "I tried. I apologized, but she wouldn't give me anything to work with."

Angel understood. "A girl has her pride."

"So does a man," he told her softly.

She knew he wasn't talking about apologizing to Danielle. He had no issues saying he was wrong when it happened. It was one of the many things she loved about him.

She missed a step when the word flitted through her thoughts.

Love.

It was the very word she'd been hiding from. Frightening, dangerous...wonderful.

She thought she might love Colton, but she didn't have any experience with the feeling to be sure.

At one time she'd thought she was in love with Lucas Stone, but that hadn't been love at all. He had manipulated her into believing she was important to him. But it was never real.

This feeling she had with Colton *felt* real.

But was it truly love?

Should there have been some definitive way to know? A line she passed. One moment she didn't, then something happened and she did? Or was it more subtle? Something she just noticed over time?

She'd always imagined she would know. If for no other reason than the terminology was *falling* in love. One certainly knew when they fell. It was a shocking, painful jolt. Nothing subtle about falling. You didn't do it without noticing.

"I'm going to the restroom," she managed to say when the song ended.

She needed a moment to collect her thoughts. She knew making sense of them was beyond her—collecting them was the best she could do.

He kissed her, and she fled the banquet room, being careful not to run. She was so sick of running from everything. She'd thought herself strong, brave, but that was just another lie.

She looked in the mirror at another farce. The person staring back at her was not real. She was a fake from her flowing hair to her brown eyes.

As she washed her hands, someone came into the restroom. She wasn't surprised to see Danielle in the reflection.

"How do you like Oregon?" the woman asked, sounding polite.

"It's very nice. But I'm not used to being in such a small town." Angel was laying the path for her exit. Colton would be able to explain her absence as them not being able to work it out. Cassie could go back to Baltimore and city life.

Danielle stepped closer, her heavy perfume leading the way. "Duncan mentioned he likes living in a small town."

"Yes. He does."

Not true. He'd grown up in a small town in Illinois and moved to Philadelphia when he joined the DEA. He'd told her how much he liked the anonymity of living in a big city, and the way he could get food delivered at two a.m.

"I'll still be here when you decide to leave," Danielle said, her chin coming up, but her eyes were unsure.

It was good to see Colton had options here. He wouldn't be alone if he didn't want to be. Danielle had spunk. If his interest in Angel was any indication, Colton liked women with spunk.

Angel should have simply smiled and walked away, letting Danielle have the moment, and sending home the story that she loved the city life more than she loved "Duncan."

But she couldn't do it.

Instead, she tossed the paper towel in the trash and met the other woman's eyes. "If I decide to leave, I might take him with me back to Baltimore."

With a smug grin, she left to go back to the man she'd just claimed…but had no idea what to do with.

Chapter Sixty-Eight

Colton wasn't sure what had happened in the restroom, but Angel was quiet. Too quiet. She hadn't said much as they'd said their goodbyes to his friends and left.

"You okay?" he asked when they were in his truck, heading for home.

"Yeah." She nodded as if to sell it, but then gave up. "No. I messed things up with Danielle."

"How so?" He couldn't imagine. Angel had been nothing but friendly to the woman despite the way Danielle had practically glared at her all night.

He hated that Angel was taking the punishment for his sins. It was his fault Danielle felt she had been pushed aside.

"I should have let her believe I was thinking of leaving again, but instead, I told her you might come with me," Angel confessed.

He pressed his lips together to hide the smile that threatened. This was uncharted territory, and the worst thing he could do was to push her into admitting *why* she might have done that.

But inside, his heart was doing a victory dance. A small one, but still.

"Don't worry about it," he said. "I should probably move again, anyway. Just in case. That'll give me a good cover story for leaving."

He kept his eyes glued to the windshield, even though he could feel her studying him. Would she let it go, or fess up? He felt as excited as he did as a boy on Christmas morning.

Would he get the thing he wanted?

Or would it be the thing he needed instead?

Chapter Sixty-Nine

Rather than respond to Colton's comment, Angel placed her hand on his thigh and moved it up until she was grasping his length firmly through his khakis.

Yes, she was using sex as a distraction—again—but she didn't know what else to do. And it always seemed to work.

Her emotions were running all over the place. She didn't know what was going on with herself, and until she did, it wouldn't be a good thing to make any promises—or even to talk.

She wanted to go away with him forever. Someplace quiet, and theirs alone.

Apparently, one glass of wine made her delusional.

Because she knew damn well she wasn't brave enough to go for any of that. To take a risk and try for a real life.

And even if she did somehow muster the courage, Colton wouldn't want any part of it. Not a boring life where the height of excitement was grilling dinner or going to a movie.

"Be careful," he warned. "We're still fifteen minutes from home. If you keep doing what you're doing, I'm not going to make it that far."

"Maybe we should pull over, then," she suggested, gripping him tighter.

He gasped and removed her hand, putting it back in her own lap. "And risk having the cops find us in a compromising position?"

She felt a sharp stab of regret and envy and frustration. *Danielle* would have been able to pull over with him. If the police caught them messing around, he and Danielle would have gotten a warning with a laugh. But being caught with Angel would mean jail time for aiding and abetting.

"You should have left with Danielle." It just popped out of her mouth without her permission. "Less complicated."

Damn that glass of wine.

"If you remember correctly, Danielle would have been leaving in her own vehicle, so there'd have been no chance of her hands roaming."

Angel pressed her lips together. "I guess not."

My God. She was *pouting*. Ridiculous. She'd never been one to feel sorry for herself. It was much better to find a way to manage with what she had. Wanting more was selfish.

Especially if what she wanted put Colton in danger.

"Drive faster," she ordered, making him laugh.

"I can't drive faster. I have a wanted fugitive in my vehicle."

"Drive faster." This time she undid his pants and slid her hand inside.

"Yes, ma'am." His voice squeaked as his foot pressed down on the gas.

Chapter Seventy

When they pulled into the garage, she released him and turned to open the car door, but Colton stopped her.

"What's going on?" he asked, sensing it was more serious than simple horniness.

Now that her hand wasn't on him, he was able to think again. She was trying to distract him. He was on to her tactics by now.

She pushed out a breath. "I'm not sure. I've never been to a wedding before. I guess it got to me."

He glanced over at her in surprise. He'd attended his older brothers' weddings, even taking on the role of groomsman when requested. He'd been in the weddings of friends and other family members. A dozen or more. He couldn't imagine how she'd been spared.

Then he remembered her family wouldn't have attended family weddings. And she didn't have close friends, other than the Phoenix team.

"Do you miss your team?" he asked, wanting to give them

both a minute to think about something else. He wanted her, and he had no doubt they'd get back to it soon enough. But something was bothering her, and he didn't want to take her to bed if she was hurting.

She had a habit of brushing off the hard feelings with sex. He'd let her do it in the past, but he knew it wasn't healthy. The bad stuff didn't go away, even when you felt good physically.

"You want to talk about my team when I just had my hand down your pants? I must not be doing something right," she joked. She was still trying to brush off the heavy emotions.

He leaned across the seat to kiss her.

"I want to know everything about you," he whispered, and saw the pulse at her neck kick up. "Come on. Tell me what's going on."

Chapter Seventy-One

Angel's plan to ignore her feelings was demolished by Colton's request to talk. He hadn't even budged from his truck, as if it was safer there.

Her team. He wanted to talk about the other members of Task Force Phoenix, the people who were like a family to her. The people who had been there for her when she'd had no one else.

"You've met pretty much everyone who's still active. Garrett does some odd jobs here and there when needed, and Donovan does a lot of international stuff, but we're fairly small."

"Plus Dane, Justin, and Thorne?"

"There are a few people on the inside that provide intel, and there are other tech agents. But yeah, the five of us are it right now. When Garrett left, Thorne started looking for a replacement. But he hasn't found the right person yet."

She thought she might have found the right person for him. Though, she wasn't sure she'd be able to stand it. Waiting for Colton to come back from a job she wasn't working would be torture.

Still, she knew he'd be a perfect fit, and it would give him the excitement he so desperately wanted. It wouldn't be right to hold him back. Besides, there was no guarantee she'd ever be able to go back, even if this whole mess ended well.

If she didn't find the real killer, she'd be exiled forever.

Or in prison.

"Garrett left the team so he could be with someone?" Colton asked, his voice quiet.

She knew what he was thinking. Garrett left Task Force Phoenix to be with Samantha, but Angel hadn't made the same decision. She hadn't taken the chance with Colton.

"Yes. Garrett is Thorne's son-in-law now." She still found it funny. Especially on the few occasions she'd heard Garrett call Thorne "Dad." Thorne seemed less than amused by the endearment.

"And Dane?"

"Dane and I have worked a lot of missions together." They were like a single unit when they worked. They rarely needed to speak out loud, using just a gesture or a look to communicate. He was dependable and steady. Like a machine.

"And the two of you never…"

It took a full ten seconds to understand what Colton was asking. Then she burst out laughing. "Dane and I? Together? No. Never. It's never even come up."

"For you. I'm sure it's come up for him."

Angel laughed again and shook her head. She couldn't imagine Dane ever looking at her in that way. "He's the older brother I *should* have had. The kind that offers protection along with teasing and annoyance." The laughter faded and she frowned. "We're all wounded in some way. Everyone on the team comes with baggage and sadness. Dane had to walk away from his wife and young son to protect them. I doubt he'd ever get close to anyone again."

Somehow, that seemed a lot worse than never having the courage to get close to anyone in the first place. He'd once been normal, and happy, and knew exactly what he was missing.

Which only made Angel even more wary of putting herself in that position.

"Why didn't his wife and son come with him?" Colton asked.

"I'm not sure. He's never said, and I don't want to pry. We're like a family, but there are still things we don't tell each other. I'm not sure how he did it, though. For me, it was easy. My family was gone. There were no tough choices to be made. I can't imagine walking away on my own."

Although, true, she'd come close when she'd left Colton.

"It's a bitch, let me tell you," he said.

"Right. I guess you know very well." Although he hadn't been given many choices, either. He'd been fighting for his life at the time.

"Not on that level. It's one thing to leave my brothers and my mom. It hurt like hell, don't get me wrong. To know I would never see them again just about killed me for real. Fortunately, by the time I figured it out, I was on a lot of pain meds to numb everything."

He laughed, but she could still see the pain in his eyes when he spoke of his family. "They all had lives with other people. They were married or had girlfriends. My mom has the grandkids. But to walk away from the woman I love—" He swallowed and shook his head. "Like I said, I can't imagine."

Could he not imagine because he'd never loved anyone, or because it was too painful to think about? She knew he would answer if she asked, but she remained silent, not really wanting to have her fears confirmed.

So she changed the subject. "Justin is a different story. He asked me out the first day on the job. He's always been a flirt and the happy-go-lucky one of the bunch. But it's just an act."

"What's his story?"

"Don't know. He's never shared. Thorne hasn't said. No one really knows, but it's there, plain as day under the surface."

"And Thorne?"

Angel smiled and shook her head. "He's the reason I'm not sitting in prison. He gave me a chance to change my life. To use my skills to help people instead of causing them a lot of inconvenience when I stole their identity."

Colton chuckled.

"I was having trouble dealing with being the sole survivor. I guess I didn't think I deserved it, so I was going out of my way to punish myself and sabotage my own life."

He reached over and squeezed her hand. "You deserve happiness, Angel."

"I'm starting to get that." Slowly but surely, she was coming around to that way of thinking.

"It's also okay to care about people," he whispered. "Not everyone goes away, or hurts you."

She wanted to allow herself to care, to want, to commit fully and be more than she was, but she didn't know how. She didn't know how to give herself over to feelings she couldn't address in words. Not without being terrified.

She leaned over and kissed him. Silently telling him how much she cared about him, when she didn't dare say it out loud.

Instead of getting out of his truck on her side, he pulled her over onto his lap then out the door. They were kissing and walking—or stumbling—toward his bedroom. He stopped in the kitchen long enough to open the door and let Pudge out, then they kept right on going.

But rather than lead her straight to the bed, he stopped at the bathroom.

"Take them out," he said while kissing up her throat.

She had no idea what he was talking about, her mind in a daze. "What?"

"The contacts. Take them out. I want to look into your eyes."

She choked on the air caught in her throat. She'd known men who never even noticed what color her eyes were. But Colton wanted *her*—the real her.

Or as much of the real her as she was able to give.

With a quick nod, she rushed in to take out the contacts. She pulled a brush through her hair to release the curls, and when she looked in the mirror she was startled by how much she looked like her old self. Her real old self.

Cassandra. Not Angel.

Her hair was this color naturally, and it suited her better than the platinum blond or the jet black. As Angel, she was all about extremes. But now...she had mixed emotions about all the things she once thought black and white.

Not everything had to be black or white. There was a whole bunch of gray to be had, too.

She could be a good deputy marshal and also want a quiet life with the man she—

God.

She swallowed down the thought before it blossomed, and let out a breath.

Taking off her bra and panties, she went to the bedroom in just the flowy dress. He was waiting for her on the bed, gloriously naked and ready for her.

She practically fell onto the bed, and he pulled her on top of him. As he moved his hand under her dress to her ass, he moaned when he found no obstructions.

"Were you like this the whole time? Hell, if I'd known, we

would have found a dark corner somewhere at the reception. Then we wouldn't have had to worry about getting home so fast."

She kissed him again. "I just took them off. For you. I didn't want anything in the way."

They worked together to cover him first with a condom, then with her body. A slow breath left both of their lips in unison as they joined.

She moved on him as he bunched up her dress and pulled it over her head to expose the rest of her.

His gaze brushed over her, and she felt more than naked. She felt…vulnerable.

Normally, that wasn't a good thing to feel. But like every other time she was with him, she also felt safe.

Wrapping both feelings around her, she smiled down at him and lowered her body over him in one easy slide, until he filled her completely.

They fit together perfectly, and she took a second just to enjoy the delicious sensation before she started moving on him faster. His large hands moved up her thighs to her hips and her waist. Never restraining or demanding, they followed her movements as she rose up and down in an enticing rhythm.

She felt pleasure building in her body, and moaned in anticipation of the orgasm that was bearing down on her. As the first spasms hit, he groaned and arched up off the bed to thrust deeper into her with his release.

When they'd caught their breath, he slipped off to the bathroom. She didn't move when he got back in bed and flipped the covers over them both, kissing her hair.

"Please be here in the morning," he whispered before his breathing evened out in sleep.

And her heart squeezed.

They were not new words. He said them nearly every night. But tonight, they really hit her hard.

She'd hurt him when she left before, but she'd hurt herself, as well. She could admit that now, even to herself.

Leaving the way she had gave her no closure, and was surely one of the reasons she had ended up back here. When she left again, she would have to do it differently. She would have to face him, and explain why they couldn't be together.

But for the life of her, she suddenly couldn't remember any of the reasons. She didn't know how she would convince him leaving was the best thing for both of them.

Not when she couldn't even convince herself.

Chapter Seventy-Two

A week later, Colton woke to the smell of coffee infiltrating his slumber. He smiled and rolled out of bed, knowing Angel was the one who'd made it, since Pudge hadn't quite mastered hot beverages yet.

The living room was as empty as the kitchen, but he didn't panic. When he peered out at the backyard, he found what he was looking for.

Carrying his mug outside, he walked up to where they were sitting. Pudge raised his head from his spot on the blanket next to Angel, but didn't bother to get up.

"You're in my spot, asshole," he joked. But the dog simply rolled over on his back and rubbed against the blanket, marking the spot as his.

We'll see about that. Colton pulled a squeaky plastic cheeseburger from his pocket, giving it two squeaks before he whipped it down the yard.

Ha. So predictable.

Pudge took off like a dart and Colton brushed the dog

hair from the blanket and took the spot next to Angel.

His spot.

"If only I had a nickel for every time a male left me to chase a plastic piece of meat," Angel joked.

Colton leaned over to kiss her good morning. "I would never leave a piece of Grade A top sirloin for a rubber burger. Let me assure you."

She chuckled, and he linked his hand in hers. It was a clear morning, and the birds were chirping. Perfect.

Looking around the yard, he frowned down at the blanket. "You checked for dog bombs before you laid it down here, right? Since *some* of us can't go in the corner as instructed." Pudge was back with the toy. He dropped it between his paws and barked. "Yes. I mean you."

Colton picked up the slimy cheeseburger and threw it again.

"I picked my spot perfectly," Angel told him, her arm blocking the morning sun from her eyes.

"What, exactly, are you doing out here?"

It was a nice day, but her spot seemed a little too open for his liking.

"Redgamer3 sent me an email. He said he was watching me. I wanted to see if it was true." Her voice was as calm as if she'd told him she wanted waffles for breakfast.

He was not so calm.

"Fuck, Angel!" He shot up, looking around for danger. Hell, he hadn't even brought a gun outside with him. "*E hele mai!*" He called the dog back, though he wasn't sure what Pudge could do if this Redgamer3 asshole started shooting.

His dog dropped the toy and came to his side, awaiting the next command. But Colton didn't know what the next command should be. "We need to get inside," he told her.

"I like it out here," she said.

Damn it! He wished she listened and obeyed as well as

his dog. "Angel—"

"If he's here, I want to face him now. I'm sick of playing by his rules. He's toying with me, and I'm calling his bluff." She was her normal calm self. While he was freaking out.

"I don't like the idea of taunting a diabolical killer," he said, still surveying the yard and what he could see past the fence. "Let's go inside."

"I have a better idea. Let's go out."

He stared at her, nonplussed. "Out? As in, for dinner?" he asked in confusion.

"No. It's only eight in the morning."

"Then, where? You're kind of still wanted for murder, and all. It's not as if we can go hang out at the mall, or go for breakfast."

Unless she planned to change into her disguise. The thought didn't appeal. As attractive as she'd been at the wedding, that woman wasn't her. He wanted to look into her eyes as much as possible. Before he couldn't anymore.

He'd thought he remembered the correct color of blue all those months without her, but when she was there in front of him again, he'd realized he hadn't done her eyes justice. They were far more beautiful than he'd recalled.

"I don't think we should go anywhere if Redgamer3 is out there," he said firmly. "Maybe we should call Thorne."

There. That was a good plan.

But of course she didn't agree.

She shook her head, still not getting up. "I need to be outside. I need to walk around. Let's go. Pudgey, do you want to go for a walk?" Of course the dog went to her, tail wagging, eager to please his queen. "Do you want to go for a ride?" she asked in that annoying voice people only used for babies and pets.

Pudge barked his approval. Then to make things worse, he ran around her in a circle.

"You're embarrassing yourself. You should play a little harder to get," Colton told the dog as he reached down to pull Angel to her feet. He tugged her close for a kiss. "Are you sure this is a good idea?"

He didn't want to lose her. He especially didn't want to lose her because they did something stupid like get caught by the cops or killed by a maniac. Being reckless with his heart was one thing, but risking her life was another.

"It's an excellent idea. We'll be fine. I know he's lying. Why would he be watching me? And how would he have found me? I've selected a park to go to that is secluded, and we can use the hiking trails. By the time anyone has the chance to report me, I'll be long gone. And if he does show up, it would be nice to be somewhere unpopulated, instead of your nice, peaceful neighborhood."

She had a point.

A hike in the mountains did sound like fun.

He was rethinking his acquiescence an hour and a half later when they still hadn't arrived at the park she'd selected.

Another half hour went by, and she continued to give him directions from the printout she'd brought along. It didn't take much longer for him to realize she was up to something. He might have thought she was just playing it safe by not selecting a park close to his home, but this was getting ridiculous.

This was not a random destination.

"Here. Turn down this lane."

"Is this really a park?" he asked, frowning at the overgrown path. Vegetation pinged the sides of his truck. Great.

"It's the back way in."

"I only have one clip of ammo in my gun. The rest is in my bag," he shared, hoping they weren't about to get into a gunfight he wasn't prepared for. After being shot six times because he didn't realize he'd been compromised, he liked to be prepared for anything.

If this was a meeting between Noah and the killer, she would have prepared him. Wouldn't she?

"You won't need your gun. I promise," she said.

Okay, so something was really up. Something he suspected had nothing to do with Redgamer3. He just couldn't figure out what the hell it could possibly be.

He was going to carry his gun, anyway. If for nothing else than the possibility of bears. They were pretty remote, and the road that wasn't really a road continued to climb up the mountain.

He knew having a gun was useless if the feds or local law enforcement showed up. They'd already agreed she would go peacefully if they were ever caught. No use going out Bonnie and Clyde style.

She'd come up with a silly plan to spare him any punishment for aiding her. She actually thought if she pulled a gun on him, he could say he'd been forced to help her. Even now he rolled his eyes.

He'd had countless opportunities to get away. Even the day after she arrived, he'd gone off to work as usual. Surely, he would have been able to contact the police sometime over the past several weeks if he were being forced.

So no gun was needed for a shootout with law enforcement.

But if Redgamer3 showed up...that would be another thing.

Eventually the rough lane leveled off, and she pointed to a gravel parking lot by a trailhead. According to the carved wooden sign, they were at Otter Bend Park. Still in Oregon, at least.

Pudge practically crawled over him to get out first.

"*Hoike*," he commanded, and his dog ran off.

"What did you just tell him to do?" She looked worried.

Her reaction only confirmed his suspicion that she was up to something.

"Why? Are we meeting someone here?" He tilted his head, wanting to know why he'd been brought to the edge of nowhere just to go for a walk.

"There could be other hikers. Kids."

Clearly, she wasn't ready to tell him. Thankfully, she didn't look nervous, so hopefully it wasn't dangerous. He frowned and let out a breath.

Fine. He'd go along with this farce for a little while longer. It was a beautiful day and he did need the exercise.

"I told him to check things out and report back," he answered.

She made a face. "Does he have a little camera on his collar?"

"He doesn't need a camera."

He'd had plenty of time to train his dog. The hours he'd spent each night had paid off. He had a companion who was also a partner in many ways.

It took a few minutes, but Pudge returned to sit in front of him and bark once.

There was one other person here. Okay. He had enough bullets to cover one other person.

"Thanks, buddy." He gave Pudge a treat and a scratch on the neck. "You're such a good boy." He looked up at Angel and smiled. "Should we go meet your friend?"

She didn't deny it. She simply shook her head and smiled back. "Lead the way," she said with a wave of her arm.

"Are you going to tell me what this is all about?" he asked, lifting a brow. It wasn't like her to be this obvious. Or this cagey.

"You'll find out soon enough." She gestured toward a larger parking lot where a truck was parked at the far end. A man was leaning against the unfamiliar vehicle.

When the man stood and turned in their direction, Colton's stomach fell to his feet.

Holy shit.

Holy, fucking shit!

Chapter Seventy-Three

It was clear to Colton that this was no random meeting. Angel must have reached out and asked him to come. He would have had to fly here, and rent the truck.

When they were only ten feet from each other, Colton couldn't stand it any longer. "John!" he said, his voice cracking with emotion.

They rushed to close the distance and grasped each other tightly. Then Colton stood back to take his brother in from head to toe. He couldn't believe it was really him.

Oh my God, such a welcome sight!

John wiped tears from his eyes while laughing, and Colton had no idea what to say. "I'm not dead," he eventually managed to squeeze past the giant lump in his throat.

"Yeah. I guessed that when you asked me to meet you here."

Words wouldn't come. Colton opened his mouth and made a few strangled noises, but it was Angel who explained.

"Actually, that was me." She gave a little wave and a

smile. "I wanted to surprise him."

"Thank you," Colton said before kissing her hard with gratitude and a bunch of other emotions he couldn't identify at the moment. "*Thank you*."

He was definitely surprised.

"I'll leave the two of you to catch up. You know the rules," she said as she turned to go.

"I'm not allowed to tell you where I'm living," Colton told his brother as he soaked in the sight of him and grinned ear to ear.

God. John was really there. In the flesh.

Unable to help himself, he pulled his older brother into another big hug and pounded him on the back.

"Not a problem," John said, his voice muffled by their hug. "I don't really care *where* you're living, as much as *that* you're living." He pulled back and wiped his eyes again. "I had a feeling when I saw her at the cemetery, but she wouldn't confirm." He nodded toward Angel who was walking away from them.

"Because it wasn't safe," Colton explained.

"I get that. But it meant I wasn't really sure. I was left hoping I wasn't delusional. I wanted you to be alive so much, but I didn't want to lie to myself, you know? I wouldn't have been able to get past it when I still had hope."

Hope was a vicious son of a bitch.

"Not delusional. I'm alive." Though that was up for debate. Until Angel showed up, he wasn't sure if he had been living as much as simply existing.

"Were you really shot six times, or was that just to sell it?"

Colton's answer was to pull up his shirt so his brother could count the round scars.

John let out a low whistle. He'd been shot once on the job. He'd taken a hit to the arm. Carson and Brock also had battle scars. They all liked to show them off. Back then, Colton had only owned a few scratches. Now he would have won the competition hands down.

"They all go through?" John asked.

Only a cop would ask that. Colton grinned wider. "This one got stuck. They had to go in after it." He pointed to the scar that was bisected by a thin line and the telltale trace of stitches. "This one almost finished me off." That one had nicked his lung. It was the worst one. Or so he'd been told when he woke up.

John shook his head in awe. The only good thing about it was that Colton didn't remember a damned thing. He didn't remember being shot or being left for dead as he bled out onto the cement.

He still didn't know what had tipped Viktor off. For two years, the man had treated him like a son.

"Damn. It was a close thing," John whispered as Colton pulled his shirt back down to cover the scars. His brother's eyes had gone shiny again.

Colton wanted to hug him close and never let go. But he resisted embarrassing them both. "It was touch and go for a few days in the hospital, but thankfully, I don't remember any of it."

"Probably for the best." John's gaze moved over Colton's shoulder so he turned to see Angel throwing a stick for Pudge.

"Are you sure this is safe?" John asked.

"Coming to see you? I don't see what it will hurt, as long as you keep your yap shut." Colton grinned to let his brother know he was joking.

John was a cop, he knew how to keep things quiet. Even the normal exception of sharing with one's spouse didn't apply when it came to something like this.

"That's not what I meant. I've seen her picture all over the news for the past month. Her hair color might be different, but she's Angel Larson, The Mantis."

Colton grimaced. Not surprised a cop would have recognized her immediately. "I'm hoping you'll keep your yap shut about that, too. And whatever you do, don't bring up that stupid nickname to her face. She might be small, but she can take you down, for sure."

John nodded. "No problem. She brought my brother back from the dead, so I owe her big."

"She didn't kill him." Colton felt the need to defend her.

John raised his brow skeptically. "They never do, do they?"

At that moment, he reminded Colton of their dad. The same look paired with the same comment. How many times had their father told them how well people lied?

Which was all true, but—

"I know her," he said resolutely. "I trust her. She *didn't* do it."

"I see." John pressed his lips together and nodded slowly, a different look taking over his features. It was the same look John had given Colton when he came back from the prom with Jenna Buckley—and without his virginity.

"What do you think you see? You don't see anything." It was like old times. John was older than Colton by two years, but he acted as though he had decades of experience over him. "You've been with the same woman since eighth grade. You don't know shit."

When it came to women, Colton had his fair share, while John had always only had eyes for Robin.

"I see someone being awfully defensive. Why would that be, unless you like her?"

"I swear to God, if you start singing about kissing in a tree, I'm going back to being dead."

John laughed and held up his hand. "Relax. I'm not going to sing." When he got himself together, he slapped Colton on the shoulder once. "It's good to see you. I wish I could have brought Tyler."

"I saw pictures. He's a giant," Colton said of his nephew. "Are you still going to name the new kid after me?" He remembered Robin's Facebook post.

"Yeah. I think I will." He nodded. "You gonna marry her?" He nodded in Angel's direction.

Colton looked over his shoulder again. Angel was sitting on a picnic table, Pudge had his head on her thigh. "Doubtful. She's not up for that."

"But you would be?"

Colton shrugged. "Maybe. I'm living a normal life now. You settled down and had some kids. Why not me?"

John searched his face. "It's the best. I mean, I like all the action on the job, but it's nice to come home and sit on the sofa with my wife, and have my son crawl up in my lap to tell me about his day. Some guys might say it's giving up the good life, but it's not. It's getting a hell of a lot of great stuff instead."

"Maybe someday. We have a couple of things to take care of first."

John choked out a laugh. "I'd say. By that, I'm guessing you mean a murder rap, and being technically dead."

Colton laughed, too. A bit of an understatement.

"Yes. But aside from all that, I'm still figuring things out." He gave another glance at Angel, and imagined what his life could be like if she would stay.

And really, really hoped he'd get the chance to find out.

Chapter Seventy-Four

Angel tossed the stick for the hundredth time so Pudge could chase it. She didn't begrudge Colton's time with his brother. Not a bit. She wanted to give him as much time as he needed. Though she should have thought to bring something to do.

With no internet access, it wasn't as if she could monitor her situation or check in on Redgamer3.

She'd talked to Thorne this morning before Colton woke up. She'd shared what she'd done to prompt a response, and he'd warned her that her initiative had been a bit rash.

No shit. She knew she was getting desperate. Patience had never been one of her skills. But her life was suspended until this issue was resolved.

She still didn't know what she would do when this situation was behind her, but she wanted to be free to move on with whatever she decided. Not wanted by the law.

None of this was fair to Colton, either. He was stuck, too.

Thorne did have some good news. FBI Special Agent Markel had made a play on Thorne in an attempt to connect him to her escape. He'd been greedy, and when it fell through, he'd been taken off the case. In fact, Task Force Phoenix had been cleared of being in collusion with her. No investigation ongoing.

With the federal watchdogs backing off, the team was now able to launch a deeper investigation of their own. Thorne shared what they'd come up with on the killer, which so far wasn't much. She'd sent them the emails from Redgamer3 to run through crypo. Maybe there was some hidden message she'd missed. So far, nothing.

In the end, Thorne had made her promise she would contact him when she was ready to make a move on a target. With anyone else, she would have been able to evade his request, but Thorne knew her too well. He'd been the one to train her, so it was easy for him to ensnare her with words.

She was left with no other option but to lie to him. "I promise," she'd assured him. It was the first time she'd ever lied to her friend and mentor, and guilt over it twisted in her stomach.

But this was her fight. If she couldn't prove the other person was the killer, her whole team could be entangled in her mess. Her team was her only family. She wouldn't risk their careers and futures until she was absolutely sure she had a way out of this for everyone.

Pudge came back and dropped the stick at her feet, then flopped over on his side to pant. He'd been running nonstop for the last half hour.

"Tired of running, boy?" she asked as she scratched him behind the ears in that place he loved. "Yeah, I am, too."

If only she could drift off to a quiet life in the woods somewhere. She could order everything she needed online and have it delivered. She could live off the grid and out of sight.

It sounded appealing. Except for one missing piece.

Colton.

She had really enjoyed their time together. They had fun both in and out of the bedroom. And she liked talking to him and watching him cook. With him, everything was easy.

Except when he looked at her as he was looking at her now.

Even from across the park, she could tell he was talking to his brother and thinking about serious things. When John glanced her way, too, she knew they were talking about her.

She could just guess what they were discussing. Most likely Colton's feelings for her, and her propensity for disappearing overnight. And all the things she wasn't able to give him.

But, oh, how she wanted to.

Chapter Seventy-Five

Colton hung on every word his brother shared about the family. Even the most basic things, such as how Tyler had stuck a rock up his nose and they were in the ER for hours. This was real life. This was his family. Colton couldn't get enough.

"So, tell me what you're up to. At least the parts you're able to share," John said with a wry smile.

After hearing all the excitement of John's life, Colton didn't want the spotlight focused on him and the boredom of his own.

He puffed out a breath. "I'm a high school math teacher. Can you believe it?"

"Actually, I can. You were always a whiz at math."

"It's an anybody job," Colton said, kicking at the dirt with the toe of his shoe.

"The hell it is. You sound like Dad now." John seemed disgusted by the thought.

Colton studied his brother for a moment. "What's wrong

with sounding like Dad?" he finally asked when John didn't elaborate.

His brother swiped a hand over his mouth. "Dad was a great detective and an honorable man, but now that I'm a dad myself, I can see some areas where he failed us."

Colton was taken aback. No one had ever spoken ill of their father. He had always been a saint and a hero. "Like what?" he asked. He wasn't a father, so maybe he couldn't see what John saw.

"All five of us are in law enforcement. What are the odds of that?" John held out his hand as if that explained everything.

It didn't. "And?"

"And he molded us into the thing he knew rather than get to know us as individuals and encourage each of us to be what we excelled at, or what we were passionate about. From the time we were able to understand, being a cop was the only acceptable thing to do if we wanted to be *somebody* instead of just *anybody*."

Colton had never thought about it like that, but hearing it now, he realized it was true. He'd never been asked what he wanted to be when he grew up. It had always been assumed, so eventually he assumed it, too.

"Carson has high blood pressure and a stomach ulcer," John said with a frown. "Brock and Rachel are getting divorced, and Kody is just plain miserable. Being a cop is hard enough if you love it, but if you get in and figure out it's not for you, it will slowly destroy you."

Colton stared in bewilderment into the trees around them, seeing nothing.

His brother had just turned his entire universe on its axis.

John shook his head. "I'll be damned if I'm going to force Tyler into this life, or tell him he's not somebody if he's an artist or an engineer." He grinned. "I got him this really cool set of blocks. He mostly knocks them over, but I've been building some kickass shit. Robin says I have a gift for design. She thinks I should look into some classes." He acted like it was no big deal, but Colton saw the pride in his expression.

"I guess I never thought about it like that." Colton laughed once. "To be honest, I do like teaching. I'm just not used to being so...well, bored."

"Are you truly bored, or are you just lonely?" John looked past him to where Angel was playing with Pudge.

Colton followed his gaze. "Admittedly, I haven't been bored since she showed up, that's for sure."

"Well, then. That's what you want. Find yourself a wild woman and hold on tight." John winked and waggled his eyebrows.

Colton covered his eyes and shook his head. "I do not want to hear this about the mother of my nephew. Stop."

John laughed, the sound comfortingly familiar. "I bet you're a damned good teacher. Kody would never have made it through the academy if you hadn't patiently prepared him for the test."

True. Colton had forgotten about that. Or rather, he'd never noticed. There had only ever been one path for him. "I do like making a difference in a kid's life," he admitted, thinking of Kenny and how he'd just needed someone to care about him and encourage him.

"I hate that you're not able to be in our lives," John said with a wistful expression, "but this might be the best thing that happened to you. A wake-up call. A chance to do what *you* want to do instead of what has been expected of you since you became the son of Detective Jack Williamson. Let yourself enjoy teaching. Don't think of it as an *anybody* job. Because, trust me, *nobody* can do it the way you do it."

Colton thought about that for a long moment. And admitted to himself that he *did* enjoy teaching. His new life wouldn't be so bad if he had someone there with him. Someone to come home to every day. He liked helping kids, seeing their eyes light up when he explained something in a way that led them to understand. And yeah, he *was* good at it.

John had a point. It might not be the action and excitement he missed as much as having someone to share his life with. He looked over at Angel again, and hoped he wouldn't have to let her go.

Because she was the one he wanted to be there with him.

Chapter Seventy-Six

It was almost dark when John looked up at the sky and let out a sigh of regret. Colton knew what he was going to say before he spoke, and not just because of their brotherly bond.

Angel was walking toward them. It was time to go.

"I guess we have to wrap this up, huh?" John said, watching her approach.

It was difficult not to be greedy. Colton had been given this enormous gift, but he wanted more. He wanted to be able to go grab a beer with his brothers—all of them. He wanted to be able to stop in to see his mother whenever he wanted, and snag a piece of whatever she'd baked that afternoon.

He missed his family desperately, and being with John had brought it all back to the surface. Angel had done a wonderful thing. But he'd never tell her how much her kind gesture had killed him inside.

"I guess we do. The park closes at dusk. Two-thirds of us shouldn't be here when the park ranger comes by." Colton kicked a stone with his foot, letting out some of his acute frustration.

"Do you think it would be okay to keep in contact through Messenger?" John asked.

Colton made a face. "I don't know what that is, but I'll ask Angel and my handler." Whatever he had to do to keep in contact with his brother, he'd do it. Even if it meant touching a computer.

Angel came up to them. "I can make sure it's a secure link on Colton's end. As long as it isn't a constant thing, and Colton uses an alias, it should be okay."

Colton wrapped his arm around her and kissed the top of her head. "That would be great." She fit perfectly against him, and she smelled like his soap.

"I'm sorry, but we need to get going," she said.

"John, this is my Angel." That one extra word "my" made a world of difference.

She looked up at him in surprise. "You told him who I am?"

He gave a wry smile. "John's a cop. He recognized you right away."

She looked immediately uncomfortable. "There's a very large bounty on my head, you know."

She didn't need to spell out what was worrying her.

"It's fine," Colton assured her.

As expected, John took offense at her hint. "I can't be bought. My brother says you were set up, and I believe him. Which means you're under my protection, the same as you're under his. I don't care if your whereabouts are worth a hundred thousand dollars, I'm not turning you in."

"Ten million," she said with her brow cocked. "I'm worth *ten million* dollars."

John swallowed. "Holy shit," he choked out.

Colton's eyes widened. "Really?" He hadn't realized it had gotten this bad. He knew his brother still wouldn't be tempted, but anyone else was a wildcard. The stakes had really been raised.

Angel grimaced. "Yeah. Heath's company put it up, thinking finding me will get the prototype back. The board sees it as a sound investment."

"Idiots," Colton muttered.

"I won't say anything. I owe you more than that," John said, and reached out to hug her.

She allowed it but Colton could tell she was still uncomfortable.

"My brother's happiness is priceless," John said, "so I scoff at the ten-million-dollar reward."

His brother's joke made them all laugh and diffused the tense situation.

"You're scoffing at ten million dollars, huh?" She smiled crookedly as John nodded. "Okay. I trust you." She stepped back from him as quickly as possible without seeming rude.

Colton grinned. No doubt, there hadn't been a lot of brotherly hugging in the Larson family when she was growing up. The only physical contact she'd had with her brother was of the painful variety.

"Good. And I hope you get this mess cleared up so the two of you can be happy together." John gave him a wink and a hug. "I love you, man. I'm so fucking glad you're okay." He patted the dog on the head, gave the two of them one last look with misty eyes, then jumped in the truck. With a wave, he backed out and left the park.

Seeing him drive off brought tears to Colton's own eyes, but he gazed up at the darkening sky to keep them from falling.

"I don't know what to say." Colton turned to her when he was able to speak. He held her face in his hands and tilted it up when she tried to look away. "You did an amazing thing. I can't thank you enough for this."

She said nothing, so he kissed her with all the emotions he wished he could share in words. When he came up for air they smiled at one another.

"You're welcome."

He linked his fingers with hers as they walked to his truck. This woman was in the middle of her own shit storm. She was being hunted by the FBI and provoked by a killer. Yet, she'd taken the time to do this for him. To give him time with the brother he'd thought he'd never see again.

"I envy you," she said, completely throwing him for a loop when they were back on the highway.

"Envy me? Why?"

"Seeing you with your brother, it makes me wonder what it would have been like to have a real brother. A normal one, who loved me and protected me like John does for you."

"I'm sorry. I'm just so glad your brother didn't kill you, I guess I didn't realize how much he still hurts you." He squeezed her hand, wishing there was a place to pull over without the chance of police involvement. "I have four brothers, and while we weren't always the best of friends, we never hurt one another. Not on purpose, anyway."

He thought about the scars on her body. They were part of her. He'd grown used to seeing them. He'd kissed them and did his best to take the pain of them away. Unfortunately, the pain went deeper than he would ever be able to reach.

"Family isn't supposed to hurt you," he said sympathetically. "They should always have your back. And even when you're wrong, they should help you through whatever comes. I'm sorry you never had that, but I hope someday you will know what it's like."

"I do kind of have that now," she said softly.

For a silent, joyful moment, he thought she'd meant him.

Then she clarified. "Thorne and the other marshals are my family now. I trust them all with my life. I've even tested it, and they never failed."

Maybe. But they weren't blood. They couldn't tell stories from when they were six. They didn't know what it was like to grow up with Angel. It wasn't the same as a real brother or sister. Trust was one thing. Sibling bonds were another. And a lot stronger.

"If that's true, why do you always insist on doing everything alone?" he asked. After all, she was hiding with him instead of any of them.

She stared out the window for a long moment, then glanced over at him. "Have you ever felt like a burden to your family? Like you're not worth the hassle?" Her voice was so quiet he had to strain to hear her over the tires on the road.

"No. Not once. Ever."

"Oh." She frowned and looked back out the window. "We're not going to make it home tonight. Let's get a motel room."

He nodded, wanting to be with her near a bed where he could show her his gratitude, his loyalty, and his love.

And that last word didn't even surprise him.

Yes, damn it, he loved her.

Chapter Seventy-Seven

Angel waited in the truck while Colton ran into the motel to secure a pet-friendly room. The building was four stories high, and each room had its own tiny balcony. Many had beach towels draped over them, waving in the breeze. They weren't far from Cannon Beach.

Maybe in the morning they could stop and walk along the shore. She could get a big floppy sun hat and huge sunglasses as a disguise. She smiled at the thought.

Pudge pushed his head between the truck seats and let out a whine.

"Okay. Come on." While she didn't want to risk being seen, she couldn't let the dog suffer if he had to go. "Let's be quick about it, okay?"

He was as quick as a dog in a new territory could be. He stopped a few places until he found the spot that should be his, then he lifted his leg at each place, anyway. The motel was well and thoroughly his now.

As they went back to the truck, Pudge became alert when

a car pulled in next to theirs. She should have had a leash on him. She wondered if Colton even had a leash in the truck. She'd never seen one.

She opened the door and Pudge jumped in without complaint. The window was down partway for some air, and Pudge stepped over her lap to growl at the newcomers.

"No," she said, wishing she'd learned a few of the important commands in Hawaiian.

She glanced out the window to apologize to the three college-aged boys who all seemed drunk. She wasn't sure which of them had been driving, but it was clear none of them were legally up for the task.

Deciding they didn't deserve an apology, she turned back toward the main entrance. Colton was walking out tapping a keycard against his palm and looking sexy as hell.

How had she gotten so lucky to have this amazing and hot man want to help her?

College boys forgotten, she waited for him to slide into the driver's seat, then leaned over and kissed him.

"What was that?" He laughed.

"I want you," she purred, and touched him through his jeans.

"At least this time I only have to drive to the other side of the motel."

They parked near the rear entrance. He grabbed the duffel bag she'd had him pack in case something came up, motioned to Pudge, then wrapped his other arm around her as they went through the door and waited at the elevator. They kissed the whole way up to their room on the third floor, only pulling away from each other so they could open the door.

Inside, they quickly put out the pet bed for Pudge and got him water before reaching for each other again. They had their clothes off in record speed and—after removing the bedspread because she'd read a disturbing report on the internet—they fell together onto the bed.

They were both so needy it didn't take them long to reach a mutual climax. They slowed down the second time, then stepped into the shower for round three.

They were walking out of the bathroom when Pudge alerted to the door only a few seconds before three loud *thump*s and a deep voice making the announcement, "Open up, police!"

Chapter Seventy-Eight

Colton looked down at their dripping, naked bodies, and realized they'd committed an agent's cardinal sin. Not the sex, but they'd not taken time to consider an escape plan. They were three stories up with only one door that led to an exit.

And now the police were standing outside, blocking that sole exit.

They were trapped.

Angel turned her large blue eyes on him and swallowed.

She looked ready to give up, but he wasn't willing to let her go. Not without trying everything. They didn't yet know what the police wanted. Maybe they still had a chance.

"Hide," he whispered.

She pulled on her clothes even faster than he'd taken them off. But there was nowhere to hide—only a small closet and the bathroom. If the police were looking for a fugitive those would be the first places they checked.

"In case this doesn't work," Angel said before she kissed

him quick. "I 1—"

She was interrupted by more pounding at the door.

She gasped, rushed over to open the sliding door to the balcony, and went out.

"Shit," he murmured, locked the glass door, and quickly wiped off the fingerprints. He draped his towel around his waist and ran a hand through his wet hair.

The police banged again and he opened the door, hoping this worked. He smiled, ready to charm them, but one of the officers stepped immediately into the room, his gun drawn.

"Step out in the hall," he ordered as Pudge growled and barked.

"What's going on?" Colton asked the officer in the hall who had his weapon trained on him.

Pudge growled again, and pranced around the first cop.

"Tell your dog to settle," the cop ordered.

He told Pudge to quiet down. After a final bark of protest, he came and sat at Colton's bare feet.

Colton crossed his arms and watched through the open door while the other officer, as expected, inspected the closet, the bathroom, and also looked under the bed.

As if Angel would have hidden there after her anxiety about the cleanliness of the bedspread. He would have laughed at the thought if he weren't so worried about her.

The officer then unlocked the door to the balcony and went out. Colton had to fight every instinct not to react. He concentrated on staying calm and waited until the man was done and came back out in the hall.

"Where's the woman?"

"What woman?" He knew if they were asking about a woman, it was because they were sure one existed. But he'd come up with a plan.

"Someone reported seeing a woman with you."

He raised his brows. "Since when is that illegal?"

"Where is she?" the cop demanded again.

Colton narrowed his eyes. "She told me she was of age."

The officer looked briefly confused.

"I didn't have any reason to doubt her," Colton continued, holding up one hand. The other was still keeping the towel securely closed. "Though, admittedly, I didn't ask for ID."

The officers exchanged a look. "We were told the woman in question was Angel Larson."

Colton gave them his best look of bewilderment, and then enlightenment. "Wait. The woman wanted for murder?" He pretended to think, then shook his head. "The chick on TV had blond hair. The girl I was with had brown."

Officer Kirkwood—according to his name badge—looked annoyed. "People dye their hair when they're on the run."

"If you say so." Colton pursed his lips. "But I don't think it was her. That Angel chick is hot. This girl was only so-so."

Pudge whined at his lie.

"Where did she go?"

He shrugged. "No idea. She left when we, uh, finished."

"She was a prostitute?"

"No!" Colton said, straightening with feigned offense. "I don't need to pay for sex, thank you very much. I can still get women the old-fashioned way."

"And where did you come by this one?"

The guy was not giving up. Colton had to check his annoyance.

"A bar down the street. We walked back here." God, he hoped there was a bar down the street, and that it was busy enough that no one would remember if he'd been there. "Is this going to be a big deal? Because"—he looked around him and dropped his voice—"I have a girlfriend back in Crystal Grove."

The officer frowned at him. "Get dressed, and come with us."

Hell.

Chapter Seventy-Nine

On the balcony below theirs, Angel took a moment to curse her carelessness. She should have made sure they selected a motel with only one floor.

No. Scratch that. They shouldn't have stopped at a motel, at all. They should have driven straight home.

It was too late to play the "should have" game now. They'd needed a pet-friendly motel, and this had been the closest one. Now she just needed to get away.

As she threw her leg over the railing, she worried about leaving Colton behind. Depending on how far the cops wanted to take this, they could check the room for fingerprints. And they would find hers. Colton would have a difficult time explaining that away. Along with her things in his room.

Hanging from the bottom of the second-floor balcony, she dangled in the air, then pumped her legs to get enough momentum to land on the patio below.

Towels draped over the railing, so the room was occupied. She hoped no one heard her land, or worse, decided to come outside. The drapes were closed and no lights came on.

She allowed herself a moment to breathe as she ducked down against the wall.

A sliding door above opened, and she heard footsteps and a scuff as one of the cops most likely looked out over the railing, then turned to go back inside after finding nothing.

When the sliding door closed, she jumped down to the ground with a *thump*. Suppressing a grunt of pain, she rolled behind a bush where she could take a moment to think…or to pass out.

The pain in her ankle caused her vision to shimmer. *Not a good time*, she told her brain as she gave it a nice, deep breath of oxygen.

She stood, and nearly fell again. She didn't need WebMD to know her ankle was sprained.

Too bad. She'd just have to deal with it. Escape was her top priority.

She stood again, and limped toward the parking lot as if she belonged there. Teeth gritted with pain, she ducked her head when she came across an elderly couple wheeling a suitcase toward her.

That was when she realized her tank top was on backward and inside out. It might not have been a problem if it hadn't been a razorback tank. And her bra was neon pink.

Crap.

She cut between a truck and an SUV before she crossed paths with the seniors. Keeping her eye on the third-floor room where Colton was handling the police, she quickly rearranged her shirt, then hurried around the building.

The car belonging to the three college-aged assholes was her first pick when considering which car to steal. She was sure this was all their fault, and they shouldn't be driving drunk, anyway.

The door was unlocked on the piece-of-shit coupe. Her initial search for spare keys turned up a few condoms and a baggie of pot. Not helping.

She kept watch on the building as her fingers moved under the dash to get to the wiring harness. A few seconds later, the car roared to life with all the decibels the modified muffler could choke out.

It was too late to change her mind now, Colton would only be able to stall the officers for so long, and they would be walking out the front door any minute.

She backed out and pulled away. No hotel curtains moved. She let out a sigh of relief.

But out on the highway, panic set in.

She was wearing a tank top, yoga pants, and sneakers. She had no money, no ID, no credit card, and no phone since she'd left all of that in the room. The crappy car she was driving had a little over a quarter of a tank. Not nearly enough to get her back to Colton's.

Then again, maybe she shouldn't go back to Colton's.

The thought twisted in her stomach as she focused on the road. As much as she didn't want to end their time together, she was nothing but a danger to him. Especially now. She would have to leave eventually, anyway. They both knew it.

She should have been prepared for this moment, but she wasn't.

She could vividly recall his face from all the times he'd left the house or gone to sleep. The way he always told her, "If you're not here when I get up, good luck, and take care of yourself."

She wanted more than his good wishes. She wanted him. And she wanted to prove to him that she could stick around. That she didn't need to keep running away from him.

But here she was, running away.

Colton had a life. It might not be as exciting as he'd like, but it was safe and respectable. It was far better than landing in jail for helping her.

Wait a second.

A memory flooded through her from when she'd left just a few minutes ago.

Had she almost told him she loved him?

Only now when she was out of immediate danger did her brain allow her to look back instead of focusing on moving forward.

Sure enough, now that she thought about it, she'd almost told him she loved him right before running out onto the balcony. The banging on the door had interrupted her, but... surely he understood what she'd been about to say?

Had it been a near-death confession? She'd been in tighter spots than that and hadn't blurted out crazy things before.

Maybe he didn't realize what she'd been about to say. She'd really only gotten out the first letter. Maybe in all the excitement he would have forgotten.

After all, *she'd* almost forgotten, and she was the one who'd said it.

Turning north, she headed in the opposite direction of Colton's place. He would probably be upset at first, but in end he would understand.

If he didn't hate her for getting him involved, he would at least be glad to have his freedom back. He could stay in any motel he wanted and not care if there was an exit. He could date Danielle and go parking in cars. He could have backyard cookouts with the neighbors.

She wasn't sure how he'd *feel* about the situation. All she knew was, the best she could do for him now was to walk out of his life.

"Goodbye, Colton," she whispered as she merged onto the interstate, her heart quietly breaking.

Chapter Eighty

When the police brought up the footage from the elevator, Colton was sure he was screwed, but fortunately their passion paid off. With his face stuck to Angel's, her appearance was hidden enough she wasn't identifiable. The angle of the camera only showed her back and his hands on her ass.

"What's that?" One of the detectives pointed toward the screen.

Colton thought he might vomit. He leaned closer to see what the man was pointing at.

"A tattoo," the other man said. "I'll zoom in on it."

It was the fake tattoo Angel had put on her shoulder for the wedding. A tree. Oh, thank God. This might be the break Colton needed.

"Um. It's a tree. I saw it when I was…you know…behind," he offered with a crooked grin.

"Does Angel Larson have a tree tattoo on her shoulder?" the detective asked another officer holding her wanted poster.

"It says no tattoos. Multiple scars."

"Did this woman have scars?" the detective asked Colton.

"Not that I saw." This was true. He didn't see her scars anymore. They were such a part of her, he didn't notice them. "She had a lip ring. I know because it got caught on my junk. You want to see?" Colton reached for the button on his jeans and all the cops put up their hands.

"No. That's okay. I think we're done here."

"So it wasn't her?" He frowned. "Well, shit. That would have been a hell of a story to tell my friends."

"You're free to go, Mr. Willis. I'll have someone drive you back to your motel."

"Okay. Thanks." When Colton stood, Pudge jumped up from his spot in the corner where he'd been snoring.

Colton kept his pace casual as he waved to the officer who'd dropped him off. Inside the motel, he pushed the floor number six times in a row in an effort to make the elevator hurry.

"Please let her be there, please let her be there," he chanted as he swiped the keycard with shaking hands.

The door opened and he hurried out to the balcony.

Nothing.

"Angel?" he called as he checked the bathroom. It only took ten seconds to verify she wasn't there, either.

"Come on, boy." He took Pudge back outside and told him to find Angel. The shepherd's nose went up in the air, then down to the ground as he moved around the building on a mission. He stopped at the place where Colton had parked earlier when he went inside to get the room.

"Find her, boy. Please find her."

Pudge turned in a circle, barked, and sat down. This was where the trail stopped.

Damn it.

She was gone.

Chapter Eighty-One

Angel let her forehead fall to the steering wheel as the stolen car drifted to the side of the road and sputtered out its last offering before it ran out of gas. Well, at least she'd had the good luck to get off the highway first.

She was now on a remote back road in the forests of deepest, darkest Oregon. Remote meant there weren't a lot of options for stealing another car. Remote meant nothing but trees for miles and miles.

She looked down at her ankle and frowned. It had swelled up to double its normal size from the sprain. Walking would be slow going.

Dawn was coming. She wasn't sure if this was on the pros or cons list.

She stared into the dark trees. Her best bet would be to walk parallel to the road so she wouldn't be seen by passing cars. Hell, if anyone else even used this road.

Walking in the woods with a sprained ankle nearly guaranteed it would only get worse. And more painful. As it was, it throbbed like the devil.

Hitchhiking was out of the question. Her lack of supplies and money were as good as wearing a T-shirt that said, "I'm a fugitive on the run!"

With a groan, she hobbled to a downed log near the car and rested her head in her hands. As dire as her situation was, she found herself worrying about Colton. Had he been arrested for helping her? Was he being watched? Would he be exposed in the news, so Viktor Kulakov would find him?

This was exactly where she hadn't ever wanted to be. She couldn't help Colton, and she couldn't help herself. If she didn't know it wouldn't help, she might have broken down and cried.

As it was, she let out a frustrated, disgruntled sigh and stood. She'd come this far. She wasn't giving up yet.

Until the cuffs were on her wrists—or a bear ate her—she still had a fighting chance.

Chapter Eighty-Two

Colton was being followed. It wasn't as obvious as the white sedan with the floppy windshield stripping. It had started out as more of a feeling of paranoia as he and Pudge got into the truck that morning and left the motel. But after a few miles of trailing him, the SUV hanging several cars back was impossible to miss.

He had a clue about Angel, at least. At the continental breakfast this morning, three college boys had been whispering about their missing car. It sounded like they'd been to a party last night and couldn't remember where they'd left it. They'd been debating the challenges of reporting it stolen when it had drugs inside.

The owner obviously wanted his vehicle back, but one of the other boys had enough money to get them bus fare back to Seattle. When they finally agreed that was the best thing to do, they'd eaten every stitch of bacon on the buffet, then left.

If his hunch was correct, Angel had stolen their car. If he was wrong and they truly were that stupid, it meant she was wandering around this small town with no way to get back home.

Either way, it was impossible to look for her with law enforcement tailing him.

His only option was to drive straight home and hope she turned up after the people in the SUV behind him gave up.

"How long do you think it will take for them to give up?" he asked Pudge, who didn't have an answer. He simply whined and put his head out the window again.

When they arrived home early that afternoon, Colton took the bag of her things and stashed it in the hiding place under his closet floor. He took a few moments to wipe down the house again, even though she'd done it before they left.

He did laundry, and tried to act normal as he waited for whoever had been following him to make contact. Was it the cops from the motel? Or that obnoxious Special Agent Markel, or one of his buddies from the feds? Probably not anyone from Task Force Phoenix. They'd just have knocked on his door.

He invited Kenny out for ice cream the next day. He wanted an excuse to get out of the house, but he wanted to talk to him, too. The SUV was still there, following at a discreet distance.

Kenny didn't notice the tail, or Colton's lack of attention. He rambled on as they ordered their sundaes and sat at an outside table in the shade at the Ice Cream Shack. Colton made Pudge sit as he waited for his doggie cone.

When the cute teenaged waitress brought the food to the table, Kenny's tongue was hanging out nearly as much as Pudge's. Colton smiled and watched the exchange between Kenny and the girl. Pudge stole all the attention—the shameless flirt—and the girl left with a smile and a handful of drool. Pudge's, not Kenny's.

"So, I've decided I want to go to the police academy,"

Kenny said after the waitress left.

"Uh-uh. We can talk about that later. What was that all about?" Colton pointed after the waitress who'd disappeared back inside.

"What was what?" Kenny's cheeks flushed pink.

The kid really needed to figure out how not to blush when he lied if he wanted to go into law enforcement.

"The girl, and the 'Thank you, Morgan.' And the watching her walk all the way back into the Shack." He made his voice all dreamy sounding in an imitation of Kenny.

"I was raised to thank people who bring me food."

Colton wasn't going to let him off the hook that easily. "There's thanking people, and there's, 'Thank you, Morgan.'" He exaggerated the dreaminess even more.

Kenny's lips pulled up on the one side and he looked away. Classic.

"You like her," Colton pushed, even bumping the kid with his elbow the way his older brothers had done to him.

"Maybe," Kenny said with apparent disinterest, but the way he then glanced longingly in her direction when she came out again told Colton it was more than maybe.

"Why don't you go talk to her? I can sit over here like a good wingman."

"Nah. That's okay."

"You should ask her out."

"No way. She would say no."

"Are you a hundred percent positive she'll say no?"

"Maybe like ninety-seven percent."

Colton smiled both because Kenny had confessed to a chance that Morgan would say yes, and because they were using math in a casual situation. The teacher in him cheered proudly.

He pulled two twenties out of his wallet and put them on the table. "If she says yes, you'll use this to take her to the movies. If she says no, you and I will go to the movies. If you don't try, no one is going to the movies."

"Seriously? You're bribing me into asking her out?"

Colton grinned unrepentantly. "Yes. And don't forget to smile. You've got a good smile." It was true. The kid's parents had probably paid a fortune for that smile, and Kenny rarely used it.

The boy took a deep breath, then stood. Two steps later, Colton stopped him. "Wait. Take the dog."

Kenny looked down at Pudge, who was sitting and staring at Colton's ice cream as if he ever shared.

"Trust me, the dog will get you in. Let her pet the dog, then say, 'Would you like to go to the movies with me?'"

"Seriously? Just straight off like that?"

"Exactly like that. Don't try too hard."

"Do I get to pick the movie when we go, or are you going to pick it?" Kenny muttered, already resigned that she would say no.

"She's going to pick it," Colton said. "Now, go."

While Kenny went to face his destiny, Colton noticed the SUV was still sitting in the parking lot. He could just imagine how annoyed they were, having to wait while a seventeen-year-old's love life played out. He snickered softly. Too bad for them.

Kenny's face was blank when he walked back to the table. Colton couldn't decipher what had happened. Was it good or bad?

Kenny sat down.

"Well?" Colton asked, curiosity getting the best of him.

Kenny snatched the two twenties off the table and smiled. "Sorry, Mr. Willis, but you're going to have to go to the movies by yourself. I have other plans."

Colton smacked him on the back and laughed. "Good for you."

"I can't believe she actually said yes." He seemed truly shocked.

"I'm sure it was the dog. Dogs are chick magnets," Colton joked, then turned serious. "Make sure to be yourself. You're going to be nervous, there's really no way around that. But just be yourself. Always. Okay?"

Kenny looked incredulous. "That's your advice? Be myself? You know me enough to know myself is not all that great." He held out a hand and let it drop.

"No. You're awesome. And she said yes because you asked. She's smiling over here at *you*, and I know it's you she's smiling at because Pudge is licking himself and no one would be smiling at that." He nudged his dog with his foot. "Cool it until you get home, Pudge."

Kenny laughed, and twisted the napkin in his hands. "Thanks for making me do that."

"I didn't *make* you," Colton protested. When Kenny raised a skeptical brow, Colton gave in. "Okay, but only because I was ninety-seven percent sure she would say yes." He couldn't help but put some math in there again. "So, you were saying you're going to go into the police academy?"

"Yes." Kenny's eyes lit up with excitement. That was a good sign. "My parents were surprised, but they seem to be onboard. But then I printed out the application and panicked. I mean, what if I can't do it? What if I suck?"

Colton ignored the men watching them from the SUV so he could focus on Kenny. This was important.

"Why do you want to be a police officer?" he asked.

No adult had ever cared to ask Colton that question. If he'd been given the chance, who knew what he might have said.

"Chicks like a man in uniform," Kenny said, and smiled.

Colton chuckled, then said, "No, this is serious. At the end of the day, you need to be okay with this decision. You can't sign up just because of what other people will think."

Colton blinked, wishing someone had given him that same advice.

"You can be anything you want to be, Kenny. You got that?"

"Yeah, okay. I know." He shifted in his chair and his cheeks turned pink. "When I was ten, I was riding home from a friend's house. It was late afternoon and it was Mill Street. The one down from your house with all the trees." When Colton nodded, he continued, "The sun was coming through the trees and I didn't see there was a car. I turned my bike onto the street and *blam*! This woman hit me." Kenny smacked his fist into his palm.

Colton frowned. "Were you hurt?"

"Oh, yeah. I was wearing a helmet, but my elbows were bleeding and my leg was broken. The woman was crying into her phone. A police officer was the first person on the scene. Everything was going crazy. I was kind of dizzy, my leg hurt, the lady was wailing, traffic was backing up, and cars were blowing their horns. But when the officer got there, he took care of everything. Even kept my dad back when he started yelling at me for not looking where I was going."

Colton nodded, remembering when he'd been a beat cop coming up on a scene like that.

"I want to do that for someone else. In the middle of all the noise and craziness, I want to be able to step up and take control of the situation so they feel better and aren't so scared. Is that dumb?"

Colton smiled. "It's not dumb at all."

In fact, it was a much better reason than what Colton could come up with for his own choice. This was the *right* reason.

Still, Colton would be remiss if he didn't help prepare the kid for what he would face. "I'm not going to blow sunshine up your ass. It won't be easy. But here's the thing. You graduated from high school, which means you successfully passed classes you don't care about. It will be different when you're learning something that really interests you, about something you really want to do."

"What about the physical part?" He looked down at his chest with a grimace.

Colton looked him over, as well. He wasn't much skinnier than Colton had been at that age. The military had whipped him into shape. "Trust me, they'll take care of that for you." He grinned.

"Do *you* think I can do it, Mr. Willis?" The boy's voice was filled with equal parts hope and fear.

"I do. If it's what you really want, you'll make it happen."

Kenny nodded and threw their trash away with an extra spring in his step. "Should we take some ice cream back to The Mantis?" he asked, his voice lowered even though no one else was close by.

"No. She had to go away for a little while," Colton said as fresh pain twisted the ice cream in his stomach.

"So I can stop by without having a gun pulled on me?"

Colton forced a smile, but didn't make any promises. "Funny."

Kenny didn't say anything for a few blocks, then he let out a breath. "It's probably better Angel isn't around right now," he said.

"Why's that?" Colton asked.

"Because there are two men in an SUV following you."

Colton shot him a surprised look, then slapped him on the shoulder with a smile. "You're going to make a kickass cop someday, kid. Come on. Let's have some fun."

Chapter Eighty-Three

The good news was, Angel now had a disguise. The bad news was, she looked like the victim in a horror flick.

After her second fall—when she hit her head on a rock—she'd decided she would only travel by day, so she could see where she was going. Her hair was now crusted with blood, and the rest of her was completely covered in mud. She hadn't eaten anything since the day before when she'd come across some raspberries. She'd found a small trickle of a stream where she could get a drink, but it wasn't large enough to clean up in.

She'd found the perfect size stick to help support the weight of her left side, since her ankle was no longer up for the task. She was still moving forward, if slowly, so she was calling it a win.

At least for now.

She'd heard only four other cars pass by on the road in all this time. Being a city kid, it was difficult for her to imagine a place this remote. Surely, she would run into civilization at some point. So far, she'd been able to suppress the panic that maybe she wouldn't.

It was early evening, judging by the blazing orange sky to her left. Her pace picked up when she saw light coming through the trees ahead. As she broke through the edge of the forest, she realized it wasn't lights she was seeing but the reflection of the sunset multiplied on hundreds of windshields.

At first she thought she'd wandered into a large parking lot, but then she saw the condition the vehicles were in.

This was a salvage yard.

A smile pulled up at her lips.

She could work with that.

Chapter Eighty-Four

Three days had gone by and there was still no sign of Angel. No word, no hint, no nothing. The only thing Colton knew for sure was that she hadn't been caught, because her photo was still being broadcast on the news along with a hotline number for tips.

He shut the TV off, wondering where she could be. Had she been abducted? That didn't seem likely. Her kidnapper would have recognized her and cashed in the reward by now.

Could she be lying in a ditch somewhere? That depressing thought must have been dredged up by some buried parental gene. He shook the thought away. Angel was a trained marshal. She would be able to get herself out of any scrape.

Which left only one other possible answer.

She'd deliberately left him.

Again.

Did she have a list of men she'd protected in the past? Was she just working her way through them, a few weeks here, a few weeks there?

No. He didn't believe that. She'd said she loved him. Well, she had *almost* said it, anyway. Angel Larson didn't just blurt things out like that and not mean them. At least he didn't think so.

But where the hell was she?

The cops or feds in the SUV had given up on him the day before. He'd held out hope that she'd known he was being followed and would turn up as soon as they were gone. He'd stayed up late last night in anticipation of her arrival, but she never showed.

He'd even opened up her laptop, but after being faced with a password he didn't know he'd turned it off again.

He looked down at the phone Thorne had left her. Colton knew Thorne would pick up immediately if he called. Wouldn't he want to know she was missing? Wouldn't he do something to help?

Colton had to try. He couldn't sit here waiting any longer. He hit redial and waited the two rings before a deep voice said, "Yes?"

"Um, Mr. Thorne, it's Colton."

"Where's Angel? Has she been taken into custody?"

"No. She's not been taken in. At least I'm pretty sure she hasn't. The thing is…" He ran his hand over his hair, thinking maybe he shouldn't have called, after all. "I lost her."

"What do you mean you *lost* her?"

"I mean, we were at a motel and the police showed up, and she jumped off the third-floor balcony, and I can't find her."

"Did you look on the ground under the balcony?"

Colton scowled at the phone. *Seriously*? "Yes." He had checked, and was very glad she wasn't there.

"She'll turn up." Thorne's voice was nothing but confidence. How could he be so damn sure?

"That's it? *She'll turn up?*" Colton burst out.

"Yeah. She's a trained marshal who can get out of

anything. If she's not lying dead on the ground, it means she's mobile and she's fine."

Colton had serious doubts about this man being like a father to Angel. Generally speaking, fathers were a lot more concerned when their children went missing. Even adult children, he assumed.

"You're not going to look for her?"

"No. She'll get in contact with me if she needs something."

"But I have her phone." Obviously. He was speaking into it at the moment. "She has no money, no credit cards, no identification. Just the clothes on her back and maybe a broken down car."

"She will find a way." The man actually sounded proud.

"You do realize she's a *human,* right? Not a real Angel, or a superhero with magical powers."

"I wouldn't be so sure. If she doesn't show up in the next week, call me again. She might not come back to your place if it's hot."

Colton knew he wasn't talking about the temperature. He meant people watching. He hadn't seen anyone since yesterday, but that didn't mean they weren't there. Were they keeping Angel from coming home?

Not that this was her home. Not really.

"I take it that SUV following me isn't your guys," he said, wanting confirmation.

"Nope. Not us."

"Okay. I'll keep you posted."

Thorne grunted, then disconnected without so much as a goodbye.

Colton tossed the phone on the sofa and poured himself a glass of whiskey. He set the bottle on the coffee table, knowing it was a waste of time to put it away.

He was officially losing it.

The woman he loved was out there somewhere and he

had no idea if she was safe. Or if she planned to come back.

The rest of the summer lay before him with no plans. He could afford to spend one of those days recovering from a night of drinking. It didn't matter that it was barely six o'clock. Who would know? It wasn't as if he had any friends or family.

He just wanted to find a way to stop his brain from playing the endless reel of horrible scenarios that could be keeping her away. Everything from human trafficking to Bigfoot flashed into his head. The worst thing he'd thought of was if Redgamer3 had been watching her and found her. If he had taken her—

Colton again tried to block the horrific thoughts.

Where *was* she?

Pudge tilted his head and let out a whine. Apparently, he'd asked that last question out loud.

"Perfect. I'm back to having conversations with my dog."

He finished off the first glass of whiskey in one gulp, and set up the next.

"You were just a puppy when she left us the last time. You used to sit by the door and cry. I envied you. When puppies cry, it's endearing. When men cry, it's pathetic."

He held up glass number four—or six—and shot it down, hoping the pain would go away soon.

Pudge put his chin on Colton's knee and looked up at him with sad brown eyes.

"I know. I miss her, too. I'm sorry you can't drink. It does help a little."

Unfortunately he knew from experience that drinking was only a temporary fix. But if he could have one night of peace, he would take it.

He'd deal with everything else tomorrow.

Or the next bottle.

Chapter Eighty-Five

When Colton woke up on his sofa, he cursed at the woodpecker that was ruining his oblivion. Fucking birds and their bird noises so early in the morning.

Except it wasn't morning. It was dark. It was only eleven.

The woodpecker tapped again, and Colton realized it wasn't a woodpecker. It was tapping. On glass.

Where the hell was his dog? He looked around to see Pudge was nowhere to be found. He usually told him when someone was at the door. Had he lost his damn dog, too? Christ, his life was a frigging mess.

An answering bark came from outside. He'd let the dog out and forgotten to let him back in. He was such a piece of crap.

He was halfway to the door when he realized Pudge couldn't have been knocking. The dog was brilliant, but knocking at the door was beyond him. Which meant a person had knocked. At his back door.

His gun was…somewhere. He wasn't sure. Oh, well. It

wasn't as if the person was going to find Angel here. Because she was gone.

He opened the door and blinked.

"Angel."

She blinked back at him. "God, you might look worse than me," she said, and pushed past him.

He put his hand out to brace himself so she didn't knock him over. He wasn't too steady. In fact, there was more than one Angel in his kitchen.

She was dressed in the same clothes she'd been wearing when she jumped off the balcony. Only, she was filthy.

Christ, this was an odd fantasy. Normally he dreamed of sexy, put-together Angel, not this mess that was limping to his refrigerator.

"Are you real?" he heard himself ask out loud.

"Are you drunk?" All four Angels tilted their heads to the side at the same time. The movement made him dizzy.

"Oh, hell," he said, stumbled out into the backyard, and threw up.

Chapter Eighty-Six

Angel spared a moment to make sure Colton was okay. He moaned from his prone position on the back porch, promising he'd never drink ever again. She smiled at his conviction while raiding the refrigerator. She was starving.

Before he opened the door, she'd been debating on what she wanted more—food or a hot shower. She probably couldn't smell much worse, but she could pass out from a lack of food. Her stomach cast its vote with a loud grumble. She was so hungry she was still able to eat the pasta salad she found despite Colton's retching off the back porch.

In an effort not to end up next to him, she halted the gorge-fest after she finished off a piece of leftover pizza. Pudge was dancing around her legs, and she had a feeling it wasn't just because she had food.

"Are you happy to see me?" she asked the dog, who responded with a sharp bark. "Yeah, I missed you, too."

He fell to his side and rolled over for a tummy rub.

"You wouldn't believe what I went through," she shared.

When she'd come across the junkyard, she'd thought her troubles had ended.

Her uncle had owned a salvage yard. On the one and only occasion her family had gone to visit him, she'd played happily in the vehicles, pretending she could drive, even trying the keys she'd found in some of them. She therefore knew from her youthful adventure there that not every vehicle was completely out of commission. Some of them still ran. Plus, no one was likely to notice if one was missing. A bit of knowledge that had saved her butt a time or two in her career.

She'd lucked out and found a minivan that still had the keys hanging in the ignition. It started right up, and she'd thought she was home free until she put it in reverse and nothing happened. No reverse.

After checking out a few other options, she finally came across a Camaro with pink fur across the dash and leopard seat covers. It smoked, but it ran. Not wanting to lead anyone to Crystal Grove, she ditched it two towns over and walked— make that limped—the rest of the way back to Colton's. It had been an ordeal, but she'd made it.

"I'm back now." She bent to give Pudge a thorough petting.

The dog was only one of the many reasons she'd come back. The biggest reason was still lying on the porch making sounds of remorse from his overindulgence.

She went to the bathroom and tossed all her clothes straight in the trash. Even if there was a way to get them clean, she never wanted to see them again.

Stepping under the warm water was heaven...for about twenty seconds. Then the burning started, identifying every scratch and blister on her body. There were many. Some she hadn't known about until that moment.

The water ran different shades of brown, gray, and red,

depending on the body part the stream was focused on. After scrubbing twice and gingerly washing her hair, she continued to stand under the water for as long as her ankle would hold her. She knew if she sat down in the tub she probably wouldn't be able to get back up.

Sparing a few seconds to the idea of sleeping in the tub, she shut the water off and maneuvered herself to sit on the edge of the bathtub.

She'd made it home.

This hadn't been her original destination, but once she'd found a moving vehicle, she didn't even bother trying to come up with a new plan. She wanted Colton. She wanted to get clean and crawl into his arms so he could make everything okay again.

Unfortunately, that plan was going to have to wait until he recovered.

She could probably guess why he was drunk—she was pretty sure she was the cause. Would she tell him how close she'd been to not to coming back? Or just tell him about her adventure and let him assume that's what had caused the delay?

A question for later, when she was better rested.

Pudge stayed with her every step as she hobbled into the bedroom to get dressed. Her clothes were all gone. Great. So she slipped into one of Colton's T-shirts and a pair of his boxers.

She checked on Colton, who was now sleeping on the porch. Deciding that was probably the best place for him, she left him there and crawled into his bed. Once there, she knew she wouldn't be able to move even if the SWAT team stormed the room to take her in.

She closed her eyes and, for once, welcomed sleep. As she faded off, she felt Pudge jump on the bed to lie next to her. And she smiled.

It felt like only a few hours later when the sound of the shower coming on woke her. It was still early. Only a hint of dawn colored the sky. She covered her head with the pillow, not ready to get up.

But she could still hear Colton moan and mutter to himself, splashing under the spray. Long minutes later, he left the bathroom and walked into the bedroom. "You're not supposed to be in my bed," he grumbled.

She'd gone through hell and back to get here. If after all that he didn't want her in his bed, she was going to lose her shit.

When she felt the mattress shift as the dog jumped off the bed, she realized Colton wasn't talking to her but to Pudge.

Crisis averted.

He slid in on the other side of the bed and let out a pathetic-sounding sigh, then she felt his hand move across the bed and touch her arm.

With a gasp of shock, he sat up and turned on the nightstand light, blinding her. "Angel! Where the hell have you been?"

Chapter Eighty-Seven

Burning Angel's retinas and acting like he had a right to demand an explanation for her disappearance was probably not the best way for Colton to welcome her home. He should have been hugging her, and thanking her for coming back.

But the pain in his heart was still fresh, and she'd caused it.

She propped herself up on her elbows and squinted at him. "Let's just say it took me a little longer to get here than it should have, and leave it at that."

"But—"

She flopped back down. "I don't want to talk about it."

What did that mean? He didn't need the play by play. He just needed to know if—

"Are you all right?" he asked, because that was the most important thing.

"I have a sprained ankle, sore muscles, and I'm exhausted, but I'll be fine."

"Okay."

Satisfied with her answer, he turned off the light and pulled her close. There would be time to talk later. She was here now. He didn't care where she'd been. The important thing was that she was home.

After several moments, he felt pleasantly relaxed. He smiled. "You said you loved me."

"No, I didn't."

He smiled wider. "You almost said it."

She let out a small huff. "I don't want to talk about that, either."

"We'll see about that," he whispered, feeling happier than he'd felt in over a year. Because she'd just admitted she *had* almost said it.

Chapter Eighty-Eight

Later that morning, Angel woke up alone in bed.

This was different. She was usually the first one up. She frowned. She didn't like this. Now she understood what it must feel like for him. That disconcerting feeling of abandonment.

Except Pudge stood and licked her face.

"Good morning." She pushed his doggy breath away, guessing hers probably wasn't much better.

She moved to get up, forgetting her ankle, and went down to her knees in pain.

"Ow! Damn you, gravity. Damn you to hell."

"You really want to piss off gravity? You know it keeps you from floating off into space, right?" Colton was already by her side, helping her back onto the bed.

"I thought you were a math teacher. I don't need a science lesson."

"I'm full service." He smiled as he bent to take a look at her ankle. The smile was replaced by a grimace. Then he looked up at her head and winced.

She knew she had about six seconds before the fussing started. She opened her mouth to tell him she was fine, but he picked her up and proceeded to carry her out to the sofa.

"I can walk," she protested.

"Yes. I saw how that went. The cursing and falling over. Very efficient. What the hell happened to you out there?"

From her spot on the sofa she noticed an odd-looking contraption on the coffee table. He picked it up and held it to her foot.

"Is that a cast?"

"It's for sprains. It says so on the box. I wasn't sure what size to get."

It was obvious he was dealing with his own issues. He looked like the poster child for hangovers, but he'd gotten up early and gone to the store to get her medical supplies. Her ankle hurt, and her head was throbbing, but it was nothing compared to the pain in her chest from holding back a flood of silly tears.

The first air cast was too big, and so was the second one.

"Angel?" he said her name while frowning at her foot.

"Yeah?

"You're so tiny. I never realized how small you are."

"Whoa. I don't need your pity. I can handle it. I *am* handling things." The assertion may have been more convincing if her voice hadn't cracked.

If Colton noticed, he didn't say anything. He simply leaned into her and put his head on her shoulder.

"That's good, because *I'm* not handling it," he confessed.

She didn't know how to respond to his tenderness. Her team looked out for one another. They cared and checked in on each other. But this was different.

"Do you want me to leave?" she asked.

She could tell her pain was hurting Colton. This wasn't just friendship, or two people looking out for each other. This was more. More than she'd ever experienced, and she didn't know what to do.

For a moment she thought about running, but she quickly pushed the idea away. Not only could she not move, but she didn't think she could make herself leave him even if she were physically able. How many times had she tried recently? How many times had she ended up right back here?

Not good. Because at some point she really would need to leave. This situation wasn't forever. But not today. They could have a little while longer.

"I'm just worried you're going to try to go on this mission alone," he said. "What if you get hurt and I'm not there to help you?"

This was the conversation she'd been avoiding. She'd known they would have to have it eventually, but she wasn't ready to piss him off and hurt his feelings.

"You can't come with me," she told him, making sure her voice was strong.

"Yes, I can. You need help."

"I'll be fine."

He sat back on his heels and gave her a level look. "If you're even thinking of setting something up all by yourself, you're not as smart as I thought. Everyone needs backup. If you insist on shutting me out, then tell me who is going with you in my place."

"This is my problem. I'll handle it." She couldn't risk her team. If they got caught helping her, they could all lose their jobs. Or worse.

"It's not just *your* problem. It's a problem for everyone who cares about you. You're tough as hell, but you're still a human being. Even if this Jim person sets something up with Noah, you don't know how many others are coming with them as *their* backup."

"I came to you for refuge, not to get you involved in my

shit."

He let out a breath, but didn't sound the least bit defeated. "I get it if you don't think you can trust me to have your back. We've never worked together that way, and you might not feel safe relying on me. But promise you'll take someone from your team. Someone you can trust."

Ah, hell. Was he serious? *He* was the person she trusted most in the world. The one she knew for certain she could rely on.

Which was exactly why she needed to keep him safe.

No matter what.

Chapter Eighty-Nine

As if mirroring Colton's mood, the sky darkened, and the first rumble of thunder sounded in the distance. It was bad enough to send Pudge running for cover to the bedroom.

Colton wanted to push Angel to let him come with her, but he realized he shouldn't become her storm. He couldn't be loud and demanding and scare her off under the bed...and right out of his life.

This needed to be her decision. And as long as she was safe, that was all that mattered. It didn't need to be him, as long as there was someone along to protect her.

She blinked up at him, and he hoped she could see how much he cared about her—loved her—and wanted her to be safe. No matter who went with her.

He knew she was fierce and capable. But as she sat there wearing his T-shirt and boxers, she also looked small and breakable.

Her eyes softened. "I trust you, Colton. Completely. You were an awesome agent, and I know you would risk everything for me. That's why I don't want you there."

He looked at his hands resting on his thighs. "You think my emotions would make me sloppy?" It was a genuine concern, but one he'd considered. It would be one thing if she wasn't trained. It would be difficult for him to protect himself and her at the same time.

But he knew she was a skilled marshal. He knew she could pull her own weight—hell, more than her own weight. He would be backing her up and she would be backing him up. They would be a team. He could handle it.

What he couldn't handle would be staying behind, sitting around hoping she came back. The waiting would be agony. But he would find a way to do just that, if she didn't trust him. The important thing was that she didn't go alone.

She shook her head. "Last year it was *my* job to keep *you* safe. I understand that's not my job anymore, but I still can't see you hurt because of me. I'm the one who failed Heath Zeller. I can't let anyone else get mixed up in this situation. I'll take care of it."

He looked down at her ankle, so delicate it looked as if he could snap it with his bare hands.

This was it. He had to make her see what she was doing to him.

Capturing her gaze with his, he swallowed down his pride...and opened up his heart.

"You're asking me to sit here while you go off to face the unknown all by yourself. Not knowing if you'll come back."

She opened her mouth to respond, but he cut her off.

"You said you don't want to see me hurt because of you. Look into my eyes, Angel. Don't you see how much you're hurting me right now? Don't you see that you are killing me by forcing me to stay behind?"

Chapter Ninety

Colton's eyes were fierce and Angel wanted to cringe away, but she couldn't. She was trapped. She was losing this battle, and it was too important not to succeed.

"I—" But she had no answer. Nothing to come back with. And it wouldn't matter, because his next words sealed her fate.

"I love you." He rested his palm on her cheek and placed the softest of kisses on her lips. "Please," he whispered and rested his forehead against hers. Waiting.

He loved her.

Her heart pounded as if it were a truth-detecting device, confirming his words were sincere.

Tears came to her eyes, stinging, burning happiness that clamped her throat shut and kept her from answering. Instead, she pulled his mouth to hers in a searing kiss.

He loved her.

He knew she was broken, damaged, and flawed. But Colton loved her, anyway.

She'd teased Garrett the last time she saw him, when he'd

told her he was in love. He'd told her there was someone out there for everyone.

She'd thought it a delusional concept—not to mention extremely futile. There were so many people on the planet. If there was one person—her person—out there somewhere, how would she ever find him?

The answer was, she and Colton had found each other. Like magnets, they had come together, and no matter how many times she pushed him away, she knew he would always come back into her life.

He loved her, and he was her person.

Her kiss became more urgent. She needed him.

His moan of assent set her off, and she pulled at his clothes as he ripped the shirt she was wearing to get to her breasts. His kisses moved up her throat to her chin as he twisted out of his pants.

Frantic to get him naked, she tugged his shirt over his head. His lips crashed back to hers after the brief separation. Thunder boomed outside as the rain started. Slow at first, but picking up at a hammering pace.

Just like them.

His hot skin pressed against hers when they were finally bare. She opened for him and he rested against her. Waiting.

They were on the sofa, and the condoms were in the bedroom. In that moment of silence he was asking her to make the decision.

She pushed upward, letting his heat sink deep inside. Filling her body, as well as her heart.

He was hers and she was his.

Completely.

Chapter Ninety-One

Angel's heat surrounded him, and Colton nearly came undone from that first thrust. This was not just sex. This was a claiming as well as an offering between them. Both giving and taking.

He'd told her he loved her. He'd laid his feelings bare at her feet, and she hadn't left him. For once, Angel hadn't run away from the difficult emotions. She'd stayed with him, and he knew that was an important thing.

He watched her and she watched him, unable to look away even when passion heightened into release. She broke apart as he came deep inside her, filling her with his love and everything he was.

The storm moved off, leaving the rain tapping quietly above them as their breathing slowed back to normal. While his breath might have returned to its regular rhythm, he knew he would never be the same.

"I want you," she said so quietly he wasn't sure he'd heard her.

For a moment, he misunderstood and thought she wanted him again physically. He didn't want to disappoint her, but he could barely move, let alone perform again.

But she swallowed and started over. "I want you to come with me," she clarified as she raised her head from his chest and looked at him steadily.

His eyes widened in surprise. He'd actually convinced her to believe in him. To let someone help her.

He tried to rein in his smile, but the triumphant feeling that overcame him was too much to hold in.

"Promise me you won't get yourself killed," she said, her eyes serious.

He remembered how many times his mother had made this same request of his father when he went off to work. At a loss for how to answer, he stole his father's reply. "I promise to do my best."

He had no doubt his father played it safe. With a wife and five sons at home, he wouldn't have taken risks. But the job was dangerous and there were no guarantees.

Colton's poor mother had to sit back and watch as one by one, her sons had followed in their father's footsteps. That last time, Colton was guilty of giving her a quick hug and telling her he would be careful. The promise was as natural and easygoing as hello and goodbye. And just as meaningless.

Because Colton hadn't come back.

He hadn't lied. He *had* been careful. He'd played his part well, and stayed close to Viktor's inner circle without calling attention to himself. He'd been a shadow.

Until Viktor figured it out.

Colton had been following the entourage through a marina. Nothing out of the ordinary about that. Viktor moved a lot of things by boat. But there was no boat docked. While Colton found that odd, it wasn't unheard of to arrive early before a boat came in. Especially if the Coast Guard or the police were nearby.

Viktor had simply stopped walking and turned to Weller with a nod.

"Get rid of our problem," he'd said, or something to that effect. Weller had pulled out a gun and pointed it at Colton.

Colton jumped up, sweaty and choking for breath. Since they'd fallen asleep on the sofa, Angel was jarred awake, as well.

"You okay?" she asked, rubbing his back as he sat on the edge of the couch.

To tell her that their plans had brought back bad memories would make her second-guess her decision to let him come with her to face the killer. He couldn't give her a reason to change her mind.

"I'm great." He stood and reached for her hand. "Let's go to bed."

"I'll just stay here. I probably won't sleep much longer."

"I said let's go to bed. I didn't mean to sleep."

"Oh." She smiled and took his hand.

Chapter Ninety-Two

After another round of too-hot sex, Angel had taken her place in the living room, searching for information in every corner of the internet.

She'd received another email from Redgamer3 after no word for weeks.

You're not even trying anymore.
I'm ready to get this over with.
See you soon.

Again with the three line messages. It was like a haiku with the wrong number of syllables. The guy probably thought it was clever. Angel just found it annoying.

When he'd told her he was watching her, she hadn't been sure, but now it was clear he wasn't, or he would have known she had been indisposed for the last few days trekking across Oregon with a sprained ankle.

But now he seemed to want to move things forward. And

she was ready.

She frowned at her ankle. The one she had propped up to reduce the swelling. Okay, almost ready.

At about ten o'clock the next night, while Colton was folding his laundry at the other end of the sofa, she finally got a break when she logged into Noah's email and saw an email from Redgamer3.

"Hot damn!" she shouted and clapped her hands in glee.

"What is it?" Colton asked.

"Redgamer3 responded to Noah. They're setting up a meeting. He's making Noah pay him at the drop instead of waiting for Noah to cash out."

"Does Noah have the money?" Colton wrinkled his nose. It made him look younger. Like the boy next door instead of the sexy DEA agent.

"No. But in his reply he said he does, so *Jim* is going to meet him." She paused for a moment before deciding to share the rest.

"You're frowning. What's the problem? Isn't that what you wanted to happen?"

She let out a slow breath. "Redgamer3 emailed me, too. He said he would see me soon. He knows I'm watching. He's expecting me to show up at their meeting. It doesn't make any sense."

This bastard had bested her and gotten away with murder. He had the ability to cover himself so well she wouldn't have seen the details of the drop. But he was luring her into the meet.

Why?

"Is it okay if I just wait for you to explain yourself?" Colton asked, shaking out a T-shirt and folding it precisely. What an excellent husband he would make someday.

For someone else.

"Redgamer3, or Jim—or whoever he or she is—is smarter than this. They planned this whole thing seamlessly. They drugged my toothpaste, for Christ's sake. They have to know Noah doesn't have the funds. Why would they agree to meet him and send me an invitation to come, too?"

"Maybe they want to kill him. To shut him up so someone else will buy it. With Noah out of the way, there won't be anyone to threaten his potential buyers."

Colton had come to the same conclusion she'd just reached, but that didn't explain why Redgamer3 would involve *her*.

But Colton wasn't finished. "And he's made sure you're there so he can set you up to take the fall for Noah's death, as well."

She swallowed. She hadn't pieced that part together yet, but it made sense. She nodded slowly as she played the idea through her deputy marshal filter. "Yeah."

Colton cleared his throat. "He could be setting it up as a deal gone bad. With you and Noah there together, he could kill you both, making it look like you killed Noah and he shot you as you were getting away. It would wrap things up nicely, and he would be completely in the clear."

Oh God, he was right. It all made terrible sense now.

"We have to protect Noah," she said reluctantly.

Protect the asshole who had hired someone to kill his own brother. She almost wished she could close the email and pretend she hadn't read it.

But she couldn't.

Colton rubbed his palms together, no doubt in anticipation for the coming action and excitement, and said, "I guess it's time to make a plan."

Angel was glad to have the chance to do something. But she didn't feel excited. She wanted it to be over with so she could get on with her life.

A life she dearly wished she could spend with Colton.

But she couldn't do that, either.

Chapter Ninety-Three

Thankfully, the meeting had been set up for next week, which would give Angel's ankle time to heal.

She'd been good about keeping it propped up and not using it. Which seemed to be working. The nasty purple had faded into a yellow-green color. And it looked like an ankle once again. It didn't hurt when she put weight on it anymore, but running was still a bad word.

"I'm going shopping," Colton announced after lunch. She knew he didn't mean for groceries. "If you're good, I'll get you something extra special." Colton grinned as he leaned in to kiss her.

"I'm never good."

"Which makes you amazing." He pulled her close for a kiss, and soon his hands moved to her hips. She expected him to take them to the bedroom, but instead, he used his grip to push her back. "We'll continue this when I get back." He gave her an evil grin and left.

Well, hell.

If this was his new plan to keep her from leaving, it was working. Although, of course, she wasn't with him just for the amazing sex. It was the man himself she wanted most of all.

She shook her head and let Pudge out before going back to her computer. A few minutes later, the back door opened and Pudge came running over to her.

"How did you do that?" she asked the dog, worried she'd been drugged again.

"Oh, hello," a woman said from the kitchen. "I didn't realize anyone was here. I saw Duncan leave a little while ago. I just wanted to put some apple dumplings in Duncan's refrigerator. Don't mind me."

Don't mind me? That would be easier to do if Angel weren't a fugitive and the woman weren't looking right at her.

"I'm Deb. From next door. You must be Duncan's girlfriend."

"Uh, yes. I'm Cassie Benton, Duncan's ex— Er, girlfriend. It's nice to meet you. I've heard many good things about the apple dumplings." Angel wanted to turn the frantic smile on her face down to a normal level, but she had a gun sitting out on the coffee table and no way to move it without calling attention to it.

The woman simply smiled and turned to shove a foil-covered tray into the refrigerator. Angel made her move. With a quick motion, she tucked the gun under the sofa cushion.

"Is Duncan teaching you to shoot, too?"

"Um. Yes." Her pride twisted a bit just to say it. She was a much better shot than Colton. Even he had said so. Which didn't matter at the moment. She needed to relax and try not to look like the girl plastered on every TV screen across the land.

"Kenny has been going on and on about it. It was good of Duncan to spend some time with him. I think it made an impression. The boy might actually turn out okay. And if he does, he has Duncan to thank for it."

"Yes." That was easy to agree with, since it was true.

"A single woman needs to be able to protect herself," Deb said airily.

"Yes. Definitely."

"I used to watch those crime dramas on television, and the horrible stories would worry me into a panic. Now I don't even watch the news. It's better not to know."

Oh, thank God.

"You're right about that." Angel relaxed, hoping the woman hadn't seen her face anywhere else. Colton told her she'd been on the front of one of those gossip magazines at the grocery store last week.

"Should I leave one of these out for you? I don't have to tell Duncan how many there were originally." The older woman winked, and Angel smiled.

The woman didn't watch the news, so she probably hadn't seen her photo. Besides, who would jump to such an outlandish conclusion when they first met someone? Especially if the person didn't put you in mind of a killer.

"He won't mind sharing his dumplings. He's great that way," Angel said as she stepped closer to take in the delicious scents.

"Yes, he's one of the good ones. And so handsome. I'm pointing that out in case you haven't noticed."

"Oh, I've noticed."

Many, many times. It would be hard not to. For months after she left the first time, she'd catch herself thinking about the muscles of his back bunching under her palms, or the way the sun glinted off the gold strands in his light brown hair, or those eyes. Serious as an ocean storm and the same color.

"That's good. Because Mrs. Sutherland—at the end of the block—has also noticed him, and she's going through a divorce. I've heard talk that she's set her sights on our

Duncan."

Our Duncan?

"Okay. Thanks for the heads up." End of the block. *Got it.*

"The women all plant themselves at their front windows every morning when he goes for a run."

Seriously? "I bet."

"They're all pretty disappointed he's missed his runs lately."

"Maybe I should charge admission," Angel joked. She couldn't wait to tease Colton about this. He was absolutely going to die of embarrassment.

"You would be a wealthy woman." Deb bent to pet Pudge. "I'll spread word that he has someone living with him. That should give him some room to breathe. For a few days, anyway."

"Wow. Not much excitement around here, eh?"

"You have no idea.

Angel suddenly understood why he was so bored.

They laughed together, and she realized this woman reminded her of her mother, and how funny she had once been. The pain took Angel's breath for a moment. She hadn't remembered that. When she thought of her mother, she only saw the sadness and worry that had plagued her last years as her son had plunged farther into the abyss.

Normally, she saw her mother the way she'd last seen her—staring lifeless toward the door as her oldest child continued stabbing her while dripping with her blood.

Tears sprang to Angel's eyes, but she blinked them into submission and pasted a wobbly smile on her face.

Justin had warned her she couldn't have this. That she couldn't have friends who made apple dumplings. She couldn't have innocent chitchat and jokes.

She couldn't have a future with a man who filled her

heart with love and happiness.

"Take care of our boys," Deb said as she moved toward the door. "And Pudge, you take care of Cassie."

Angel twitched at her real name. It made her feel small and vulnerable. But…not necessarily in a bad way.

Pudge's only reply was to paw at the woman's leg, begging for her to pet him again.

"It was nice to meet you," Deb said cheerily. "I'm sure we'll have time to talk more at another time, but I have a doctor's appointment I need to get to."

"Sure. Thanks for the apple dumplings. You've made Colton's day. Mine, too."

When the woman was gone, Angel slumped onto the sofa and let her head fall to her knees. She focused on her breathing so everything else could spin away.

She had a mission to plan. She couldn't be distracted by how much she wished she could set up a time to have tea with the neighbor lady.

But she couldn't have that.

Not as long as a killer was still on the loose.

Not as long as her job still took precedence.

Not as long as her past still haunted her.

Chapter Ninety-Four

Angel was ready.

Scratch that—*they* were ready. Because she had a partner for this job. Possibly the most important job of her life.

Over the past few days, she'd tried again and again to talk Colton out of coming with her. But he was unshakable. It didn't help that she understood. If their roles were reversed, she wouldn't have backed down, either.

It was almost fun seeing how much he enjoyed being a part of the plan. He seemed to come alive. Colton had all their supplies packed, and with her help he'd even used Google Maps to route their trip.

"Deb next door is going to watch Pudge and pick up my mail," he said while standing in the kitchen going over their gear. "Am I forgetting anything?"

To anyone else, it might have looked like they were planning a different kind of trip. But instead of packing beach towels, they were checking rounds of ammo.

She smiled at his honest-to-God list of things he

was checking off. *Take out the trash* was right after *pack bulletproof vests*. Each had a little checkmark next to it.

She shook her head indulgently. "I think you've covered everything."

"When I was a DEA agent, I didn't have a home and a pet to be responsible for," he said, a tad defensively. "Which isn't a bad thing. I'm still one hundred percent in the game. Now that I know my dog is taken care of."

As often as Colton complained about his mundane life, she could see how much he valued it. She had to admit, she enjoyed the quiet home life as well. It was something she'd wanted for a long time, but every time she'd considered leaving Task Force Phoenix, another job would come up that needed her skillset.

She could never turn her back on Thorne when he needed her. Not after what he'd done to give her a decent life. At twenty, she'd been heading down a bad path. She'd been in jail for a month, with almost two years of her sentence left to go. She'd made a lot of mistakes and gotten mixed up with the wrong crowd. But Thorne had given her another chance, and had offered her a home, of sorts. She would never be able to repay him for that.

The last thing to go in the truck was a big bag of snacks. Just like a real road trip. Colton had selected her favorites, and she was touched. They had a long drive ahead of them.

As he checked the back door again and turned off the lights, she swallowed. This wasn't a vacation. This was a mission.

A dangerous mission.

To kill or be killed.

Chapter Ninety-Five

After an hour on the road, Colton was still surprised he'd been allowed to come along. Over the last week, Angel had made a few attempts to change the plan, but he'd won every argument.

Not that it was much of an argument. He could see the struggle behind her blue eyes. She wanted him with her. She just didn't want him in danger. But she couldn't have one without the other.

In the end, he'd made the decision for her. He just hoped it didn't end in disaster for either of them.

He knew she was a trained U.S. Deputy Marshal. He knew she could put down a man twice her size. He knew she was a good shot. He was proof that it didn't matter how big you were when the other person had a gun.

But his heart knew how much he loved her, and how badly he would break if something happened to her.

He reached across the console and took her hand, giving it a reassuring squeeze. He would keep her safe, even if he had to die doing it.

"Thank you for coming with me," Angel said, her voice so low he thought he might have imagined it.

He had no choice but to take his eyes off the road to check to see if she was joking, or if he was having auditory hallucinations. Maybe his body wasn't processing all the adrenaline properly.

"Please don't say shocking things when I'm driving," he joked, just in case.

"I mean it." She looked almost embarrassed. It was adorable.

He shook his head in surprise. "Yes, I could tell how happy you would be to have me along all those times you told me I couldn't come with you."

She scowled over at him. "Are you going to let me thank you or not?"

"No. I'm going to thank you, instead." He glanced over again to see if he'd surprised her.

He had.

"What for?"

"For letting me come with you. For not making me stay at home worrying about you." He didn't know how he would have survived that.

She shrugged it off. "Okay."

"Can I ask you a favor?" he said a few minutes later.

"You can ask." It didn't mean she would oblige.

"Please call for backup." It was a long shot, but he had to try.

From the beginning, she'd insisted on going alone. As much as he didn't like it, he understood why she might not have wanted to take him. But she'd been reluctant to ask anyone else to help, either.

Despite her claim that it was her own mess so she should fix it, he was certain part of her reluctance was sheer stubbornness and a need to prove she was capable—to herself and everyone else. Colton knew her well, but he couldn't figure out why she wasn't moving past that to do the right thing.

She was brilliant. It wasn't like her to take unnecessary risks. Going in with no backup was a huge risk. The two of them could easily be outnumbered, and this whole plan and their lives would be at stake.

She didn't even pretend to think about it. "I'm sorry. I can't ask the team."

"It would be the smart thing. The safe thing. You don't have to do everything alone."

"I'm not alone. I have you."

She did have him. Did he have her?

"We don't know how many others this Redgamer3 is bringing with him," he pointed out.

"I don't know who I can trust."

What? This was new. "Not even Dane and Thorne?" he asked.

She shook her head. "Dane has an injury, and I can't ask Thorne."

"Why not? You said he was like a father to you. If my father was alive, and I called and asked him to come, he'd be sitting in the back seat right now eating all of our Twizzlers." He smiled at the thought.

"Thorne's already done enough for me. I can't ask him for anything else."

Ah. So, not about trust.

While Colton wasn't a father himself, the fathers he knew didn't put limits on what was asked of them when it came to their children.

He didn't push her. That wouldn't get him anywhere. She'd made up her mind, and he should just feel lucky she'd given in and let him come along.

They were silent for a few more miles.

"Would you be interested in joining Task Force Phoenix?" she asked out of nowhere.

His jaw dropped and his eyes went wide. "Are you *trying* to get me to drive off the road?"

"No." She laughed. "I'm just thinking you were with the DEA, and there's no reason why you couldn't switch agencies, right? We're down a man since Garrett left. We could use someone dependable."

All this time, he'd believed he only had one path—hiding. He'd wanted her to come with him into WITSEC. He hadn't thought about the other way around—going with her.

But...it made perfect sense.

He could see how it might be possible to have everything. He could have her, *and* a life with excitement, meaning, and purpose.

Chapter Ninety-Six

Angel could see she had shocked him with her question. That much was obvious. To be honest, it had surprised her, as well. Not just that she'd blurted it out, but that she hadn't thought of it a year ago.

Colton would make a great addition to their team. Like the others on the team who were officially "dead," he wouldn't be able to take on any high-profile cases. But he would be great at extraction and long-range protection. Those jobs were somewhat less dangerous, too, which suited her just fine.

Maybe that's why she'd never mentioned it before. She'd selfishly wanted him hidden away where he was safe.

And where she could keep him at a distance. So she wouldn't be forced into anything...serious.

She opened her mouth to apologize for her subconscious, but he spoke first.

"I think I might like to join your team," he said. "It would be great to be in the action again. And it would mean working with you, right?" He glanced over at her. "Would that be a problem for you?"

She frowned down at her hands, and he turned back toward the windshield again.

Would she be okay if they worked together? That was not the question he was really asking. There was another question hidden in the layers. What he was really asking was if she was willing to have a future with him.

Rather than promise anything, she took the cowardly way out. "We need to survive this mission first. Why don't we wait and discuss it when this mess is all straightened out?"

"Sure," he said with a nod.

They didn't speak again for probably an hour. It was an easy silence. She could tell he was considering all the details of her suggestion. She was doing the same thing.

He deserved to have the life he wanted. She wanted to make sure he was safe. They wanted to be together. This one idea seemed to solve everything.

So why was she still reluctant to commit?

Every time she pictured them together, it was in a more domestic setting. Like his home, sitting with Pudge on the sofa watching movies. Leaning on the counter while he made their frittatas. She couldn't picture them spending the night in a van during a stakeout, or stretched out on a roof ready to shoot anyone who made a move on their asset.

Maybe after this mission, she could see them together like that.

Maybe.

They pulled into a hotel parking lot at ten that night. She'd been driving the last four hours and her shoulders were stiff. The hotel had been chosen beforehand. They even had a blueprint of the property in their bag.

If something happened, she had multiple ways to get out of the room. None of which would result in a sprained ankle, or a three-day excursion through the wilds of Oregon.

She sat by the hotel room window watching the parking lot, while Colton went to pick up dinner. She longed for the chance to go to dinner with him in public. To be able to sit across from him at a restaurant table, order a glass of wine, and be normal.

Instead she was stuck here, tense and restless. She wished they'd been able to bring Pudge. She missed her dog. But he was safer with Deb.

Her apartment in DC didn't allow dogs. And she didn't even know her neighbor's name. If she and Colton decided to go with the Task Force Phoenix plan, they would need to find a new place. Their things would be mingled together. Would he like her coffee pot better than his? Hers was clearly superior, but maybe he liked the old style of his.

They would be making a home together.

The thought both excited and terrified her.

Even more than what they faced next.

Chapter Ninety-Seven

Colton wasn't sure what had happened while he was out getting their dinner, but Angel seemed out of sorts when he returned. He'd asked, and she'd told him she was fine, but he wasn't buying it.

Something had spooked her.

Checking the window himself, he watched as she set out dinner on the small hotel table. Normally he was the one who did that while she was online. She was always in another dimension when she was on her computer. He'd always wondered if she even noticed she hadn't eaten in hours when he disrupted her attention with food.

He forced a smile and sat across from her. Then jumped up and went to the door where he'd set one other bag.

"I almost forgot. I got us a bottle of wine." He opened it and carried the bottle and two little plastic cups to the table. Most of the soldiers and law enforcement agents he knew had a standard routine as they prepared for a job. For him, it was all about the meal the night before.

He'd never thought of it as a last supper, but more that it was the last time he had control over what and where he ate. Once he went undercover, he assumed a role and his decisions were based on the part he was playing. Even when it came to his meals.

Angel stared at him while he filled her little cup.

"Sorry about the cups. We'll just have to pretend they clink when we make a toast," he joked, earning only a slight smile from her lips.

What was wrong? He wanted so much to ask again, but he'd already asked twice.

"I was just thinking about this. Eating together. A glass of wine. But at a restaurant."

He nodded and held up his cup in a toast. "To being able to eat in a restaurant again."

Her smile was genuine when she tapped her cup to his. "Soon," she said, and took a sip.

They would be in Dallas by the next afternoon. Redgamer3 was meeting Noah at nine tomorrow night, which would give them plenty of time to get ready, but not enough time to relax and enjoy a meal together.

So tonight they ate and talked as they finished off the wine. Laughter came easier by the time they tossed the takeout cartons into the trash. He reached for her at the same time she stepped closer to him.

She stood on tiptoes to kiss him, as if she couldn't wait the fraction of a second it would take him to bend down to meet her lips.

He'd been thinking about her offer. If they worked together, they could have this all the time. Dinner and loving each other at night. Granted, there would be times when they were sent off on separate jobs and they wouldn't see each other for months. But he would know she would always come back to him. There would be no need to worry she would leave in the middle of the night.

No, that worry would be replaced by a new worry—whether she would ever come home again.

Shaking the thought away, he focused on the moment they had together right now.

He undressed her slowly while he touched and tasted the skin he exposed. His normal process before a job had been to enjoy an excellent meal. He mentally updated that to include enjoying an amazing woman. Not just any woman, but *his* woman.

"I love you, Colton," she whispered as he slid inside her. Their fingers linked above her head as he moved on top of her. Their eyes locked on one another.

"I love you, too."

So much it nearly broke him.

Chapter Ninety-Eight

After all the years of facing down criminals, Angel still felt a rush of terror in her chest as she stepped out of the truck the next night to go and face what awaited them in the warehouse where Redgamer3 and Noah were to meet.

She should be better at this. She should be stone cool and calm. But she wasn't. The best she could do was act like she was.

She swallowed down her nervousness and checked her ammo again.

"It's not too late to call in reinforcements," Colton reminded her.

"No. We're good. We've got this."

He nodded, but she knew it wasn't in agreement. Rather, it was a nod of resignation.

It was definitely protocol to have backup, and she'd nearly caved and called Thorne. But she couldn't.

This wasn't a sanctioned mission. They would be considered rogue, like her, if anyone found out. She wouldn't do that to them. However pissed off they'd be when they found out.

She could deal with angry friends. She couldn't help them, or herself, if they were all arrested together. Going alone was the only way.

She stepped into the cool darkness of the warehouse. How cliché. Everyone knew bad things happened at warehouse meetings. Why Noah would ever have agreed to this place, she couldn't fathom.

They arrived an hour before the meeting. They listened, and waited. Expecting that Noah, Redgamer3, or both, would have brought their own people ahead of the meeting.

No one came.

Which made her even more nervous.

"What is going on?" she whispered when they heard the door open and a single set of footsteps enter the building.

Colton shook his head. "Maybe they're planning to have a normal meeting, not a shootout like we're expecting." He frowned down at his gun as if discouraged that he wouldn't have the chance to use it.

She smiled and looked away, adjusting her Kevlar vest. She hated wearing it, it felt too restrictive, but it was the safe thing.

They hid behind a pallet as a man walked out into the large open area. It was Noah.

Across the warehouse, she heard another door open and close. Another single set of footsteps approached.

Angel let out a little breath of relief. It seemed Redgamer3 hadn't come with an army, after all. Colton would never let her hear the end of it if they'd been outnumbered.

"You're Jim?" Noah's voice echoed in the expansive space.

"I'm here." The other man had a southern accent, and a low, calm voice. Recognition stirred, but she couldn't place it.

"Did you really come alone?"

"You told me to," Noah said.

"Yes, but— Never mind. Where's the money?" Jim got right to business.

"Where's the prototype?" Noah asked as Colton made a face that he was impressed by Noah's snappy retort.

She recognized the two clicks of a briefcase being opened, and rubbed her forehead. She hadn't expected Redgamer3 to actually bring the prototype to the drop. This guy was not doing anything the way she expected.

"The money?" he asked, almost pleasantly.

Noah's feet shuffled. "I was hoping you'd accept a better offer. I'll pay you twice what we agreed upon if you'll give me a chance to sell it first."

"You don't have the money." The other man's voice was now flat and dry.

A chill ran down Angel's spine. It was the voice of a killer. A sociopath with no emotion.

Angel nodded to Colton. It was time to move. This was going south, and Noah was blowing it.

"Well, no," Noah said. "But you know I'm good for it. I just need—"

Noah was silenced by a single gunshot.

Angel jumped at the loud *bang* that echoed through the building, and again at the quieter *thump* of Noah's body falling to the floor.

"Jesus," Colton whispered.

Redgamer3 hadn't even considered the counteroffer.

Angel hesitated for only a second, wondering for the first time if she'd bitten off more than she could chew with someone so unstable. But he was snapping the case shut and would be leaving. They had to act now.

Motioning to Colton, she indicated they should split up to move around each side of the pallet and join up on the other side with guns drawn.

"Freeze!" Colton yelled as earlier agreed upon...after a round of rock, paper, scissors.

"Hello, Angel."

There was no southern accent now. She recognized the voice at the same time she identified the man standing across from her, gun raised and pointed straight at her.

He had been expecting her to come to the meet.

But she had not expected this.

"Lucas," she choked out as ice water rushed through her veins.

Chapter Ninety-Nine

Colton kept his gun drawn on the shooter, but didn't know what to do next. It was as if Angel was under some kind of spell. She still had her gun up, but she looked almost… terrified. He'd never seen her like this before. At such a mental impasse.

It was clear she and this man knew one another, but Colton hadn't been able to hear the name she'd muttered upon seeing him. Who the hell was he?

Shooting the guy was not a choice until he knew exactly what was going on with Angel.

However, the man still had a firm hold on the case containing the stolen technology, which most likely meant he was the one who'd killed Zeller and taken it.

So why wasn't she acting? The asshole was going to get away.

"It's nice to see you again," the man said. "Sorry we don't have more time to catch up." He laughed.

Colton gripped his gun tighter. Jealousy now heightened

his need to shoot this son of a bitch.

"But… You're dead," she whispered.

Colton frowned. What the hell?

"Angel?" he called steadily, hoping he could bring her back. He might have shaken her if she had been closer. "What's going on?"

Nothing.

She just continued to stare at the man who was now turning to leave, his weapon still at the ready in his right hand and holding the case in his left.

Colton made a decision and pulled the trigger.

A split second after the killer did the same.

Chapter One Hundred

At the sound of gunfire, Angel was finally shaken from her moment of stupidity.

She whipped up her gun and shot him.

Normally she was an excellent shot, but she'd been so stunned to see him, her hands weren't as steady as she would have liked. She managed to hit him in the arm, causing him to drop the case and run for cover.

The door slammed, but she didn't want to assume he was gone. It would be just like Lucas Stone to pretend he'd left and sneak back to ambush her.

She followed him outside just as he jumped into a silver sedan and sped off. She took note of the license plate, but was sure it would probably come back to a rental, or stolen. It would never lead her to his home base. He was much too smart for that.

Walking back inside, she called out to Colton, letting him know their target was gone. She turned the corner only to see him slump to the ground.

"Colton!" She rushed over to him and dropped to her knees. "Oh my God."

Blood was spreading across his gray T-shirt. He was still breathing, but his breaths were shallow and quick. Ripping open the T-shirt, she exposed the Kevlar vest he was wearing.

The vest with a big hole in the chest.

"Armor-piercing bullets. Oh God. Oh God."

She pulled Colton's phone from his pocket and called 911. She told them to hurry, even knowing it wouldn't help. They would get there as soon as they could.

She just prayed it would be soon enough.

"Colton, I'm so sorry. This is all my fault." The words tripped out of her in a rush. He was badly hurt, and it was all because she hadn't acted when she should have. She'd blown it, and he was the one paying for her mistake.

Just as she'd feared all along.

"Please don't die," she repeated over and over as she held pressure on the wound and prayed luck was on his side one more time.

He'd survived six gunshots.

Please let him survive this one, too.

Chapter One Hundred One

Angel didn't care about hiding or being recognized. She'd already called Thorne, and hoped he would be able to get her out of whatever trouble she might be in after riding to the hospital with Colton. Her freedom was secondary to Colton's survival. She had to stay with him, no matter what happened to her.

Heath Zeller's prototype was safely tucked in her back pocket, and she could only pray Thorne would get there before she was arrested so she could hand it off to him.

"We have to call the police for GSWs." The paramedic eyed the two guns in Angel's waistband—Colton's and her own.

"That's fine. We're both undercover officers. He's DEA, I'm a U.S. Deputy Marshal."

"Oh," the woman seemed relieved.

"Is he going to be okay? He's losing a lot of blood." Angel wanted the woman to focus on saving the man she loved rather than the armory in her jeans.

"We're working on it."

The other paramedic was speaking into a radio in what sounded like a different language. He relayed Colton's blood pressure, which sounded low, and his heart rate, which sounded high. She heard the words "collapsed lung" and "breath sounds."

"Did he gain consciousness at any point?" the EMT asked.

"No. He didn't." And with that answer, tears flooded into Angel's eyes, preceded by a tight burning in her throat. "Please save him," she begged the medical professionals. "Please don't let him die."

The tears were running freely now, and guilt wasn't far behind.

The sirens suddenly shut off and they pulled into the hospital bay.

And that was when Angel realized that no matter what happened next, she was going to lose this man.

Chapter One Hundred Two

Angel stood by the door, afraid to step inside Colton's room. It didn't take long for Thorne to get there. He must have taken the jet, which meant people would take note that he'd suddenly jumped on a plane to rush off.

She didn't care what happened to her now. She'd gladly spend the rest of her life behind bars if it meant Colton was okay.

"How is he?" Thorne asked.

"He's stable for now. It'll be touch and go for the next twenty-four hours." She had been watching every breath, every blip on the heart monitor.

He was alive. *For now.*

"He made it through surgery," Thorne said with a nod. "That's a good sign."

She didn't answer. She wasn't ready to rest easy. Not until he opened his eyes.

Not that she would be there to see that happen…

"The police will be looking for you," Thorne said at her

side.

"I don't care."

"You're not going to be any help to him in jail."

She knew that. But she hadn't been any help to him, even standing right next to him. She'd done nothing but cause him trouble and pain. She could only hope she wouldn't cost him his life.

She'd been so stupid. She'd done nothing to stop Lucas Stone while she'd had the chance.

She'd thought he was long gone. She'd *killed* him. Or so she'd been told. When he showed up in that warehouse, walking straight out of her nightmares, her mind had seized up and she hadn't been able to move a muscle.

"I didn't help Colton when I had the chance. This is my fault. I froze when I saw Lucas."

"You're sure it was him? We were all certain he was dead."

Killed, the night he'd shot her for betraying him. She'd managed to get off a shot, too—a good shot from the amount of blood he'd left behind. He'd stumbled backward and tumbled over the edge of a bridge. A very high bridge.

She'd been told he would definitely have died from the gunshot, the blood loss, or the fall. Apparently, none of those things had actually ended the monster.

"Right. I guess I'm not very dead, either, am I..." Angel murmured.

"Not so much. Neither is Samantha." Thorne's daughter was alive and well in the witness protection program, married to Garrett. "Or Colton."

God, she hoped he stayed that way.

She remembered his concern that no one would come to his funeral when he died the next time. Tears filled her eyes, but she refused to let them fall.

"Let me guess. You're going after Stone." Thorne

sounded almost bored.

"I have a plan." At the moment, that plan consisted of many dangerous things. But she knew once she calmed down, she would be able to come up with a way to track Lucas and bring him to justice. Now that she knew who she was dealing with, it wouldn't be as difficult. She knew Lucas Stone as well as anyone could know him.

"Is there anything I can say to talk you out of going it alone?" Thorne asked.

"And risk more people I love? No, thank you."

He looked a little startled at her words.

She managed a weak smile. "That's right. I love you, you stubborn old grump. You've been like a father to me. I'll never be able to repay you for what you've done for me. You saved my life."

He smiled back. "I seem to remember you telling me you saved your own life."

When he'd showed up at the hospital the night of her brother's attack, Thorne had told her how lucky she was. He'd said her guardian angel must be working overtime.

She'd been bouncing from anger, fear, and the pain of losing her parents. She didn't know the man who'd walked into her hospital room and said he'd known her father long ago, and that he was there to help.

She'd lashed out and said something disrespectful. Something about how he was a little too late to help her. Then she'd told him she didn't need a guardian angel because she could take care of herself. She was her own damn guardian angel.

That was when he'd given her the nickname Angel, and when she finally got her shit together and joined his team, that was the name she'd taken.

"I'm mature enough now to give you credit for saving me from myself," she admitted. "I was on a path of self-destruction."

Thorne crossed his arms and gazed down at her. "Yet you're not mature enough to let me help you with this."

"If he wakes up, give him a job on Task Force Phoenix. He'll make a good marshal. And you may need someone to replace me."

A muscle worked in Thorne's jaw. "Where are you going?"

"I'm going to rid the world of a diabolical killer."

She gave him a quick hug, and spared a long look at the man lying in the bed with all the tubes and wires. Her chest hurt at having to leave him again. If she were a different person, she might have been able to have a happy life with him. She wanted it so bad, but it was out of her grasp.

There was a killer out there, and he needed to be stopped.

With that, she left the hospital to go plan her next move.

Chapter One Hundred Three

Colton was sure he was having a bad dream. After he'd been shot by Viktor Kulakov's goon, he often dreamed about his awful stay in the hospital—the pain, the smell, the noises.

Usually, he'd force himself awake and it would go away.

Except that didn't work this time.

He really was lying in a narrow bed with nothing but a hospital gown covering him. The IV in his arm was real, and the beeping didn't go away with the last traces of sleep.

"Fuck," he said with a gravelly voice as the memories of what had happened filled in the gaps.

"Yes, but it could be worse."

Colton turned his head to see a man sitting in the chair next to his bed. It took a few seconds for him to recognize him. They'd only met one other time.

"Supervisor Thorne."

"How are you feeling? Should I call in the nurse?"

Rather than answer those questions, he asked one of his own. A very important one. "Angel?" He managed to get out of his dry throat.

"She's fine. At least for now. She's off to find the man who shot you."

Colton's heart sank. "By herself."

Thorne didn't answer. Hell, he didn't need to.

How stubborn could one person be? Did Angel not realize what would happen to him if she got herself killed to avenge him? Did she not realize the insane amount of pain that would cause him?

"She thinks she needs to prove herself to you," Colton croaked as Thorne took pity on him and poured a glass of water from the pitcher beside his bed.

"Me?" Thorne seemed genuinely surprised. But, surely, he had some idea how she felt. "Why would she ever think that?"

"She said you saved her."

Thorne ground his teeth. "She told me the same thing, but it's nonsense. I offered her a job. She took it. End of story. She's been a valuable deputy marshal. She's proven herself time and time again. How big is this debt she thinks she owes me?" The man shook his head and looked up at the ceiling.

"She had no one, and you gave her a family. How big do you think that debt feels to her?"

Thorne's brows rose then drew together in a frown. "She's wrong. I used her."

"What?" Colton wasn't expecting that response.

"I had no access to my own daughter. I'd given up my wife and child for my job. I'd given up so much. Angel is only a little older than Samantha. And when I showed up at the hospital to offer my help to Angel, it was Sam I saw lying in that bed. I used Angel to fill the hole in my heart."

Colton swallowed the water gratefully. "I think you both

got something out of the deal."

Angel had no father. No family at all. Thorne was the perfect fit.

"Yes, and now she's worked a deal for you." Thorne flicked a piece of lint from his dress pants.

"What deal?"

"She told me to give you a job. So, it's yours when you're up for it. We'll give you another identity and bring you on as undercover protection. Angel said you were bored. We probably should have explored this option before. You're welcome to join Task Force Phoenix as soon as you can stand up and take a deep breath without pissing yourself."

Colton chuckled, and wondered when that might be. Not today, for sure. He was barely handling the pain. He knew when the nurse came in she'd up his meds and he'd sleep.

He didn't want to sleep. He wanted to go find Angel and stop her from doing something so stupid. He wasn't quite ready to plan out his future on Thorne's team, either. But it was nice to have the option.

"Thank you for the offer. I'll let you know."

Thorne nodded and stood.

"Who was the guy who shot me?" Colton asked. He half expected Thorne to brush off the question and leave, but instead he came back and sat down.

He crossed his ankle over his knee and sat back. "His name is Lucas Stone."

Colton recognized this name. He'd been Angel's partner. But she'd said she killed him. Colton frowned at the IV in his arm, hating the way the drugs jumbled his thoughts.

Thorne let out a breath and added, "He's my biggest regret."

Colton could tell that wasn't the end of it. If he'd only planned to say that much, he wouldn't have sat down. Colton waited for him to continue, and hoped the drugs wouldn't keep him from hearing the entire story.

"He was one of my agents. I thought he was the best. Very effective. Then I started getting complaints that he was rough with suspects. It's different with the marshals than with other law enforcement. We already know without a doubt the person we're bringing in is guilty."

Colton nodded in agreement. It was often the same way with the DEA. Yes, there would be a trial, but so much agent time had been spent with Viktor, there was no doubt the guy was bad to the core.

"He'd come to Task Force Phoenix from the army because he'd had disciplinary problems with his sergeant. After interviewing him, I chalked it up to different personality types and decided he had a lot to offer."

Thorne didn't look at Colton, but Colton could see the guilt on the man's face.

"When he started having more kills than collars, I became concerned. I decided to give him a partner. It was about when Angel joined the team. I knew she would learn a lot from him, and I thought having her around would make him more careful."

"But it didn't," Colton guessed.

"Actually, it did. But not in the way I'd imagined. He became a textbook marshal, and I was pretty proud of myself for managing the problem. Except, I'd created a whole new problem, instead." The man shook his head.

"How so?" Colton asked.

"Angel was only twenty. She was impressionable, and Stone was like a god to her."

Colton remembered the man in the warehouse. He could see how women would find the guy attractive. He had sharp features and a smile that was as dazzling as it was evil. "They got personal." Angel had told him so, and Colton had seen as much for himself at the warehouse. He'd sensed something between them. Something in the way the asshole had smiled at her.

Thorne blew out a breath. "Yes. Stone took advantage of the situation. And her trust."

Colton knew the story was going to take a turn. A bad one. He felt awful for her. This woman had gone through so much in her life. All he wanted to do was love her and keep her safe, so there wouldn't be any more horror stories in her future.

"Stone used his job to hunt down bad people and kill them. And he greatly enjoyed the killing part." Thorne rubbed his forehead. "He and Angel were together for two years before she figured it out. Stone had explained to her how he wasn't really a killer, that it was another person who lived inside of him and came out at the worst times." Thorne snorted. "Nothing but a bunch of bullshit, to get her to go along with his behavior. To feel sorry for him. But one thing Angel isn't, is indecisive. Or a pushover. It didn't take her long to come to me and tell me what was going on."

Colton knew Angel was a good marshal. She respected the agency too much to break the rules. Or allow anyone else to do so.

"She saw him kill someone who was handcuffed, then remove the cuffs before he called it in, to make it look like resisting arrest. He didn't know she saw what really happened."

"I'm glad she came to you." Things could have ended much differently if she hadn't.

"She helped us set him up so he could be stopped. I didn't see anything to make me think she couldn't handle it. She was rock-steady the evening of the operation. She had him trapped on a bridge. One team was waiting on one end, another team on the opposite. But as I hurried toward them, I saw she'd frozen."

Just like what had happened at the warehouse. She'd frozen up on Colton, too. If only he had gone with his instincts, and shot the guy right off. Colton wouldn't be lying in the hospital now while the woman he loved was out there planning a superhero move to bring the murdering psychopath in.

"On the bridge, Stone rambled on about her betraying their love, and then he shot her. I was too far away, but I pulled my gun. Even with a wound, she was quicker, and she shot him first. Stone fell over the railing and landed in the water. It was much too high for him to survive, especially after being shot. There was so much blood on the bridge, even without the fall he wouldn't have survived."

"Except he did survive," said one dead guy to the other.

"And he's waited five years for revenge, and planned it carefully." Thorne shook his head and looked out the window. "It's not going to be easy to take him down."

"Do you know where she is?" Colton asked as Thorne stood and made his way to the door again.

"No."

He wasn't sure if the man was telling him the truth or not. But it didn't really matter, since Colton couldn't get out of bed, anyway. Just breathing was a painful struggle.

"She's not coming back," Colton whispered, hit by the sudden certainty. It wasn't a question.

How many times in the last few months had he expected this to happen? He should have been better prepared.

Thorne let out a breath. "She mentioned not wanting to put anyone else in danger."

"If you find her, you'll let me know?" Colton asked.

"Will it alter your decision to join my team?"

"Possibly," Colton said, and revised it to, "Probably," when Thorne raised a brow.

"I'll let you know if I hear anything."

When Thorne was gone, Colton lay in bed staring up at the ceiling, feeling helpless. The woman he loved—and damn if she didn't love him, too—was out there hunting a killer, all by herself.

The beeping on the monitor next to him kicked up, and soon the nurse came in and asked him to calm down.

He didn't think he would ever be calm again.

Chapter One Hundred Four

Thorne had given Angel a clean credit card and lined up a safe apartment for her. With her hair pulled up in a bun and a pair of large sunglasses covering her face, she was ready to head out of Colton's place for the last time.

She'd double and triple-checked that she hadn't left anything behind. She'd wiped down everything one more time.

It wasn't safe to stay here. At any moment, one of the paramedics or nurses could put it together and call the police. It wouldn't take long for them to track Colton—or Duncan—to this house.

She'd already caused him so much pain. She couldn't put him in prison on top of it. She had to make sure there was nothing left behind that would link her to him.

As she walked out the back door, she knew his home was clean of all traces. It was as if she'd never existed.

Suddenly, someone stepped out of the shadows.

She reached for her gun. Then realized who it was.

"Damn it, Kenny! Are you *trying* to get yourself shot?" she snapped.

Kenny grinned, but didn't look all that worried. "I'm just checking your reflexes."

Pudge ran up, and she dropped to her knees to hug him and give him some love.

"Mrs. Bosley asked me to take him for a walk," Kenny explained. "Naturally, he took off for here, no matter what I said."

"He wanted to come home." She understood. That was the real reason she'd been here, too. Because she was scared and lonely, and just wanted to be home. Unfortunately, it hadn't helped. The house was cold and empty. Just a shell of what had made it feel like a home.

Colton was missing.

"Do you know when Mr. Willis will be back?" Kenny asked.

"I'm sure he'll be back soon."

Kenny's gaze focused on the bag in her hand. "You're leaving before he gets back?"

"There's something I have to take care of," she explained, but the boy didn't seem convinced.

"You're running away." Disappointment clouded the boy's solemn face.

There had been many jokes regarding Kenny's intelligence, but Angel saw how bright he was. This kid had instincts that would make him a great detective someday. He could read people, even when they were doing their best to hide the truth...even from themselves.

"He'll be back soon." She deflected his comment with her own bit of truth.

She'd gotten word yesterday that Colton was awake and out of critical condition. The relief of Thorne's announcement had brought on another wave of tears, and she'd hurried the conversation along so she could get off the phone and let them fall.

"I wanted to thank both of you for taking me shooting," Kenny said, and grinned. "I made it into the academy."

"I'm proud of you. You're going to do great," she told him. "Really. I'm sure of it."

"I hope you're right." He kicked the dirt with his foot, then looked up at her. "I think you should stay until Mr. Willis gets home. You didn't see how sad he was when you were away the last time. If you leave, no amount of ice cream is going to fix it. Not that I'm not willing to try."

She hugged Kenny and gave a watery smile into his shoulder. "He's pretty tough. He's going to be okay. I promise." She pulled away, patted Kenny on the arm, then crouched down to deal with canine guilt. "Take good care of him for me, okay?" she said to the dog, who whined his reply. "Good boy."

With a pat on the head, and a smile for Kenny, she stood to go face her biggest fear.

Putting the violent past behind her...in the only way she knew how.

Chapter One Hundred Five

A guy by the name of Garrett showed up at the hospital to drive Colton back to Oregon. Angel had told him a little about the man. How he'd left the team to marry Thorne's daughter.

"You worked for Thorne?" Colton asked when he had caught his breath from the exertion of getting in the vehicle and buckling up.

"I used to. Now I'm his son-in-law."

No doubt there was a good story there, but before Colton got the chance to ask for details, Garrett turned to him.

"How deep are you in with Angel?" Garrett asked, his eyes narrowed on Colton's face.

Colton let out a sigh. This must be the "What are your intentions?" conversation. No problem. He was prepared. She'd said often enough her team was like her family, so it wasn't surprising they acted the part.

"All the way," Colton said. Not only was he in love with Angel, but after their moment on the sofa with no condom, she could be pregnant. Would she tell him if she was? Would he get the opportunity to be a father to his kid?

Garrett searched his eyes, apparently believed him, and gave a short nod. "Good. She needs someone who's willing to go all the way."

Colton nodded. "I'm willing." He raked a hand through his hair. "Not that it will matter. Even if she survives her next stupid stunt, she still won't give me a chance. She'll just come up with more reasons why we shouldn't be together."

For the last few days as he lay in the hospital, he'd tried his best to push her out of his thoughts. He'd figured he would be better off if he could exorcise her quickly from his mind and body. And he'd already been on pain meds. But they hadn't helped. Nothing had.

He couldn't just give up on her. Not yet.

Love made people do really foolish things. Like set themselves up for rejection again.

Or get themselves killed.

"Take it from me," Garrett said. "If someone loves you enough, they won't be able to stay away. I couldn't. When I finally figured out that I couldn't go back to the way things were without Sam, I came back to her."

"The whole 'let something go, and if it's meant to be, it will come back to you' thing?" He might have rolled his eyes if it didn't hurt so much.

"Something like that." Garrett let out a breath. "Angel's had it rough."

A huge understatement. Colton laughed, causing a wince of pain. He wasn't quite up for laughing yet.

"If she doesn't get herself killed, and if she decides she wants me, I'll be ready."

That statement had way too many ifs to be hopeful.

"She won't get herself killed. We'll make sure of it. We all plan to work the mission from our end," Garrett said with a wink before he left Colton sitting on his living room sofa with a wave.

Only a few minutes later, there was a knock at the door. Pudge nearly knocked him over with jumps and big doggy licks as soon as he hobbled to the door and opened it.

"Oh my!" Deb said worriedly when she caught sight of Colton. "That motorcycle accident was far worse than they said. You look absolutely terrible."

There was nothing like having someone confirm you looked as bad as you felt.

"I'm going to be fine. Just a little sore," he assured her.

"I brought you a nice piece of cake," she said as she bustled past him to the kitchen.

Things were looking up.

Except, his neighbor was frowning back at him. "I'm sorry to say your lady friend left. I saw her pack up her things, and Kenny spoke to her as she was leaving."

Colton kept his face blank. Barely. "Oh. Uh—"

She put the cake on the table, and went back to the door. "It's okay, dear. You don't want a woman who will just up and leave when you need her. You want someone who stays loyal in sickness and in health."

"You're right, ma'am."

If he thought for a moment Angel had left him because she didn't want to help him through his injury, it might have been easier to let her go.

But he knew the reason she'd left.

Guilt.

She believed it was her fault he'd been hurt. It was easy to replay something after the fact and see where you'd fucked up. In the heat of the moment, however, it came down to instincts, training, and shit luck.

Luck hadn't been on his side when Viktor Kulakov's lackey shot him. And it hadn't been with him in the warehouse when his partner froze up at the sight of her ex-lover-thought-dead. He didn't blame her. Despite their understanding of how the system worked, it was still daunting when someone you thought was dead greeted you while pulling a gun.

Her main reason for not wanting Colton to go with her was that he might get hurt while helping her. And that was exactly what had happened.

If he'd had a chance to talk to her before she left, he might have been able to convince her she wasn't to blame... but he had his doubts.

No, Angel hadn't left him because she didn't want to be bothered with his recovery. She'd left because she couldn't handle seeing the pain she was convinced she'd caused him.

If only she realized how much worse the pain was, caused by her absence.

Deb smiled at him. "My daughter is divorced, and a nurse. I should invite you both over for dinner."

Colton laughed and shook his head. "You're going to have to give me some time, okay?"

"Sure, sure. You let me know when you're ready to move on."

The woman patted his bad shoulder and left.

When he closed the door, he let out a wince at the pain. Both the external kind as well as the internal variety.

He scratched his dog's ears and sighed. "The problem is, I don't think I'll ever be ready to move on."

Chapter One Hundred Six

Angel tossed her Kevlar vest in the back seat, not bothering to wear it. What was the point when the person she was trying to bring in was using armor-piercing bullets? The vest hadn't helped Colton.

Just thinking his name made her clamp her jaw in frustration and regret.

She needed to mentally prepare for what came next. She would be facing down a heartless killer. She knew from past experience that Lucas didn't act like a normal person. He didn't have feelings like remorse of curiosity. He fed on death and blood.

She slid a knife into the sheath inside her boot and got out of the car. She was a walking arsenal, but no way was it overkill. Not when going up against someone like Lucas Stone.

It had taken her over a month to track him down. The little weasel had been on the move, but now it seemed he was settling down.

She'd managed to infiltrate his computer network and use it to track him. Knowing who she was dealing with had given her the insight she'd needed to find him.

The feds now had the prototype, but she'd still seen a hefty sum deposited in Stone's bank account. Was it upfront money for a hit? If so, he'd probably be moving on when the job was done. It was time to finish this.

She'd hidden her vehicle among the trees and shrubs at the end of the lane. With shaky hands, she closed the trunk and turned toward her destiny.

This is stupid. So stupid, Angel told herself as she stared up the farm lane in rural Oklahoma, working up the courage to make her next move. She'd checked satellite maps and done surveillance, and come up with a foolproof plan—if there was such a thing as a foolproof plan when hunting a crazy person.

All that was left to do was to walk up there and implement it. Come what may, it would all be over in the next hour.

Striding down the lane in the dry heat, she pulled her gun from its holster. Each step she took sent up a small cloud of dust. There were no trees closer to the house. She would be approaching the house and barn on foot, in a fairly open space. She would have to hope Lucas wasn't looking through the front windows as she moved in.

It was never good to be pinning the success of a plan on hope. Hope was as useless as luck.

Fear pumped through her body, making her light and quick. She allowed herself a moment in between cover to catch her breath and work out the next leg of the approach.

If felt as though it took days to reach the front of the house. She peered in the first window.

An empty living room.

The next was a bedroom. Also empty.

As she moved swiftly and quietly around the house, she heard an engine roar to life in the barn. The sound was as good as yelling his name and having him answer.

She hid behind a large tree in the backyard and counted to three before making her move—which was to run like hell to the barn. Once there, she maneuvered around it, looking for alternate exits. The last thing she wanted was for Lucas to get away again.

This needed to end, here and now.

Using the edge of her shirt, she cleaned a small area at the corner of a window in the back. Even after cleaning the window a second time, she wasn't sure what was happening inside.

It was fairly dark. The only light was coming through the open doors behind Lucas, whose back was to her. The engine she'd heard came from a chainsaw, and he was using it to cut up something.

Her heart jackhammered. No. He was cutting up some*one*.

He was covered and dripping with blood while standing over the dead body. She nearly choked on a surge of nausea. Seeing him like that brought back a flood of memories from the night her brother had murdered her parents.

She swallowed down the disgust and fear, and forced herself to focus on the man in the barn without seeing her brother.

Nicholas's hair had been dark, and Lucas was blond, but in that moment they looked like the same person. Maybe it was the emptiness in their eyes, or the tension emanating from them, she wasn't sure. She only knew they were both the same kind of monsters. And at one time, in different ways, she'd loved them both.

Her phone vibrated in her pocket, but she ignored it. Instead, she moved in to put an end to this nightmare.

She held up her gun, ready to shoot him.

While she couldn't help the person scattered in pieces on

the floor, she could help the next person, and the next after that. Because one thing was for sure, Lucas Stone was not able to stop killing.

Her entrance created a shadow in the light coming in through the door behind her. Lucas jumped, dropping the chainsaw, which abruptly stopped running. The silence in the barn surprised her as much as the screwdriver he threw at her before taking off at a run.

With no other thought than to stop him, she chased him to the other end of the barn, which was lined with hay bales. Dust choked her throat and brought tears to her eyes, but she was focused and rushed on, her gun out, blood pumping.

Her only warning was a slight shuffle on the floor. Then he lunged, grabbed her gun hand, and pressed a blade to her throat.

She knew there wouldn't be a lot of talking. Lucas wasn't driven by the dramatics of it. He needed the blood. The death.

It would be over quickly.

Chapter One Hundred Seven

To Angel's surprise, Lucas didn't kill her immediately. Instead, he said disgustedly, "I was eventually going to get to you. You just can't wait for anything."

"Who was she?" Angel knew the victim in the barn was female.

"No one you knew."

He used his weight to drag Angel back to the body. The head was gone, so she couldn't be sure he was telling the truth.

"Did you bring your friend or did I kill him?" he asked conversationally. "It felt like a good shot, but in the heat of the moment you never know."

"He's fine. Thank you for asking."

The knife pressed more firmly into her skin, and she held back a squeak of pain as it pierced her flesh. He liked hearing the pain. She wouldn't give him that.

"Always a comedian." He squeezed her arm tighter,

cutting off the circulation.

"You're getting dramatic in your old age," she taunted. "I always thought you were less talk and more action."

"Only because I was forced to hurry. Back in righteous days, I had to rush through the best parts before my partner found me. You remember." He pulled the knife even closer to her throat. "But now I have all this space to work, and because I know you never call for backup, I have unlimited time."

"Lucky for me"—she made her move, pushing the knife away just as a shot rang out through the barn. Lucas fell to the ground with a stirring of dust—"I learned from that mistake," she finished.

Thorne stepped out around a stack of bales, as Dane holstered his gun and limped closer.

"Thanks, guys," she said breathlessly.

Thorne moved in to hug her, but then frowned at the blood on her clothes and patted her shoulder instead. Fair enough.

"Thanks for not being stupid this time," Dane said. "Check his vitals. I want to make sure he's not going to do a surprise resurrection scene. I really hate those."

"He's not going anywhere," she assured. It was pretty obvious Lucas was dead. But she did check for a pulse in what was left of his neck. "Good shot."

"Wasn't me," Dane said with a shrug, and glanced at Thorne.

Thorne smiled, shook his head, and turned toward the sound of another set of footsteps.

"Great job, Deputy Marshal Williamson," Thorne said as Colton stepped into the room.

Chapter One Hundred Eight

Seeing Angel being held at knifepoint by a madman had scared Colton more than anything he'd ever lived through. Somehow, he'd managed to steady his trembling hands enough to get off the shot to drop the guy.

After taking a brief moment alone to put his head between his knees and make sure he wasn't going to do something silly like puke or pass out, he strode out from his hiding place to go check on her.

She was walking and talking, but her hands shook, and he wanted nothing more than to go to her and hold her. He wanted to feel her alive and warm in his arms, and never let her go.

It was the letting her go part of that plan that kept him in place as the sound of sirens filled the hot summer air.

He couldn't keep doing this to himself. Stepping into her life, only to look around and find he was alone again—it was killing him.

When she thanked him for coming, he nodded but didn't

say anything. He didn't trust himself to speak. He worried if he opened his mouth, the only thing that would come out would be begging.

Fortunately, he was relieved of the possibility when the building was swarmed by the local police. As was normal protocol, each of the marshals gave a statement of what had happened, then they were asked to come to the station to tie everything up.

It was a good shoot, and the mutilated body on the floor was pretty solid proof of the man's guilt.

Colton kept his eye on Angel as he gave his statement, and he was glad to see Dane get in the driver's side of her car to take her to the station. Her family was taking good care of her. That was as much as he could hope for.

Since he didn't have any other choice.

Chapter One Hundred Nine

The body in the barn had belonged to a local woman who'd been seen with Stone two nights before.

"Maybe if I'd gotten here sooner, she'd still be alive," Angel said sadly as she stepped out of the police station bathroom in a clean shirt they'd lent her. She and the others were free to go, so she followed Thorne outside to the parking lot. The blue sky above them should have made her feel happy, at least, if not hopeful.

But all she felt was unsettled.

"You can't save everyone, Cassandra." It was the first time Thorne had used her real name since the night he came to recruit her. "And you couldn't have saved your parents if you'd woken sooner. Nicholas would have killed you. You do know that, right?"

She felt him beside her. Strong and steady, and waiting for her to answer. She couldn't speak. All these years, she'd thought if she'd only woken up sooner, maybe as Nicholas was heading to their room with the knife, she would have been able to stop him.

There wouldn't have been time for help to arrive. She'd seen the police reports, and knew it had taken them eighteen minutes to respond to her call. She wouldn't have survived eighteen minutes unarmed and untrained.

But her parents might have had a chance. She might have saved them.

"I'm a father." He grasped her shoulders and turned her to face him. "At times, I've allowed myself to pretend I was your father, because you were here and my own daughter wasn't. And believe me, Cassie, I love you like my own."

Damn it, now she was crying.

"So I can say this to you with all sincerity. The last thought that went through your parents' minds was not that they wished you had been there to sacrifice yourself to Nicholas's blade. I guarantee you they were hoping and praying you were safe. Because that is what parents always want."

He hugged her tight and kissed the top of her head just like she remembered her dad doing when she was little.

"Now." He cleared his throat, back to business. "What do you want, Cassie? Because you're not coming back to Task Force Phoenix."

Her heart sank. But she'd known that was a possibility. "I guess I'm not going to be much good to you, now that my cover's been blown."

He shook his head. "No. That's not why. You're out because you need to find your own life. I thought I was helping you by offering you this job, but I didn't realize it had become an anchor."

She stared at him incredulously. "Are you kidding? I would probably still be in and out of jail if you wouldn't have given me this chance."

"True, I'd intended it to be a *chance*. But at some point, it became an *obligation* to you. All I want is for you to be happy, Cassie. Find someone to love, and have a few kids I can spoil."

Her eyes went wide in surprise as Thorne nodded toward the man standing in the parking lot by a black SUV.

Colton.

"But—"

Thorne held up his hands to interrupt. "No. I don't care what you think *I* want. You're wrong. It's *okay* to have a family. It's safe for you to love people outside of our team. You can't keep hiding behind this job because you're afraid to live and love. You can't keep running away from your life. So, I'll ask you again. What do *you* want?"

Though the question was *what* and not *who*, her thoughts went immediately to man in the parking lot. And the peace she'd felt at night while he'd held her in his arms. The laughter. The way she loved him.

But being with him wasn't possible.

He was a marshal now. He wouldn't be content having a day job like teaching. Hell, he was still wearing a shoulder holster, even after everyone else had disarmed. And she knew damned well she wouldn't be able to relax knowing he was in danger and she wasn't there on the team with him, ready to help.

She swallowed and looked up at Thorne. "I'm going to take some time to think it over, but I think I want a new identity. A home, a dog. Maybe I'll start my own software consulting business so I can work in my pajamas whenever I want to."

Thorne's brows rose. "That's it?"

She could tell he was asking about Colton.

"Yeah. That's everything."

Thorne let out a sigh, and nodded. "All right. When you're ready, I'll make it happen."

"I see you offered him a job." She nodded in Colton's

direction.

"Yeah, and he accepted." Thorne shook his head, then walked away.

Breathing out a sigh of relief, she felt better knowing she'd helped Colton get back his life of action and adventure. Despite getting him shot, at least she'd managed to redeem herself by getting him everything he wanted.

Chapter One Hundred Ten

Colton knew how this was going to end before Angel even opened her mouth. He'd expected it to go down like this, but still, he'd hoped.

Why hadn't he learned his lesson by now?

"Please don't thank me again," he said as he held up his hand in a stop motion.

She nodded. "Okay. Then—"

"Or apologize."

"Then what should I say?" she asked with a small huff.

He had so many answers to that question.

He wanted her to say she wanted to give their relationship a chance and see what happened. He wanted her to say she loved him, and couldn't live without him.

But she wouldn't say that.

And he couldn't say it.

Mostly because he wouldn't survive her telling him she wasn't willing to stay with him.

He knew it all already. He'd lived through it before.

The first time, he'd thought it had been harder because she'd left without a word. He'd stupidly thought it would have been better if they'd had a chance to discuss things first.

He'd been wrong.

This was much worse.

The only hope was that he might be able to wear her down in time. He'd figured if he took the job Thorne offered, they would see each other from time to time. So he had. Maybe he'd be lucky enough to be partnered with her occasionally.

"I guess I'll see you at team headquarters when I'm released for active duty," he said, watching her intently to see her response.

When she frowned and shook her head, his heart sank. And his small hope died.

"No. Thorne took me off Task Force Phoenix," she said softly.

Colton looked at her in surprise. True, she'd been exposed in the news, so she couldn't do undercover work. Still, he thought she'd come back in a different capacity. Maybe something with computers, or intel. The team was her life. Her family.

"What will you do instead?" he asked in surprise.

"Not sure. I'm taking some time off to figure it out."

Only his shredded pride kept him from falling at her feet and begging her to stay with him. His pride, and the fact he knew begging wouldn't change anything.

She was obviously determined to leave him. Again.

And this time, he was determined to let her go.

Forever.

Chapter One Hundred Eleven

The silence grew uncomfortable as Angel stood with Colton in the parking lot. He was looking at her so intently, but didn't say another word.

There were so many things she wanted to say to him, but she knew it would only confuse the situation even more. It wasn't fair of her to ask him to give up this new opportunity with Task Force Phoenix.

She didn't deserve his sacrifice, if he gave up what he wanted for her. Not when she'd been too scared to do the same for him a year ago.

"Well, I guess I need to get going before the news vans show up." She couldn't handle a bunch of probing questions about her past *or* her future.

He gave a short nod. "Sure. Good luck in whatever you end up doing."

He started to turn away, but she struck like a snake before

he could, her body moving without her brain navigating.

She stood up on her toes and pressed her lips to his. There was a moment of hesitation before his mouth softened into what she interpreted as permission. His hands moved up her back and over her shoulders, to hold her face in his palms as his tongue mastered hers.

With a gasp, he pulled back and rested his forehead against hers. "Angel—"

Yes, she silently answered whatever he was going to ask.

"Take care of yourself." He stepped back and opened the door of the SUV without looking at her. "Goodbye."

"Bye," she said, but he'd already closed the door. Her heart pounded hard, the rhythm begging her feet to move.

Instead, she stood there in agony, watching him drive away.

Taking her heart with him.

She heard the uneven scuff of a boot on the pavement, and swallowed down the tears that were brimming.

"I've seen you do some pretty stupid things, but that was seriously painful," Dane muttered.

Dane was the older brother she wished she'd had. She loved his protectiveness, and didn't mind the teasing. But the best part was his brotherly advice.

Except when he didn't agree with her.

"I don't know what you're talking about," she managed to say through her tight throat. She prayed he'd play along, but she wasn't that lucky.

"Seriously? That's how you're playing it?"

She let out a sigh and gave up the innocent act. "What was I supposed to do? Beg him to come with me into a life of oblivion? I don't know where I'm going or what I'm doing? He has a future with the team. It's what he wants. But it's not what I want anymore."

"What *do* you want?" Dane asked, looking steadily at

her.

Good question. Once being with Colton was off the table, there wasn't much left. "I don't know."

"That's a lie. You do know. You're just afraid."

"Maybe." She shrugged it off. "But it's too late now."

Dane sighed and shook his head. "Fine. Whatever. You want to stay with me until you get things figured out?"

"Would you mind?" She really didn't want to be alone.

She'd been roommates with Dane in the past. While he didn't cook and he played video games way too much, he was neat and didn't ask her questions about her past.

"It would be nice to have some company," he said as he glanced away.

Wait. Something was wrong. She'd been so immersed in her own misery, she hadn't noticed his.

Until now.

"What's going on?" she asked, ready to spring to his defense, whatever it was.

"Caroline got married this weekend." He winced as if the statement caused him physical pain. It probably did.

Angel's problems were difficult and her past was painful, but Dane's story had always been utterly heartbreaking.

Caroline was Dane's widow. The woman who thought her husband had been killed in a fire, and had gone on to raise their son while Dane saved other people so they could go home to their families.

It wasn't fair.

"I'm so sorry," Angel said, and pulled him close for a hug.

"Come on," he muttered. "Let's go get drunk."

Chapter One Hundred Twelve

Something was wrong with Colton's dog. Pudge hadn't been eating. He didn't want to play catch. He didn't even try to get up on the bed.

Colton didn't feel like doing any of those things, either, but he wasn't a dog.

He was a man getting over a broken heart.

"Mr. Willis? You can bring Pudge back now." The vet tech hovered by the door separating the lobby from the exam rooms.

"Are you going to come willingly, or are we doing this the hard way?" he asked his dog, who was stretched out on the floor as if already dead.

"Pudge, my boy!" an older gentleman in a white coat called to him in a cheerful tone. Pudge raised his head for a moment. His tail made two whole thumps, then he went back to his earlier position.

"Fine. No problem. I'll carry you," Colton said as he bent to pick up his lethargic—and very heavy—German shepherd. "It's not like I was shot, or anything." Though his wound had healed over the past two months, his chest was still tight.

He settled Pudge on the black vinyl table and stepped back so the vet could fix his best friend.

"How long has he been like this?" Dr. Westcott asked.

"A couple of months. It's been getting worse over the last week."

"She's gone?" the vet asked as he placed the stethoscope on Pudge's side and tilted his head.

Colton looked at him in surprise.

"I saw the news. She's been cleared."

Colton knew this was the vet who'd helped Angel when Pudge ate the bee. He'd stopped in shortly thereafter to settle the non-existent bill for his services.

"Yeah," Colton said evenly. "She left a couple of months ago."

"The timing seems suspect." The man raised a thick gray eyebrow.

No shit.

"Yes."

Dr. Westcott gave Pudge a thorough workup and scratched him behind the ears before delivering his diagnosis. "I don't see anything obviously wrong with him. I could do some more tests, but my guess is it's not a physical problem. I think he's suffering from the same condition as his owner."

Colton let out a long breath. "Will he get better in time?"

"Will you?" the vet asked.

Colton dragged his hand over his face and shook his head. "I'm not sure. I hope so."

"I'm not going to pretend to know the girl, but she seemed like a catch."

Perfect. As if he wasn't already worried about his dog.

Now the man was going to throw salt in his wounds.

"Yeah. Too bad she doesn't want to be caught."

Dr. Westcott tilted his head. "You ever notice the best stories are about the one that got away?"

Colton pressed his lips together. Really? The man thought this was helping?

The vet tossed a treat, which Pudge snatched up quickly. "I guess you need to decide if you want something more than a good story."

Colton sure as hell hoped he wouldn't be charged extra for the advice. Because it wasn't worth shit.

Angel didn't want him. She'd left. Again.

He couldn't spend his whole life chasing after someone who would never stop running.

"Get up, you big faker. I'm not carrying you around anymore." Colton pointed to the door, and Pudge lowered his head but walked out under his own power.

Pudge sat on Colton's foot in the lobby as he paid the bill, and rested his chin on Colton's leg on the drive home, rather than have his head out the window as usual.

Damn her to hell.

She'd broken his dog.

She'd broken him.

Chapter One Hundred Thirteen

Angel wasn't pregnant. She'd known that since the week after Colton was shot. It was stupid, but it had taken until yesterday morning for it to finally catch up with her. She'd curled into a ball in the spare room at Dane's apartment, and cried until he came in and threatened to call the entire team to come help.

She didn't know what had caused her emotional overload. A baby would only have complicated things.

Or maybe it would have simplified everything.

Without her permission, a vision came of her and Colton walking at a park with a baby strapped in one of those ridiculous carriers on his back, Pudge loping along, chasing after a toddler.

Her chest seized as if it was a picture of something she'd lost, rather than something she'd never had. And never would have.

She didn't tell Dane why she was crying. And eventually, she got herself together enough to pack her things and say goodbye.

She should have been relieved that her strong sense of duty to Thorne was gone. She'd finally realized he was right. She was holding onto her job out of obligation, as well as the sense of family.

But as much as she loved the team, they weren't her real family.

She stepped up to the gravestones bearing her parents' names for the first time since they'd been placed there. Her brother's marker was a few feet from theirs. Thorne had helped her make that decision. Anger had made her want him buried on another planet, as far from them as possible, in an unmarked grave. But Thorne had convinced her to put Nicholas there with them because they'd loved him.

She'd given in because she'd been too overwhelmed to argue, but now she realized he was right about that, as well. And if they still loved Nicholas after what he'd done to them, she knew they still loved her, too, even though she hadn't been able to save them.

Instead of pouring out a stream of apologies to her parents as she'd planned, she sat down in the grass and spent the next two hours telling them about her life. She was surprised by how much of it included her feelings for Colton.

She found herself feeling the same way she'd felt a year ago.

Wondering what it might have been like if she hadn't left him.

If she hadn't been afraid to try a real relationship.

Chapter One Hundred Fourteen

It wasn't a surprise to see a black sedan waiting in his driveway when Colton got home. Thorne got out of the driver's seat and followed him inside without a word.

Pudge flopped over on his side under the front window. He hadn't even begged their visitor to pet him. It was a testament to how sad he was.

How sad they both were.

"What's wrong with him?" Thorne asked.

"He's trying to get attention. Just ignore him." He didn't want to explain that he and his dog were heartbroken over the same woman.

Thorne laughed, then sobered as he looked around the living room and the stacks of moving boxes. "You're packing."

"Yeah."

"I don't remember planning a move for you."

"I have to get out of this house."

Every time he came home, he expected to see her sitting on the sofa. He couldn't sleep because he was still hoping she would sneak into his house. Into his bed. Every time he let the dog in, he prayed she'd be waiting on his porch.

He needed to find his own place. Without ghosts. Somewhere she wouldn't be able to hack the address and show up just as he was trying to make a new life. He needed to cut the remaining thread between them.

Thorne nodded. "What does this mean for your position with the team? The doctor's about to clear you for active duty."

"I'm sorry. I've done some more thinking, and I've changed my mind about that. There's something else I want more."

Thorne just nodded, and didn't push for details, which was a good thing because Colton didn't have any. All he knew was it was time to start over.

Completely over.

After a few more minutes, Thorne stood and let out a breath. "Let me know where you want to go and what you want to do. I'll do my best to set it up."

"Thanks. I appreciate that." He opened his mouth to ask about Angel, but then closed it. He didn't want to know.

He walked the man out and waved goodbye.

Thorne was just pulling out of the driveway when another visitor showed up.

Kenny practically bounced into the house carrying a piece of paper with him. Pudge came closer and flopped over on the boy's feet looking up with sad puppy dog eyes.

"Don't fall for it. He's taking advantage of the situation."

"Are you sure? He looks legit miserable."

"And you look legit excited about something. What's up?"

"I'm top of my class." Kenny held out the paper with a wide grin. It was good to see him excited about his future.

"Good for you." Colton smiled, genuinely happy that

something good was happening for someone. "I'm so proud of you."

"Thanks." The kid's cheeks flushed and he glanced away. There was something else.

"And?"

"And Morgan is my girlfriend. Like official. She even changed her relationship status on Facebook."

Colton really wasn't sure what that last part meant, but if Kenny was happy, Colton was happy. "Wow. That's big. Congratulations."

Kenny took in the state of the living room, and looked back at Colton in surprise. "You're moving? Did you get back with The Mantis? I hear she got cleared and everything."

"Yeah, I'm moving. I'll miss you, kid."

"Have you talked to her?" Kenny asked eagerly.

"Nope."

Kenny's expression turned puzzled. "Are you going to tell her you want her back?"

"No. I'm not."

"Come on man. I am 99.753 percent sure she will be happy if you reach out to her."

Colton couldn't help chuckling at the exaggerated prediction. "Too bad. I might have been willing if it was 99.8 percent."

"Don't you know about rounding?" Kenny wagged his finger at him, making them both laugh.

Kenny pulled out his wallet and handed Colton two twenty-dollar bills.

Oh shit.

It was never good when people used your own advice against you. Especially smart-ass kids.

"Find her and ask her out to dinner," Kenny ordered, as though he were the adult. "If she says no, you can use this to buy yourself a steak dinner. If she says yes, you can take her"—

he looked at the twenties and made a face—"for a burger."

If only it were so simple.

Colton shook his head and admitted, "I don't know if I'll ever see her again."

Kenny looked genuinely disappointed by that. "Promise me, if you do, you'll try your best."

What the hell. It wasn't like he *would* see her.

He ruffled the kid's hair. "Yeah, okay. I promise."

"Thank you for helping me," Kenny said after Colton reluctantly took the money. "I wouldn't have figured out what I wanted to be if it weren't for you. And I wouldn't have known how to start if you hadn't helped me fill out the application. You're the best teacher ever, Mr. Willis."

Colton swallowed down a lump of emotion at the unexpected praise. The best teacher ever, who'd held a gun on him, and intentionally sabotaged his ability to construct a bookcase.

But... Despite his questionable tactics, Colton had managed to help this kid. He'd guided him to a path where he could excel and succeed.

He smiled, and slapped Kenny on the back.

And knew they'd *both* found their purpose.

Chapter One Hundred Fifteen

Angel sat in her hotel room looking through the files in front of her. Each one contained a new life in the form of a different house and community. All she needed to do was pick one, and she would be able to move and start living like a normal person.

Or as close to normal as someone like her could get.

Did she want to live by the beach, or in the mountains? The northeast or the southwest? It was a bigger decision than she'd expected, and she found herself wishing she had someone to discuss it with.

There was one area of the map that had been moved off to the side, removed from the options before her.

Oregon.

She knew if she was close enough to Colton, she would end up at his house. He deserved better. He deserved an exciting career. He wanted a life full of adrenaline and danger, and she was done with both of those things. She wanted peace and quiet. She wanted to snuggle up on the sofa in front of a fire and know she was safe.

She pursed her lips, perused the choices again, and cleared out the homes that didn't include a fireplace.

She let out a sigh, the selection still too daunting.

Normally when people went into protection, they weren't given options. They were simply placed where they knew the fewest number of people. Where there would be the least chance of running into someone from their old life.

For Angel, that wasn't a concern. For one thing, she didn't have any family, and her friends were all deputy marshals. Secondly, her face had been spread across every media outlet in the country, so there wasn't anywhere she could go where she didn't risk recognition.

After eliminating everything that didn't have a fireplace, privacy, or a moderate year-round climate, she was left with five choices. Employing the methodical way of making a decision, she shuffled the files, closed her eyes and pointed to one.

"Good. That's done," she said to no one.

Instead of being happy to have made a decision—however random—she was stunned by the feeling of emptiness that overwhelmed her.

She was all alone in the world.

Again.

She'd have to get a dog. As soon as she was settled, she'd head to the shelter and pick out a companion. Maybe she'd get a female and name it Pudgette.

Before she changed her mind, she texted Thorne her choice, and waited for his instructions.

Three days. See you there.

Three days later, she was standing in front of her new home. It was a log cabin deep in the woods. A large deck took up the right side of the house and wound its way to a hillside that ran along the back side. She knew from the photos there was a workout room in the basement and a bunker off in the woods.

The whole front of the structure was glass. The entry door led into a great room with a two-story stone fireplace as the centerpiece of the space.

"Welcome home." Her unenthusiastic voice echoed back at her, reflecting the loneliness she was suddenly feeling.

She walked in, and frowned at the overpowering scent of bleach.

Great. Someone had probably been shot in her new home. She pushed the thought away to focus on the positive.

The house was furnished and clean—obviously—but she would clean it again and bring in some pieces that fit her style better. Maybe that would help make it feel like home.

As expected, a manila envelope waited on the island.

She knew what was inside. Her new identity and the credentials to back it up. What would her new name be?

Please don't let it be as bad as Dunking Willies, she thought to herself as she opened the flap and pulled out the document.

"What the hell?" She read the words two more times. They hadn't changed.

Cassandra Larson.

It was her old name. The one she'd been born with. Except the middle name, Angeline. Thorne had assigned her her old name. Tears filled her eyes, and she laughed at how emotional she was feeling.

But the laughter fell away when she flipped to the next document. There were two identities in the envelope.

The second one was for a man.

Jack Colton.

Without wanting to, she read the address. Trying her best to shake away the knowledge of where she could find him, if she so chose, she pushed the paper away and went back to her vehicle to start unpacking her things.

She stood in the parking area, looking at the trees around her. She'd wanted someplace secluded, but now that seclusion felt a bit like...solitary confinement. There was no nice next-door neighbor who would bring her apple dumplings. There was no neighborhood kid to take to the shooting range.

There was no one.

Damn. This was not a home.

It was a prison.

Chapter One Hundred Sixteen

Colton's new home reminded him of the place he'd just moved from—a modest rancher on a quiet street in a rural neighborhood. The backyard was fenced and shaded.

He would start working immediately on an escape plan. Old habits, and all.

Justin, his handler, showed up the first morning to make sure everything was in order.

"You're all set up to start teaching in the fall," Justin announced as he plopped onto the sofa. "I have some great news. You might want to sit down."

Colton fought the urge to run out of the house screaming. What if the great news was about Angel? What if she was getting married? He wanted her to be happy, but he didn't know if he was ready for her to be quite *that* happy.

It had only been a few weeks. Not enough time to meet someone and fall in love.

Not that it had taken him long to fall for her.

"Viktor Kulakov was arrested yesterday."

Colton whipped his attention back to Justin. "Are you serious?"

The other man nodded with a grin. "It will be a few months until he goes to trial, but once you testify and he's locked up, we might be able to relax some of your cover enough to make contact with your family."

Colton wouldn't mention he was already in contact with John via Messenger. It still wasn't the same as seeing his family in real life.

"You're sure the charges will stick?" he asked hopefully. Viktor was a slippery bastard.

"Yes. It was a good arrest."

Which meant he must have been caught with hard evidence. The trial wouldn't just come down to Colton and his testimony.

He let out a breath and rested his head back against the sofa in relief. At least this part of his life was working out. "Thank you."

After a beer and some more easy conversation, Justin smacked him lightly on the leg, stood, and headed for the door. "Let me know if you need anything else to settle in."

For a brief moment, Colton almost asked about Angel. But he let it go, knowing it wouldn't matter. She was gone from his life. He was moving on.

When Justin left, Colton slumped back onto the sofa and turned on the television.

Pudge sniffed the house and came back to stand in front of him, looking unimpressed. The dog was getting better with time. They both were. They were still a little gloomy, but he hoped they'd be all good in a month or two.

"Yeah, I know. But it'll be okay. We'll make some friends in the neighborhood and soon you'll be the center of attention again."

Colton swallowed, unable to talk about his other plans. Especially the one that included finding someone to move on with. He wasn't ready now, but he was making it a goal. Maybe in a year or two. He didn't want to be alone for the rest of his life, pining over someone he couldn't have.

Pudge whined at the back door and Colton opened it to let him out onto the large deck. Pudge trotted down the steps and ran across the yard as Colton went back inside to start the task of unpacking.

He was just opening the first box when Pudge was already barking at the back door. The quickness of his excursion could only mean one thing. Colton rolled his eyes and opened the door, ready to stop the dog from running inside with some dead offering locked in his jaws.

But Pudge was just sitting on the deck looking at him, his tail wagging.

"Where is it?" he asked the dog. "Where's the disgusting carcass you're so proud to show me?"

Pudge barked once and went to the steps.

It wasn't a dead squirrel.

It was Angel.

"I know I'm not at my best," she said with a lopsided smile. "I've been driving for twenty straight hours. Even so, 'disgusting carcass' is a little harsh, don't you think?"

My God. She was here. Grinning at him.

He didn't grin back.

How could she do this to him? Rip his heart out over and over and over?

"You broke my dog," he accused, unable to give voice to what he was really feeling.

Though, it looked like Pudge was fixed now, his tail wagging and that sparkle in his brown eyes as he gazed lovingly at his true master.

Damn her.

"I didn't break him. He loves me," she said.

So did Colton, but he didn't say it. He was trying so hard *not* to love her.

"Did you wake up next to another dead guy?" he asked.

He was only half joking. With Angel, you never knew what she might get into.

"No. I woke up alone. And I don't like it much."

He swallowed. She looked...serious. Like she had something to say to him. That maybe involved not waking up alone.

A trickle of optimism ran through him.

"I don't like it much either," he said honestly. "Do you want to come in and tell me about it?"

She stepped into his kitchen and looked around, brows hiked. "I thought you wanted an exciting life. This is not going to be exciting."

"I changed my mind," he told her. Then he decided to take a big risk with the truth. She was here, and he'd be damned if he let her walk away without knowing how he truly felt. "I decided I want a normal life. No guns. No excitement. Well, no excitement other than maybe my students winning the next State Math Bowl, or something."

"So do I. Want a normal life, that is." Her voice was casual, but her eyes were serious and intent on his.

This was too good to be true. He tamped down the hope that surged through his body.

"What if you change your mind again?" she asked. "About the guns."

"Then we'll figure it out." He shook his head. "But I won't."

"I don't know if I can sit here waiting for you to come home after some dangerous job. I'll worry myself to death."

His heart swelled. She'd worry. About *him*.

That must mean—

"Can you wait for me to come back from class?" he asked, his whole body filling with a brand-new kind of excitement. "I generally get home about four, but I was thinking about maybe coaching basketball. I was always good at it. That might take me away some evenings. Of course, you're welcome to watch. Do you like basketball?"

"Yeah, I like basketball. A lot."

They gazed at each other. And he wondered what she was really trying to say.

Then he remembered his promise to Kenny. That he would go for it if he had the chance.

This was his chance.

"I love you," he said. *That* was what they should be talking about. Not basketball. "I love you. And I need you in my life." He swallowed and kept going. "I don't need action and danger to make my life exciting. I need the challenge of helping my students achieve their dreams. I need someone to talk to about my day when I get home. I need an engaging sex life, and someone to hold at night. I need *you*. You're everything I want. And hopefully, you'll be my everything for the rest of our lives."

Her eyes grew shiny and a wobbly smile broke out on her face. "I love you, too. I wish I would have stayed with you when you asked last year. I wish I would have shown you how important you were to me. How important you still are. I'm ready to show you now, if you let me."

He stepped up to her and took her hands in his, joy filling his entire being.

"Hell, yeah. The last time I asked you to stay with me, I wasn't clear about what that meant. I know now. Will you marry me, Angel?"

Somewhere in one of the moving boxes was the diamond ring he'd purchased in the hopes of convincing her to stay with him. He'd find it later. Now it was just about them. This moment.

"Yes. God, yes, I'll marry you. But actually, it's Cassandra now."

He shook his head and smiled down at this woman who was his life. "Maybe. But you'll always be my Angel," he whispered. "You were sent to save me."

She smiled and pulled him closer. "We'll save each other, every single day for the rest of our lives."

Epilogue

As soon as she woke, Angel realized something wasn't right. It was still dark, and her husband was pressed up against her back, his arm draped over her like every other night since they'd moved here.

His hand rested protectively across her stomach. Not that his large hand had been able to cover her stomach for months.

Pudge lifted his head and whined from his spot at her feet.

The alarm clock next to her reported it was only two in the morning. She'd been sleeping through the night since she'd been pregnant, but now she was wide awake.

Unlike all the times she'd awoken in the past, it hadn't been a dream, a worry, or a sound that had stirred her. Not this time. She wasn't sure what it had been.

Pudge jumped down from the bed and came up to her face to lick it. He wasn't alerted, so she knew no one lurked in the darkness. She was safe.

But there was something…

The something revealed itself in a tight pain across her abdomen and wrapped itself uncomfortably around her back. She let out a gasp of surprise and closed her eyes.

"What is it?" Colton asked, his voice rough with sleep.

"It's time."

• • •

It was time.

Every agent worth his badge had at least three escape routes planned out at all times. But Colton was no longer an agent. He was a teacher.

Still, he'd mapped out seven ways to get to the hospital. He was prepared for everything from bad weather to traffic, from construction to alien invasion. No matter what happened, his son would not be born in the back seat of a police cruiser, as Colton had been.

He was ready. Or he thought he was.

Now that the moment was upon them, he couldn't seem to breathe right and his chest hurt.

His wife was in pain, as evident by the way she'd made a new word, "Ohmygodohmygodohmygod!"

"I can't believe I did this to you," he said, jumping out of bed. He had no idea what to do next.

"Who do you *think* did this to me?"

She'd never looked so scary. He had no doubt she could kick his ass and give birth at the same time. His wife was tough like that.

"No. I know it was me, but what was I thinking?" The only answer was a dry look. "Right. I wasn't really thinking."

When he'd suggested they make a baby, she'd said okay. So really, this was *her* fault. Though he would wait for another time to share this incredible nugget of wisdom.

"Colton?" she called.

He came back in the room after realizing he'd nearly gotten in the car and left without her. "Sorry. Sorry. What should I do?" he asked, all seven plans long gone.

"Kiss me." She was smiling at him, no doubt amused by his panic.

How the hell could she be so calm?

He kissed her. Taking a deep breath, he pulled back to smile at her. "We're going to have a baby," he said, bright waves of happiness coursing through him.

She smiled, and he knew she felt exactly the same way. "Yeah. We're going to be a family."

About the Author

One very early morning, Allison B. Hanson woke up with a conversation going on in her head. It wasn't so much a dream as being forced awake by her imagination. Unable to go back to sleep, she gave in, went to the computer, and began writing. Years later it still hasn't stopped. Allison lives near Hershey, Pennsylvania. Her contemporary romances include paranormal, sci-fi, fantasy, and mystery suspense. She enjoys candy immensely, as well as long motorcycle rides, running, and reading.

Discover more Amara titles…

Reckless Honor
a *HORNET* novel by Tonya Burrows

Jean-Luc Cavalier has only ever cared about three things: sex, booze, and the dangerous missions he undertakes with HORNET—until the night he rescues virologist Dr. Claire Oliver. Someone wants her research and they're willing to kill anyone and everyone it, but that's the least of HORNET's concerns. An ultra-deadly virus with all the markings of a bioweapon is decimating the Niger Delta, and Nigeria is only the testing grounds…

Fair Game
a novel by Taylor Lunsford

Vivien Monroe couldn't be more out of place in the video game company she inherited from her eccentric father. Not only does she have to sort out her father's last request and deal with a younger sister she barely knows, she has to go toe-to-toe with her father's gorgeous, geeky protégé—a man who makes her think about the *last* thing she should be thinking about right now.

THE MAN I WANT TO BE
an *Under Covers* novel by Christina Elle

DEA agent Bryan Tyke hates weddings. He hates them even more when he's forced to travel to a hot as hell resort to watch his best friends say I do, while acting happy about it. Forever isn't in the cards for Tyke. It hasn't been since he joined the army years ago and lost everything. That is, until the woman he's never forgotten shows up as a bridesmaid and puts herself into immediate danger.

CAUGHT UP
a novel by Rya Stone

Cassie Mitchum is only interested in closing a deal on the Lucas property. Until she sets eyes on Jameson Lucas. She's never been one for tattooed roughnecks, but she's willing to make an exception. Jameson Lucas needs Cassie Mitchum to stay the hell off his land. He wants her, but being close to her would put her on the radar of the most dangerous person Jax has ever known.

Made in the USA
Middletown, DE
26 February 2020